It happened in a flash

Richard caught Elizabeth roughly by the waist and pulled her to her feet in a crushing embrace. His mouth covered hers in a hard passionate kiss that stunned Elizabeth and seared her to her toes.

Never had she experienced anything like this. This was sheer lust, an explosion of attraction and desire. While his mouth plundered hers, she couldn't think, she could only feel and ache and want. It was the most totally physical moment of her life.

Only the knowledge that she was seconds from surrendering brought her to her senses. If she didn't stop this right now, she was lost. Her hand came up and she slapped him hard across the face.

He stood facing her, legs wide apart, his breathing labored. "Ye belong to me," he said in a hoarse voice, his eyes glittering on her. "Ye called me and I came. You're mine."

Dear Reader,

From the creative and talented Margaret St. George comes yet another innovative, compelling love story, *The Pirate and His Lady.*

The idea for this book—and Captain Richard Colter himself—lived for many years in Margaret's head before she found the perfect showcase for them. "Taking this brash, arrogant eighteenth-century privateer and throwing him two hundred years ahead to 1992 was particularly fun," Margaret says.

Indeed, Captain Colter *is* special. He has captured the hearts of all of us who have read his story—and has shown us that when a love is meant to be, nothing can stand in its way . . . not even time.

"I loved writing a time-travel romance," Margaret tells us. "And I especially love Captain Colter."

We hope you do, too.

Warm regards,

Debra Matteucci
Senior Editor & Editorial Coordinator
Harlequin Books
300 East 42nd St., 6th floor
New York, NY 10017

MARGARET ST. GEORGE

THE PIRATE AND HIS LADY

Harlequin Books

TORONTO • NEW YORK • LONDON
AMSTERDAM • PARIS • SYDNEY • HAMBURG
STOCKHOLM • ATHENS • TOKYO • MILAN
MADRID • WARSAW • BUDAPEST • AUCKLAND

This book is for Shelagh Larkin, a friend and the
most loyal reader an author could have. This one
is for you, She, with appreciation and gratitude.

Published November 1992

ISBN 0-373-16462-9

THE PIRATE AND HIS LADY

Prologue

His ship was sinking.

The forward mast sail burned against the sky. A dozen fires raged on deck. Arrows of flame raced toward the sail that had billowed across the ship's waist when the main mast came crashing down.

Shaking with fury and frustration, Richard watched through clouds of dark oily smoke as the last of the cutthroat Spaniards ran back to the *Madre Louisa* which was coupled to his ship by grappling hooks. A loose cannon wheeled drunkenly through the deck debris as the bow of the *Black Cutter* shuddered from another hit at waterline; seawater poured into the hull at a deadly rate. The screams of dying men rose in his ears.

A flaming yard fell from the after mast and crashed at his feet, showering him with smoke and fiery splinters.

Richard wiped the blood from his eyes, then threw back his head and bellowed his rage to the sky.

"Richard!"

Instantly he dropped into a crouch and swung his sword up, straining to see through drifts of stinging smoke. "Who's there? Show yourself!"

"Jump! Come to me!"

The voice was inside his head, all around him, above and below the screams and crackling fires.

"Show yourself, damn it!"

As the bow sank hissing into the sea, the stern rose beneath his feet. Wind whipped his long hair about his face and spun the smoke away. What he saw caused Richard's jaw to drop and his sword to fall from limp fingers.

This, then, was the face of death.

Chapter One

Struggling with the cumbersome ankle-length skirt of her colonial costume, Elizabeth Rowley hurried across the beach and approached the water lapping the shore. She raised a pair of binoculars to her eyes.

"How on earth are they doing the lighting?" she murmured, staring at two eighteenth-century tall ships maneuvering in the breeze about a half mile off shore.

It was truly an astonishing scene, a sea battle such as the Florida Keys had not witnessed in two centuries. Although twilight shadowed the shore, the two ships were lit in such a way that they appeared to be fighting in late afternoon sun. Whoever had devised the lighting had produced a stunning effect.

Elizabeth lowered the binoculars briefly and cast a hasty glance up and down the deserted beach. It was a shame that she was the only person watching this. Someone had spent megabucks to construct the ships, bring them to Key West, then stage a sea battle. She couldn't believe there hadn't been a hurricane of publicity.

She scanned the ships through the binoculars, gasping with pleasure at the authenticity of detail. Whoever had planned this spectacle had spared no expense. The costumes and weaponry were historically correct to the smallest item.

When Elizabeth eventually focused on the names of the ships, she started and her heart turned over beneath the low-cut bodice of her costume. The smaller and more severely damaged of the three-masted ships was the *Black Cutter.* Capt. Richard Colter's ship.

Elizabeth knew that ship and she knew Capt. Richard Colter, a privateer out of Boston. Now she recognized the battle being reenacted before her eyes. She should. God only knew how many weeks, how many hundreds of hours she had spent researching Richard Colter, the *Black Cutter* and this particular sea battle.

This would have been Colter's final voyage. He intended to return to Boston and retire, a rich man. But it hadn't happened that way. On this day in 1792, the *Black Cutter* had gone down with all hands aboard.

Elizabeth grimaced as she watched blossoms of fire explode across the *Black Cutter*'s decks. Trust her to fall for a guy who had been dead for two hundred years.

"You've got it bad, girl," Elizabeth muttered, focusing in on the replica of the *Black Cutter.* "Uncle Cappy is right. You're fixating on Captain Colter."

She knew she was. But she couldn't help it. Every time she studied Capt. Richard Colter's portrait something happened to her. She looked into his direct, challenging gaze and her breath stopped in her chest. Her stomach tightened, then looped in a slow roll. She felt— she couldn't explain it—a surge of excitement, or déjà vu. Destiny, maybe. Followed by depression brought on by the knowledge that she and Richard Colter had missed each other by two hundred years. She had a visceral feeling that they could have been explosive together, they would have loved each other with a passion to rock the heavens. It was a crazy obsession, seriously off the edge, and Elizabeth knew it.

She also suspected she knew why she was infatuated with Capt. Richard Colter. He was a myth, and a long dead myth was safe. She didn't have to deal with the real man.

A sigh lifted her bare shoulders, straining the laces of her corset. She gripped the binoculars tightly.

The *Madre Louisa* was maneuvering in for the kill. The *Black Cutter* foundered badly.

The scene was a chillingly accurate reproduction and Elizabeth shivered in the warm night breeze, wondering what Capt. Richard Colter had thought in these final moments. Had he thought about a woman as the grappling hooks flew and the men from the *Madre Louisa* prepared to loot his vessel? Had he thought about the riches he would not live to enjoy? Had he experienced any regrets as the Spaniards poured onto his dying ship?

Sudden tears glittered in her eyes at the terrible beauty of the scene, two wounded ships locked together in their final death throes, masts broken, hulls fatally damaged, exhaling smoke and gunpowder. Elizabeth's nostrils stung with the pungent scent. She heard distant shouts and the eerie squeal of the two hulls scraping together.

"Oh, God," she whispered. Capt. Richard Colter lay dying on the decks of the *Black Cutter*. Felled by a musket ball or a Spanish broadsword, it was impossible to say. History had not recorded his final moments.

"Hi, babes!"

Bill Trowbridge clattered down the steps to the beach. "You look great," he said with a low whistle, but his expression sobered as he peered at her in the deepening darkness. "Hey, are you crying?"

Elizabeth lowered the binoculars, then wiped her eyes and gestured toward the flaming ships. "I can hardly bear to watch this." When Bill didn't reply, she explained, "It's a reenactment of a sea battle that took place near here two hundred years ago. Isn't it spectacular?" The sound of musket fire and clashing swords made her wince.

Bill scanned the sea, then raised a puzzled eyebrow. "I don't get it. I don't see anything out there."

Elizabeth frowned, irritated. "I'd have thought a navy officer would be interested in this," she said coolly.

"I'd be very interested in something like that," Bill said. "Is this some kind of joke?"

"You tell me," she said sharply, brushing past him. Lifting her skirts, she moved up the stairs to the deck. Bill followed at a slower pace.

"I'll fix drinks," he said, moving toward the patio doors.

"Good. You do that." This wasn't a good beginning to the evening. Elizabeth sighed, then raised her eyes to the peculiar radiant light bathing the sea.

The grappling hooks had been released and the *Madre Louisa* drifted free of the *Black Cutter*. Fire consumed the decks of the *Black Cutter;* within seconds the ship blazed like a torch. Smoke stung Elizabeth's eyes as the wind shifted. Bits of ash floated on the warm air. A tremendous explosion rent the night and a shudder trembled down her body. Richard was dying.

Richard!

Mind and spirit fused, flinging her anguish across space and time. She felt his name rip from her body, as if her silent scream were physical, a part of her own spirit erupting forth on rocket wings of yearning.

Reason insisted that what she watched was not real, but emotionally the blazing ship was as real as the railing that splintered beneath her grasp, as real as a woman's timeless passion. A man she knew was dying on that ship. The knowledge clawed her heart.

By now the actors were long departed, whisked away by some theatrical magic. The shapes that ran through the flames were an illusion created to shock. But the illusion was so damned real.

Jump! Come to me! Richard, come to me!

The *Black Cutter* sank so swiftly Elizabeth could hardly believe her eyes. One minute it was there, blazing like a flaming brand upon the sea—the next minute the ship was gone and there was nothing but hissing steam and foam churning the water.

As she lifted her fingertips to wipe the tears from her eyes and cheeks, Bill stepped through the patio doors.

"All I could find was rum. Is rum and Coke all right?" He stared at her wet eyes, uncertain what to do.

"I'm sorry, I just..." Embarrassed, she blinked rapidly and shook her head. She had planned to make grog, but her heart wasn't in it anymore. "Thanks." The drink tasted overly sweet, a reminder of early college days when she had actually liked rum and Coke.

"Whatever's troubling you—you can tell me." When she didn't answer, Bill touched her arm, his fingers disappearing in the tumble of lace at her elbow. "We don't have to go to your uncle's party. We can stay here and talk."

"I think I'm losing my mind"

"I beg your pardon?"

"Never mind. Look, they've turned out the lights." Moonlight shimmered on a calm sea. There was no trace of the boiling waves or the *Madre Louisa*. Whoever had staged this was a theatrical genius, Elizabeth decided.

"Beth—"

She stepped away from his grasp. "It was so *real!* I've done so much research on Colter and that battle, that it was like watching the real thing. It was like being present when he died." Fresh tears stung her eyelids.

Bill looked as if he didn't understand a single word she was saying. She saw now that he also hadn't understood the requirements for his costume. This year the rules for Cappy Haleburton's famed Pirates' Ball decreed colonial dress, and Elizabeth's uncle was a stickler for authenticity.

Bill wore a pair of khaki pants rolled up to the knee, loafers without socks, an old suit vest over a button-down shirt opened to the waist, and a bandanna twisted around his navy crew cut, pseudo-pirate style. For effect he had pasted a black patch over one of the lenses of his glasses. The costume was so awful that Elizabeth winced, anticipating Cappy's reaction. One thing was certain. Bill would not be invited to next year's Pirates' Ball.

Abruptly Elizabeth gathered her heavy brocade skirts and stepped inside. "I'll be back in a minute," she called over her shoulder, heading for the bathroom to repair her makeup.

She looked better than she felt, she decided, examining herself in the mirror. Tonight she had pulled her glossy dark shoulder-length hair high on her head and had formed dozens of fat springy curls that hung to the tops of her shoulders. The luxuriant hairstyle framed her oval face and offered a soft counterpoint to her intense dark eyes.

She swallowed two aspirin, hoping the tablets would settle her headache and her nerves. Watching the demise of the *Black Cutter* had devastated her and left her feeling drained and depressed. The last thing she felt like doing was attending one of Cappy's raucous parties.

"We're running late," she called as she came down the hallway, her skirts swaying. She gave Bill a bright artificial smile, hating his costume, wishing she could fall in love with him, knowing she never would. He called her Babes. Or Beth, for heaven's sake, a gentle name that reflected his hopes and expectations more than it reflected Elizabeth Rowley.

If only Richard Colter had been born in her century or she in his. If only she hadn't taken the *Black Cutter* assignment. If only she weren't infatuated with a portrait. If only she weren't losing her stupid mind.

TONIGHT THE BEACH near Mallory Square had been transformed into a scene from a bygone century. The parking lot in front of Cappy's wharf had been screened off with rolls of high fencing, blocking any glimpse of automobiles and city distractions.

Elizabeth stood at the railing of the replica of a Spanish galleon that served as the offices for Golden Dreams, a salvage company devoted to treasure hunting. The galleon replica was nowhere near authentic, but few of the tourists who came to view Cappy's mini-museum knew that. What the tourists cared about were the collections of golden doubloons and silver pieces of eight, the gold chains, and medallions, the silver cup and plate and Cappy's most prized find, a large Bolivian emerald framed by diamonds. Although Cappy had found the treasure, very little of it actually belonged to him. Most of the items were on loan from the state of Florida. The emerald was a paste replica.

By and large the tourists were indifferent to the offices on the lower deck, including Elizabeth's, and oblivious to the dive boats that crowded the *Sante Oro* when the weather was too uncertain to risk going out.

Tonight the dive boats were nowhere in evidence; the twentieth century had vanished. Bonfires dotted the beach, surrounded by lords and ladies, pirates and wenches, all quaffing ale or rum punch from wooden tankards. Lobster pots hung suspended over the bonfires and here and there tables slowly sank in the sand beneath the weight of platters containing carefully authenticated colonial dishes.

"Where did you find that guy?" Cappy demanded, stepping up beside Elizabeth. His voice roughened with disgust. "He's got a rubber knife stuck in his waistband. Good God."

"It's my fault," she said, eyeing Bill on the beach. "I guess I didn't explain the rules well enough."

"That gown and hairstyle suit you," Cappy commented when she turned back to discover him watching her. "You would have made a gorgeous colonial lady."

Catching one of the glossy, fat curls falling to her shoulders, Elizabeth twirled it around her finger in a coquettish gesture as she sank into a low curtsy.

"Thank you, dear uncle." She raised her lashes. "Now, what is that compliment going to cost me?"

Laughter suited Cappy. It seemed to rumble upward from his toes. He had the laugh of a big man, not the laugh Elizabeth would have expected from a lean sun-blackened man of sixty-something who was only an inch or two taller than she was.

But Cappy Haleburton didn't need physical size to be a man of stature. He possessed a presence that came from being comfortable with himself, from doing what he loved most in the world. He figured that made him unique and in fact he was. Cappy was one of only a handful of people who had made treasure hunting his life's work and managed to eke a living out of it. In actual fact Cappy was broke most of the time, rich some of the time, and happy all of the time, as long as he was hot on the scent of a new wreck, a new dream. Unfortunately he was currently in one of his broke periods.

"Did you think about our conversation?" he asked. When Elizabeth didn't answer, he continued. "We're interested in the *Madre Louisa*, not the *Black Cutter*. If, and I say if, there was any gold on the *Black Cutter*, it's almost certain the Spaniards from the *Madre Louisa* looted it." A pause underscored his point. "Honey, our bank balance is dipping toward perilous. Are you any closer to pinpointing where the *Madre Louisa* sank?"

No one could "pinpoint" a centuries-old wreck. But Elizabeth knew what he meant.

"According to my research, one man survived the sinking of the *Madre Louisa*. Assuming I can find it, verification should be in the archives in Seville, Spain. Until I can get a look at the archives, all I can offer is a rough estimate of the site."

"How many files are you stopped on?"

"Six."

Cappy nodded, frowning. "Until we can send you to Spain, we're stuck. And we can't afford to send you until we find something. It's a catch-22." He sighed. "I guess we'll just keep searching off the Marquesas.

Maybe we'll stumble across the *Madre Louisa* or one of the others by sheer dumb luck.''

"Suppose the *Madre Louisa* went down somewhere off Manhattan Cove," Elizabeth suggested without looking at him.

"That would mean everything you've dug up so far is wrong." He examined her face. "Why on earth would you suggest something like that?"

She told him about the sea battle.

Cappy frowned. "You've got Richard Colter on the brain. Now you're hallucinating about him."

"It was not an hallucination. I smelled the gunpowder. It stung my eyes. And there was ash in the air."

"Whatever you saw wasn't real. Maybe it was an apparition or something." Envy flickered in his eyes. "By God, I'd love to have seen it myself," he added softly. "Was it wonderful?"

Cappy's comments troubled Elizabeth long after the party wound down and she and Bill had said their goodbyes. Bill turned his Toyota into Elizabeth's driveway before she realized he had hardly spoken a word during the drive home.

"I'd invite you in for a drink, but it's very late," she said when he cut the ignition. "Did you have a good time?"

"To tell the truth, I felt foolish as hell. Why didn't you tell me how seriously those people take these things?"

She noticed he had disposed of the rubber knife and the patch pasted over the lens of his eyeglasses. But it rankled her that he made "those people" sound eccentric and peculiar. She was one of "those people."

"I thought I made it clear. Key West treasures its past, both the reality and the romanticized version. We feel a kinship to the early settlers. We like to think we share the same qualities of independence and self-sufficiency they had. The past is very real to us."

They sat in awkward silence until Bill stretched his arm across the backseat, resting his fingertips on her bare shoulder. Elizabeth wished his touch thrilled her or raised a tingle. But it didn't.

"It's time we talked about us." Light from the corner street lamp fell across his chest, but his face remained in shadow. "I haven't wanted to rush or to push you into anything, but we've been seeing each other for six weeks and—"

Leaning, she placed a finger across his lips. "It's late and we're both tired. We've had a lot to drink. Maybe we should save this conversation for another time."

"We're standing in front of a line, Beth. Either we cross that line and go forward or we walk away." He took her hand. "I have some leave coming. I thought we might drive up to Miami next weekend. Or we could fly over to Nassau . . ." She understood what he was saying and she appreciated his tactful approach. The time had come to confront the sexual question.

Sneaking a look at him in the warm darkness, Elizabeth tried to imagine what Bill would be like in bed. She thought she knew. He would be gentle and thoughtful, a caring and sensitive lover. He would put her pleasure first. That's what every woman wanted, wasn't it?

Most of the time.

But sometimes a woman wanted a man so transported by passion that he took what he wanted with nothing in mind but his own needs. A man who could be gentle, yes, but a man who also knew when to be rough and urgent and overpowering. Sometimes a woman didn't seek an equal role in lovemaking, she

wanted simply to be taken, selfishly, greedily, passionately.

But that wasn't Bill Trowbridge. Gently she placed
her palm against his cheek. "I'm sorry," she said softly.
"If we cross your line, I'll end up hurting you. I think
it's better if we just remain friends."

For a moment he sat stiffly, not moving. Then he
brought her hand to his lips. "Are you sure?" he asked
finally, trying not to show his disappointment.

"I'm sure."

A sigh dropped his shoulders. "I guess this means a
weekend in Miami is out."

She laughed, relieved that he wasn't going to make
this more difficult than it already was. "I'm afraid so."
Leaning forward, she gave him a sisterly kiss on the
cheek, then wrestled her voluminous skirts out of the
car door. She bent to the window. "Friends keep in
touch. Okay?"

"We could have been great together."

"Look me up in our next life and we'll give it a try."

"You're a cruel woman," he said, but he was laughing. After she watched Bill's car pull out of the driveway and turn down the street, Elizabeth let herself into
the house and turned off the porch light, wondering if
she would ever meet a man with whom she could fall in
love. She wasn't lucky with men. She wanted a strong
man, a man she couldn't steamroll, but she clashed immediately with that kind of man.

"You're hopeless." Sighing, she poured a cup of
warmed-over coffee and carried it outside to the deck.
Despite what she had said to Bill, she hadn't had much
to drink. She wished she had. Then maybe she could
have forgotten or dismissed the sea battle she had witnessed earlier. Instead, it had haunted her all evening.

Closing her eyes, she leaned on the railing and inhaled the scent of night-blooming flowers, of the moist salty air. The night was warm and spangled with stars, made for lovers. Had it been the same in Richard Colter's time? When women dressed as she was dressed now?

Tilting her head, Elizabeth contemplated the ribbons of moonlight shimmering across the waves. What had happened out there earlier tonight? What had she really seen? An apparition, as Cappy claimed? She didn't think so.

On impulse, she kicked off her slippers, then raised her skirts and pressed the hoops inward to accommodate the stairway leading to the beach. The beaches of Key West were a powdered marl, largely limestone. Tonight the marl felt cool and almost velvety beneath her not-so-authentic nylons.

Without hesitation she turned to the left, where the shore curved away from the houses fronting the beach to her right. The houses along this stretch were concealed by fountains of palms and lush stands of vegetation. With very little effort, Elizabeth could pretend this was the Key West of Richard Colter's time, a scrub-covered island scarcely touched by civilization.

Oh, Richard. I miss you. I need you.

God. She was practically certifiable. A genuine nut case. What in the hell was she doing on a deserted beach in the middle of the night, mooning over some long-dead privateer who would have driven her crazy in real life?

Angered by her foolishness, cursing beneath her breath, Elizabeth turned back toward the deck. No more Richard Colter. Damn it, she was going to put that craziness behind her and get on with her life. Somewhere out there—in the good old twentieth century—there had to be a man for her. If not—well, so be it. She'd survive. Who needed men anyway?

She had almost passed the piece of driftwood before she noticed it lying half in and half out of the dark water. It was a large piece, over six feet in length, perfect for the bare spot beneath the mimosa tree in her front yard.

If she tried to fetch it now, she'd ruin her gown. Oh, the hell with it. The gown and its time period represented an unhealthly fixation. Pressing her lips together, she lifted her hem and strode onto the strip of wet marl, tucking the elbow lace into her sleeves.

Good Lord. It wasn't a piece of driftwood at all, but a man. Elizabeth's skin prickled. She'd read about dead people washing ashore, but it had never happened along her stretch of beach.

She edged nearer, holding her breath. The man's dark head was resting in the crook of his arm, his face turned away from her. With a shock Elizabeth realized he must have been a guest at Cappy's party, because he was dressed in costume. He wore dark breeches, heavy woolen stockings, one shapeless shoe and a shirt with full, flowing sleeves. His shoulder-length hair was tied at his collar with a length of hemp.

Stay calm, she told herself. First she would check and see if he was really dead, then she would phone the police.

When she heard him groan, Elizabeth jumped and thought her heart would leap out of her chest. For an instant she was unable to move. Then he moaned again and her paralysis broke.

Running the last few steps, she dropped to her knees in the water foaming around him then brushed aside his hair to feel beneath his ear. His pulse thudded strongly beneath her shaking fingertips. She leaned over him and grasped him under the arms, holding him steady as the water sucked at his legs.

After drawing a breath, she struggled to drag him further up the beach. By the time she was certain he was well out of the water, she was exhausted. She collapsed beside him and dropped her head.

Fighting to catch her breath, she peered at him. How badly was he injured? He smelled faintly of smoke and there were charred holes in his shirt and trousers. A gash bled on his forehead and on the arm flung over his face, but she didn't think any bones were broken. To be certain, she pushed to her knees and probed his right leg.

"God's toes, but I'll thank 'e not to do that. I've enough scurvy bruises without 'e adding to them. Bloody hell! Me head feels like a busted melon."

Elizabeth snatched her hands back, as if she were touching fire. She fell backward on the marl, her mouth dropping open as he struggled to push up on his elbows. The light shining from her deck fell full on his face.

Elizabeth gasped as her world spun in a crazy arc. For an instant she thought she might faint, she who had never fainted in her life.

To anchor her sanity, she dug her fingers into the cool sandy marl and gripped hard. A tiny disbelieving sound closed her throat.

The man she had pulled from the night sea was unmistakably Capt. Richard Colter.

Chapter Two

The man was not Richard Colter, of course. That was impossible. But he bore an uncanny resemblance to Colter, enough to make Elizabeth's skin prickle as she stared at him.

This man was older than the man in Richard Colter's portrait, and much larger than she imagined Colter would be. This man was tall and raw-boned, wide-shouldered and hard as a rock. A broad chest narrowed to a lean, flat waist. His physique was big, but magnificently in proportion.

As for his face, his features were blunt and craggy. He had wide, high cheekbones, a square jaw and an aggressive chin and nose. His face, throat and hands were sun-darkened to a deep bronze. Elizabeth suspected his hair would dry into a thick wheat-colored mane.

But it was his eyes that fixed and held her attention, that sent a shiver of electric recognition through her body. Not the color especially, which was an erotic blend of gray and blue, but his expression. He looked at her with Richard Colter's bold eyes, partly defiant, openly challenging, curious and intelligent.

Elizabeth clenched her teeth and told herself to get real. All right, the man bore an incredible resemblance to Richard Colter. Or, more accurately, he looked as if he could be Richard Colter's older, more streetwise brother. It didn't really matter; whoever he was, this was a drop-dead handsome man. In need of a shave, smelling of smoke and seawater, gazing warily out of smoldering eyes—he was a man to quicken any woman's pulse. Even wounded and dazed, the guy oozed charisma and Elizabeth responded to it. She wet her lips uncomfortably, unaccustomed to instant physical attraction.

"Are you all right?" she asked.

"I know your voice."

"Have we met before?" Elizabeth couldn't imagine it. No woman would forget this man.

Instead of answering, he deliberately and insolently dropped his gaze from her face to the breasts swelling over her neckline. Self-consciously, Elizabeth raised a hand to cover her cleavage. A rush of heat flooded her cheeks. Most men were discreet enough not to stare at a woman's breasts, particularly when they knew the woman was watching. Not this man. He studied them in blatantly sexual appraisal.

Ordinarily Elizabeth would have been infuriated. But all she felt now was a hot tingle that zinged through her system as if his gaze were physical, as if he caressed her instead of merely looking at her. When his gaze finally returned to meet hers, she felt slightly breathless and confused. Thankfully she was kneeling; she suspected her legs were suddenly too wobbly to support her.

"Ye called my name," he said, staring at her. She frowned, unable to place his accent. It hovered between Boston and England, combining a little of both, but not quite either.

"You were unconscious. I might have called out, trying to rouse you. You're in pretty bad shape. You have a cut on your forehead," she said as he struggled to sit up. "And a nasty gash on your arm. You need to see a doctor immediately."

Horror narrowed his eyes and tightened his jaw. "No bloody leech-sucking doctor is going to butcher this man jack!" The vehemence behind his comment precipitated a spasm of coughing and he leaned to one side to spit out a rush of seawater. Without a word of apology he wiped a hand across his mouth, then peered into the darkness on either side. "Where am I?"

"This is Manhattan Cove." When he showed no recognition, she added, "Key West, Florida." Slowly he nodded. His gaze continually returned to the porch light burning above Elizabeth's balcony. "Look. There's probably someone you want to call. You can use my telephone." When he didn't respond, she frowned. "Are you sure you're all right? I really think—"

"What is this place? Am I dead?" His gaze returned to her face.

Suddenly Elizabeth identified pinpoints of fear and anxiety in his eyes, in the rigid set of his jaw. She heard the quaver of dread in his deep voice.

"No," she said, smiling, "you're not dead. But maybe you've got a concussion. Do you remember what happened to you?"

Pushing himself to a sitting position, he frowned and concentrated, idly examining the bloody cut across his arm. Finally he shook his head, strands of long, damp hair shaking loose from the hemp tie. "Me bloody head's in a scurvy roar, it is." His frown deepened. "There was a tunnel like, black it was, and inside whirling winds so loud as not to bear. Like a hurricane, but not. More like I was flying, but not that either.'' The frustration of being unable to explain clouded his expression. "Quick as a blink, only it couldn't have been, I found meself dumped in the water and 'twas night.'' He stared at her. "Who might you be?''

"My name is Elizabeth Rowley. You don't recall anything else?'' If he did, he couldn't articulate it. He continued to stare at her with those smoldering eyes as if—injuries and other troubles aside—he battled an urge to press her backward onto the cool night sand and make love to her. His gaze ravaged her mouth, caressed the swell of her breasts, admired the small span of her waist.

When he looked up again, their eyes held and Elizabeth felt her palms grow moist, felt her heart pound against the silly corset laces. No man had ever considered her so openly, so boldly. If asked, she would have predicted that such an appraisal would have irritated the hell out of her. Instead, his gaze did strange hot things to her nerves.

She drew a breath. "It sounds like you definitely have a concussion. I think we'd better get you inside.'' Standing, she brushed down her skirts with a self-conscious gesture, then extended her hand to help him to his feet.

Assistance was repugnant to him. He gave her a glance of disgust, as if her offer to help had insulted him. But the expression vanished the instant he regained his feet. He wobbled on unsteady legs and his face turned noticeably pale beneath the bronze sunburn. He might have fallen if Elizabeth hadn't jumped forward and dropped his arm over her shoulders.

"Lean on me," she said firmly, forgetting that he was a very large man and she was a petite woman. When his weight fell on her shoulder, she gasped and feared he would drive her into the sand like a nail. "You need to lie down," she said between her teeth.

After wrapping her arm around his waist, she found herself acutely aware of his heat and the ripples of rock-hard muscle. She gripped his hand dangling over her shoulder and kicked back her long skirts.

"See those steps? By the frangipani? That's where we're going."

One thing she had to say for him. He uttered the most imaginative curses she had heard in years. Every step seemed to jar his head and every jar elicited a groaning curse. "God's green toes! Jack in hot hell!"

Cursing, injuries, hoop skirts and all, they managed to climb the stairs. Once inside the kitchen, Elizabeth tilted him against the countertop and paused to catch her breath. Her shoulder felt as if an ox had been leaning on it.

When she looked up, he was gazing around the kitchen with wide, uncomprehending eyes. Fear and pain tightened his lips into a pale line.

"I really think you should let me drive you to a doctor. You look like hell." In the glare of the kitchen light, Elizabeth could see the bloody gash on his forehead probably needed stitches. An expression of dulled confusion suggested she had guessed right about a concussion. He didn't appear even remotely cognizant of his surroundings.

"No doctor!" For a moment the confusion blazed out of his eyes, and it was abundantly clear that he meant what he said.

"There's no reason to shout. It's your body and your decision." Had he been involved in a fight? Gingerly she touched his arm. "You're welcome to use my guest room for a while. Why don't you rest for a few minutes, then we'll sort this out."

Stumbling beneath his weight as it pressed on her shoulder, Elizabeth helped him down the hallway and into her guest bedroom. After glancing around while she folded down the spread, he kicked off his one remaining shoe and sat on the edge of the bed.

"This is familiar," he said, sounding relieved. Then he jumped when she turned on the bedside lamp.

"Does the light hurt your eyes?" Elizabeth asked. He shielded his forehead and stared at the lamp, his shoulders twitching. He had to have a concussion. "Look, why don't you take off those wet clothes while I get you some aspirin? And maybe a Valium. I think there's a robe in the closet."

She backed out of the room, leaving him on the side of the bed, staring at the lamp through his fingers. Shaking her head, she went to the bathroom and rummaged in the medicine closet.

What had she gotten herself into? She didn't know this guy from Adam. Yet she had brought him into her house, put him in her guest bed and suggested he take off his clothes. Not very smart, Elizabeth told herself, frowning into the mirror.

But there was something about him... And she knew what it was. He was dynamic. Exciting and different. He looked at her with those bold gray-blue eyes and suddenly her nerves were fizzing like the frayed end of an electrical cord. She'd read about crazy romantic stuff like this, but it had never happened to her before. If he could make her feel like this with just a look...what would happen if he actually touched her?

Heat fired her cheeks and she rolled her eyes. What was she thinking about? She didn't even know his name, for heaven's sake. Making a face at her foolishness, she reached for the mirrored door of the medicine cabinet, then paused.

God, she looked bedraggled. Long ago her makeup had faded. There wasn't a trace of lipstick remaining. Her eye makeup had smudged and it looked like she had circles beneath her eyes. The fat, glossy finger curls that had taken an hour with a hot curling iron to get just right were now sagging and limp. Her beautiful colonial gown was ruined.

She wished the guy in her guest bedroom had washed up in front of someone else's house. He was trouble; she could feel it in her bones. For one thing, he looked too much like Richard Colter. For another, he made her feel things she was not accustomed to feeling.

Frowning, Elizabeth carried a first-aid kit, two aspirin, a Valium and a glass of water back to the bedroom. And almost dropped everything when she saw he was lying on the bed stark naked. It was a double bed, small enough that his hands extended beyond the sides and his feet hung off the bottom. Stunned, she froze in the doorway, unable to move, and stared at him.

He had a gorgeous body. Elizabeth managed a silent imaginative curse of her own as her muscles tightened and a feeling like warm honey poured through her body.

He was simply magnificent. Heavy muscle swelled along his shoulders and upper arms, defined his chest in excruciatingly sharp detail. Beneath a silky thatch of golden hair, his skin was a deep mahogany bronze. The bronze color ended at his hard, flat waist. Below, his skin was pale, untouched by the sun. She noticed long, well-shaped calves and heavy thighs, and above that . . . Elizabeth stared, then swallowed and looked away with difficulty. He was a big man all over.

Striding into the room, she put down the first-aid kit and the glass of water, then gave the covers an angry twitch and threw them over him.

"I don't know what the hell you think you're doing, buster, but let's get something straight right now," she said, standing over him, hands on hips. "You're here because I'm trying to help you and that's all. Do you understand that? You're not here to play footsie with the hostess, so forget about it."

He frowned up at her as if he didn't follow what she was saying. And once again he had the nerve to let his gaze slide to her breasts. Elizabeth felt her cheeks fill with heat and she didn't know if she was more furious with him or with herself for responding to him.

"I'm warning you. Knock it off!" she snapped. "And take these." She thrust the pills under his nose.

"What are they?"

"Aspirin, you idiot. And a Valium tablet. Raise your head." She shoved them between his lips and pushed the glass of water into his hand. "Swallow." When he spit out one of the aspirin and looked at it, she glared at him. "Swallow, damn it. It's only aspirin. It won't kill you, for God's sake."

Next she tossed him a roll of gauze to bandage his arm, then released an exaggerated sigh when he looked at the roll as if the gauze was a foreign substance.

"You really must have taken a conk on the head. You're being stupid, you know." Taking the gauze, she sat on the bed beside him, cleaned his wounds and wrapped his arm as tightly as she could, pulling the edges of the slash together. "You really should see a doctor. This is going to leave a nasty scar unless you have it stitched."

Then she remembered he already had a lot of nasty-looking scars. There was one down his shoulder, another on his chest, yet another marking one of his thighs. None of them looked as though they had benefited from a doctor's attention.

"How many times must I be telling 'e, gel...no bloody damned doctor is going to kill this mother's son!"

"Tilt your head down." Maybe he belonged to one of those religions that didn't believe in doctors. She cleaned and disinfected the cut on his forehead, then slapped two Band-Aids across it, pulling the edges of the cut tightly together.

Elizabeth sat in the chair beside the bed and studied her handiwork. It wasn't a bad job. The color had returned to his cheeks and lips, his pupils were returning to normal size, and he was showing more interest in his surroundings. She had to remind herself that this was not—not!—Richard Colter. It was a genetic trick; he only looked like Richard Colter's twin.

"Where is this place?"

"I told you, don't you remember? This is Key West, Florida. You're in my house. I found you on the beach. It looks like you were involved in an accident of some sort."

Now she could see tiny burned spots on his naked shoulders and chest. Had he been in a flaming car accident? Were the police looking for him?

"Look, there must be someone I can call for you. What's your name?"

The alertness that had been steadily returning to his gaze abruptly vanished. One moment he seemed attentive and interested in what she was saying, the next instant a curtain fell over his gaze and he stared at her with a look of dulled surprise. Slowly his eyes crossed and he blinked at her. Then his lashes closed and his head fell to the pillow.

Just like that he was asleep. It was like watching an invisible blow render someone suddenly unconscious.

"Oh, come on. No one falls asleep like that. Quit faking."

A soft snore sounded from his partly opened lips. His chest rose and fell in slow, steady breaths. It didn't look like he was faking. Elizabeth stood. How on earth could someone fall asleep in the blink of an eye?

And there was something else.

Finally she made herself consider his answer to her question about his name. Just before he fell unconscious, she was almost certain she had heard him mutter: Richard Colter.

Elizabeth drew a long, unsteady breath and felt the skin prickle on the back of her neck. She returned to her chair and collapsed, folding shaking hands in her lap and staring at him.

No. It wasn't possible.

But her mind raced, leaping beyond the vagaries of possible or impossible, trying to remember everything he had said, everything he had done. No. It simply couldn't be. Could it?

She didn't know how much time passed before she bent and picked up his shoe, turning it between her hands. From the impression in the leather, she could tell it was his right shoe. But when she turned it over, the sole was cut in a straight pattern, giving no indication which foot the shoe was intended for. The shoe was authentic for the eighteenth century. So were his stockings, odd shapeless tubes with no cup for the heel.

Next she examined his damp shirt. The material was slightly coarse to the touch, flawed by imperfections in the weave. There was no label. When she inspected the seams, it was obvious someone had placed each tiny stitch by hand.

His trousers were cut from linsey-woolsey, a material Elizabeth recognized from her research but had not actually seen before. There was no zipper. The fly closed with buttons and cloth loops.

"These are crazy thoughts," she whispered, looking from the clothing to the man.

She stared at him, holding her breath. What she was thinking was simply, utterly not possible.

But she was thinking it.

The clothing, his peculiar behavior, his confused story about how he turned up on the beach. Today being the two hundredth anniversary of Colter's death. Saying his name was Richard Colter. An incredible coincidence? Or a validation of Einstein's theory? Concentrating, Elizabeth thought back to an almost forgotten physics course. Einstein had believed time was not a straight line, but more like a river that curved and twisted back on itself. Could the banks of the river meet and blend? Einstein had not ruled out the possibility.

Elizabeth stood as still as a stone, facing the man asleep in her guest bed. If an intellect as massive as Einstein's could not rule out the possibility of time travel, who was she to say that it couldn't happen?

Heart pounding, she lifted her skirts and ran to her bedroom, returning with the book containing the portrait of Captain Richard Colter. With shaking hands she tilted the lamp shade, then held the book next to her guest's face.

Good God. She sucked in a breath and gasped. For a long moment the room swayed and whirled around her. It was him. The man in her bed was Capt. Richard Colter, a man who had been born in 1760 and who had presumably died in 1792.

Wait a minute. Fingers moving feverishly, she flipped through the book until she found the page she wanted. The passage related that the *Black Cutter* had sunk on this day two hundred years ago and all aboard had been lost at sea. Nowhere could she find any mention that Colter's body had been recovered and returned to Boston for burial.

"You were lost, all right," she whispered, looking at the pale crescent lashes lying against his cheek. "But you didn't die. You came through some crazy kind of time warp." A burst of joy made her feel dizzy and she sat abruptly, staring at him. He was here. Her Richard Colter was here!

A voice inside her head shouted disbelief. Okay. Not a time warp. She was dreaming, that was it. If Richard Colter had turned up in her bedroom, it would have been a dream come true. Ergo, this had to be a dream. A damned real dream.

Naturally her dream self, like her real self, would check this out. Lifting her skirts, Elizabeth hurried down the hall and into the kitchen to the phone farthest from the bedrooms.

Cappy didn't say hello. "What the hell time is it?" he snarled into the phone.

"A little after four o'clock in the morning. Listen, Cappy, at your party... did you notice a big man—big like in six-three or six-four—with long blond hair tied back with a piece of rope, wearing linsey-woolsey trousers and a homespun shirt? Gray-blue eyes and rugged looking. A commanding presence and knock-you-dead handsome.'' Since this was only a dream, she didn't mind rousting Cappy out of bed.

''Who is this?''

''Elizabeth.'' She rolled her eyes toward the ceiling. ''Cappy, this is important.''

''You're calling at four in the morning to ask about some guy you met at my party? And you think that's important?'' He hung up.

She phoned him back. ''This man was involved in an accident. I'm trying to find out who he is. So—did you see him.? Do you know his name? Cappy, please. Think!''

He yawned in her ear. ''I know everyone I invited, and Leland checked the invitations at the gate. If the guy you're describing was at the party, I'd know. He wasn't there. Go to bed, honey. Call the police and let them handle it.''

''I see.'' If the man on the beach wasn't dressed in costume for Cappy's party, then... But, no. She was dreaming. ''There isn't much more I can do until we can afford a trip to Spain. Maybe I'll take a couple of weeks off.''

He yawned again. ''Why are you asking my permission? You're an equal partner.''

''I'm in the middle of this dream, see, and—'' But she was talking into a dead phone.

Dazed, Elizabeth stumbled out onto the dark balcony and gulped fresh air, hoping it would wake her up.

She was fooling herself. She was as wide-awake as she had ever been. She wasn't a sleepwalker; she'd never had an hallucination. This might be a dream come true, but it wasn't a dream.

She peered toward the sea, frowning and biting her thumbnail. What if it were true? What if Capt. Richard Colter was the man in her guest room?

"Oh, my God!" She started violently and spun in a tangle of damp skirts. "The Valium!"

If that really was Richard Colter in her bedroom, she had just given him a couple of powerful drugs he had never experienced before. That's why he went out like a light.

"Oh, my God! I've killed him!"

Panicked, she ran back to the bedroom, her heart pounding as she flung herself on the bed beside him. Straining to hear over the pulse thundering in her ears, she shoved back her curls and pressed her ear against his chest and listened for his heartbeat, holding her breath.

When she heard his steady, strong pulse, she sagged against him. Thank God. He wasn't dead; he was just out cold.

Suddenly, hysterical laughter swelled in her throat. She was scared senseless about killing a man whom history insisted had been dead for two hundred years. After she fought back the laughter, she leaned over him and placed a trembling hand against his cheek. The light stubble covering his jaw felt slightly coarse against her palm.

"You're in for a hell of a ride, Capt. Colter." She smoothed back a strand of hair so blond it was almost white. "I don't know how you're going to cope with what's ahead of you."

His lips were wide and beautifully shaped, slightly parted. Bending, deliberately not thinking about what she was doing, she placed a kiss on his mouth. A tingle swept through her body.

Embarrassed by what she had done, Elizabeth moved away and curled into the chair next to his bed. "Elizabeth, my girl," she whispered happily, "you are about to begin the adventure of a lifetime!"

RICHARD WOKE AS THE SKY was fading from indigo to thin ribbons of pink. For several minutes he didn't move, pretending to be asleep, studying the room through his lashes.

There were peculiar items in this room, like the magic lamp. In fact, there were hundreds of things in this strange house that Richard didn't recognize. He couldn't even guess the function of many of the items he had glimpsed.

Finally his gaze came to rest on Mistress Rowley, asleep in the chair next to his bed. Even suffering a headache the size of a cannonball, he could appreciate her rare beauty. Not a single pox mark marred her lovely smooth skin. He couldn't recall when he had last encountered a woman who still had all her teeth at Mistress Rowley's age, which he guessed to be about eighteen because she had the firm, ripe body and the dewy freshness of a woman in her prime.

Her clothing identified her as lady of quality, yet she seemed to be alone with no protector in evidence. And her language—a strange form of English laced with something else—suggested she was educated, although the etiquette and custom appeared to be different here.

The real question was: Where was here?

Not for a moment did he believe Mistress Rowley's assertion that this was Florida. He knew Florida and this wasn't it. He was inclined to believe that he was dead and this place was—heaven? No, not heaven. But if not heaven, then what?

Hell? He didn't really think so, despite an uneasy suspicion that he might well deserve such an end. But he couldn't imagine hell's new arrivals being greeted by a beautiful woman possessing the most magnificent breasts he had ever glimpsed.

As he peeked at her breasts now, swelling above the curve of her low bodice, he felt himself stirring. She slept curled in the chair like a child, her cheek resting against one hand, her lips parted as if anticipating a lover's kiss.

Her voice returned to him, and with it a memory.

Jump! Come to me.

His ship was burning, sinking, his crew dead. Then he had heard her voice inside his head.

When he looked for the voice, certain he was losing his mind, he had witnessed an astonishment. Though late afternoon sun blazed above his dying ship, on the western horizon it was night. And in the shadows of that strange, unnatural night, he had glimpsed a shoreline where he knew no shore existed.

The night on the shore expanded, rushed toward him. And with it came a demon wind that plucked him from the deck of his burning ship and cast him into a vast dark, swirling tunnel. Wind howled in his ears; colors flared and blurred, searing his eyes. Faces and images flashed past him, too rapid to comprehend, so swiftly that his mind felt scalded by the effort to focus and understand.

At the very moment he thought his mind would burst, everything went black. An instant might have elapsed, or an age. The next thing he knew, beautiful Mistress Rowley was leaning over him, kneading his leg, her succulent breasts nearly spilling from her bodice. Because he felt an immediate onrush of lust for her, he had believed he was alive. Now he wasn't as certain.

Still, he could not quite bring himself to believe that bodies functioned normally in heaven or in hell. He ached all over. And he lusted after Mistress Rowley. Now he had to urinate. It didn't strike him as seemly that men would have to urinate in heaven. Therefore, he thought it likely that he was still alive.

This last urge drove him to lean over the side of the bed and fumble beneath the frame for a chamber pot. When he found none, he frowned at his hostess. She was a breathtakingly beautiful little chit, but she ran a slovenly house.

As he stepped into his breeches, he sniffed the air for a signal of breakfast. Even in the thick of incredible events, a man had to eat. When no scents of breakfast tickled his nostrils, he frowned again at Mistress Rowley. It was almost dawn; her cook should have been at the ovens by now.

A new thought occurred. Was Mistress Rowley wed? Jealousy tightened Richard's chest, hot and immediate, and he narrowed his eyes on her sleeping face. This woman was his. He claimed her. She had called to him and he had come. That made her his.

Stepping to her chair on silent cat feet, he examined her hand for a marriage band, wondering if he would have to kill a husband to have her. When he noticed her fingers were bare, he breathed a quiet sigh of relief. It wasn't that he shied from killing—he had killed a dozen men—but he had never challenged a man who had not injured him first.

Narrowing his eyes, he gazed at her face, absorbing the satiny smoothness of her skin, the rare perfection of her beauty. Bending, he placed a restrained kiss on the velvety swell of her breast, stroking her skin with the tip of his tongue. She made a tiny moaning sound in her sleep and shifted in the chair. One of her fat, dark curls brushed the back of his hand like gossamer.

His response was hard and immediate. He wanted her. For a long searing moment, he stared at her through narrowed eyes, tempted to wake her and claim her this minute.

But he had other compelling needs. And she was his. There would be time later.

ELIZABETH WOKE reluctantly, emerging from a deliciously erotic dream. She and Richard were naked on a warm tropical beach. He had been licking her breasts, making love to her.

Richard.

She came fully awake with a start, leaning forward and gripping the arms of her chair.

The bed was empty. He was gone.

A low wild sound broke from her throat. A freak rip in time had given her a few miraculous hours with him and like a fool she had wasted those hours sleeping. She snatched his shirt from the back of a chair and pressed it to her cheek, fighting tears. Then she noticed his breeches were missing. And the bedroom door was open.

She rushed through the house, looking into each room before she ran outside onto the back balcony and leaned over the railing.

The sky was a deep pearly blue, a few stars still lingered. But there was enough light that Elizabeth saw him at once. An intense joy squeezed her heart and relief collapsed her shoulders. For a moment she could not speak, she could only stare at him, Enthralled by the miracle before her.

He stood with his naked back to her, his heavy legs bare beneath his breeches. The first streaks of dawn gave a golden cast to his profile and to his hair which had dried in a tangled halo that curled around his shoulders.

Then she noticed what he was doing and her eyes widened in shock. He was relieving himself on the exposed roots of the banyan tree.

Chapter Three

"Stop that at once!" Elizabeth shouted angrily, leaning over the railing. "What's the matter with you?"

"Stop what?" He looked over his shoulder with a puzzled expression.

"That! What you're doing!"

He gave her a look that suggested she had lost her senses. "I shall, madam, the instant I've finished."

By the time Richard had buttoned his fly, Elizabeth realized her mistake. Except for the mirror, Richard Colter would not recognize a single item in a modern bathroom. This miracle had complications she had not yet thought of. "I'll be right back," she called to him, then returned to the kitchen. While she brewed a pot of coffee, her mind raced over the problems ahead. Slightly dazed, she gazed around her kitchen, noticing the microwave, the telephone, the radio. The toaster, the coffee maker, the refrigerator. "Oh, boy," she said softly, shaking her head.

Trying to hold her fingers steady Elizabeth filled two mugs, then carried them down to the beach. Twice she almost fell over the bedraggled hem of the costume from last night. Very soon she simply had to find a few minutes to shower and change.

But not yet. These first few minutes were fragile and crucial for Richard. He would require a lot of help and understanding to comprehend what had happened to him. As if Elizabeth understood it herself.

"Captain?" Even now it surprised her when he responded and turned to face her. This was all so incredible. She handed him the coffee mug with a shaking hand and gestured toward a wooden bench near the wild orchid tree. "We need to talk."

After she seated herself and smoothed down her voluminous skirts, Richard sat beside her. He raised his coffee mug, then made a face.

"Is it too hot?" she asked.

"What is this dreck?" He frowned into his mug.

"Haven't you had coffee before?"

A look of disdain suggested she had insulted him. "Of course I've had coffee, gel. I'm not some rustic gudgeon. But none as pallid as this." Disapproval hardened his eyes to a steely color. "'Tis fortunate ye be a beauty, Mistress Rowley, as your accomplishments leave much to be desired."

"I beg your pardon?" Elizabeth blinked, unsure whether to take offense or admire his arrogance. He wasn't twenty-four hours in his new world, and already he was criticizing her as if that were somehow his obligation. Her eyes narrowed and a sharp retort sprang to her tongue. But she bit it off, reminding herself that this was no ordinary man and these were not ordinary circumstances.

"I sniff no breakfast, Mistress. It appears your cook is still lying abed." His expression stated this deplorable lapse was Elizabeth's fault. "Moreover I found no chamber pot in me quarters. Whilst it may appear unseemly to complain of your hospitality, I feel a duty to call these faults to your notice."

"And I thank you for it," Elizabeth said between her teeth. "However, I employ no domestics and we don't use chamber pots in this age. As for the coffee, next time I'll make it stronger."

His eyebrows soared. "Ye have no servants? And 'e don't use chamber pots? What manner of civilization is this?"

Elizabeth drew a breath, immediately conscious that doing so called his attention to the sudden swell of her breasts above her idiotic corset. "What I am about to tell you is going to be very difficult for you to believe."

It happened in a flash. One moment they were sitting at a comfortable distance on the bench, the next instant he had caught her roughly by the waist and pulled her to her feet in a crushing embrace. His mouth covered hers in a hard, passionate kiss that stunned Elizabeth and seared her to her toes.

His action was so unexpected that Elizabeth had no chance to resist. His mouth was suddenly on hers, hard and demanding, and she no longer possessed the will to resist. There was nothing gentle or tentative about his kiss. His lips bruised hers, hungry and urgent. His large hands cupped her buttocks and pressed her tightly against his growing erection.

Never had Elizabeth experienced anything like this. Aside from her own whirling senses, she felt from Richard a hot, raw passion uncomplicated by personalities or agendas. This was sheer lust, an explosion of attraction and desire. The impact was powerful and utterly physical. She experienced his rock-hard naked chest crushing the tops of her breasts like a sheet of fire. Felt his powerful hands holding her helpless against the heat of his erection. His mouth devoured hers as if he could not taste her deeply enough, as if his hunger for her was overwhelming and limitless.

Elizabeth's pulse thundered in her ears, her blood zinged through her body and inflamed her secret parts. She felt his hands cupping her buttocks, felt his heat scalding her. Her lips parted, opening to his exploration. While his mouth plundered hers, she couldn't think, she could only feel and ache and want. It was the most totally physical moment of her life.

Only the knowledge that she was seconds from surrendering brought her to her senses. The realization scared the hell out of her.

The instant he released her buttocks to caress her breasts, she spun from his reach, panting for breath, feeling hot blood pulsing in her cheeks. If she didn't stop this right now, she was lost. Her hand came up and she slapped him hard across the face.

"We are not animals, Captain Colter! I'll thank you to control yourself and remember your manners!"

He stood facing her, legs wide apart, his breathing labored. "Ye belong to me," he said in a hoarse voice, his eyes glittering on her. A shaft of early sunlight struck his head and chest and turned his hair to burnished gold. He looked like a half-naked pirate king, powerful and confident of his authority. His white gold hair flew around his bronzed face like a lion's mane. "Ye called me and I came. You're mine."

Elizabeth wet her lips and lifted trembling hands.

"Don't come any closer. I did call to you, but I don't know if my thoughts are what brought you here. Right now, you should just cool down. We have a lot to talk about."

God, he was sexy. Just looking at him made Elizabeth's limbs feel like limp straw. Plus, he didn't appear to be paying attention to what she was saying. Those smoky gray-blue eyes focused on her breasts. Drawing herself up on her toes, Elizabeth fought down a wave of weakness and glared at him, still feeling the heat of his kiss on her lips.

She spoke the first words that came into her mind. "Do you intend to repay my hospitality by raping me, sir?"

That got his attention. His gaze flew to her face and he scowled. His chin rose and jutted. "Capt. Richard Colter has never raped a woman in his life, madam!" Pride flared behind his eyes. "If I have offended 'e, I offer my apologies." This said, he leaned into a bow. "But I meant what I said. Ye belong to me."

"I am not chattel, Captain, I don't *belong* to—" But she bit off the words. There would be time for this later. Drawing a breath, Elizabeth seated herself again on the bench and pointed to a spot on the marl. "You sit there."

After a pause he sat on the marl, but not where she had indicated. His scowl stated that no woman dictated where he would sit. He drew his bare knees up and rested his bandaged forearm against them. The sun cleared the horizon in a burst of light as he touched his fingertips to the Band-Aids on his forehead.

"Where is this place?"

"I've told you. This is Key West, Florida. You may know it by the Spanish name of Cayo Hueso, the Island of Bones." After first lifting a hand to shield her bosom, Elizabeth drew another deep breath. "The real question is—*when* is this?" She tried to keep her face expressionless. "Captain, this is 1992. You've jumped forward two hundred years in time."

"Liar," he said flatly. "'Tis not possible."

"Wait here." After thinking a moment, she jumped up and ran up the staircase and into the house. After a moment she returned with a stack of newspapers and a handful of postdated envelopes. And a towel to cover her cleavage.

He inspected the dates on the newspaper, then the envelopes. "What manner of devil sorcery is this?" he whispered, his face white in the early light. "Are ye a witch?"

She tried to explain without referring to Einstein. For the next twenty minutes Elizabeth spoke earnestly about windows in time, of inexplicable rents in the fabric of logic. Finally she explained that in this era, the idea of traveling in time was fascinating but not amazing, not incredible.

"This . . . this time jump has happened before?" he asked in a low, raw voice that she scarcely recognized.

"I don't know," Elizabeth said after a minute. She longed to reach a hand to comfort him, but she didn't know if he would interpret such a gesture as an invitation to grab her again.

For several minutes neither of them spoke. Then Richard rose gracefully to his feet and strode to the edge of the water. Elizabeth remained on the bench beside the orchid tree, respecting his desire for privacy. She could not imagine his thoughts or feelings. If something this stunningly incredible had happened to her could she have accepted it and adjusted? She didn't know. She looked at the hard muscles flexing on his shoulders, at the rigid walls of the valley marking his spine, at the twitch in his jaw, and her heart went out to him.

His voice carried in the early morning stillness. "Will it happen again? Will I go back...will I ever see me home again and me own time?"

"I'm sorry, but...I don't know."

His body was so taut and hard with tension that he resembled a statue. The illusion shattered as he waded into the sea until water lapped the buckles closing his knee breeches. Raising his arms, he shook his fists toward the sunrise, tilted back his head and a great formless bellow burst from his chest. Elizabeth shivered and covered her face with her hands. Never would she forget the anguish in that cry.

"Richard..." Lifting her skirts, she started toward him, but her voice was drowned by the roar of an engine.

A dune buggy shot around a curve in the north shoreline, shattering the early morning silence. It hurtled toward them, spraying sand and powdered limestone behind the wheels. A bikini-clad girl tossed her flying hair and laughed at the man behind the wheel.

Richard spun in a half crouch and froze. His hands dropped to his sides and tightened convulsively. His eyes flared then narrowed. Then he whirled and sprinted out of the water toward Elizabeth. Catching her on the run, scooping her into his arms as if she weighed no more than paper, he hardly broke stride as he ran toward the sheltering branches of the wild orchid tree.

"Hide yourself!" he commanded as he set her on her feet and wheeled to face the on-racing dune buggy. His hands opened and closed as if searching for a weapon, then he cursed and ran forward to confront the vehicle with nothing but his fists.

"Richard!" Good God. He intended to protect her by doing battle with a dune buggy. If it hadn't been so outlandish, the scene might have been hysterically funny.

But it was not funny. As Richard Colter positioned himself between her and the oncoming monster, Elizabeth understood she was witnessing a display of courage such as she had never imagined. Knots of concentration rose like stones along his jaw; his mouth was a hard, determined slash across his lower face. Defenseless and surely frightened half out of his wits, he waited to fight what must have seemed like a vision out of hell.

Grabbing up her skirts, Elizabeth dashed past him and into the path of the dune buggy which swerved to avoid her.

"This is a private beach," she shouted. "Dune buggies are prohibited!"

The bikini-clad girl stood and gripped the windshield. "Sorry, dudes, we didn't know. Hey, that's a max costume." With a cheery wave, she sat down and the dune buggy veered into a tight wheelie then roared back down the beach the way it had come, shooting sand, spray and laughter behind it.

Richard grabbed her from behind, spun her into his arms and crushed her against him. Elizabeth felt the tremble in his thighs and arms.

"Never in me life have I witnessed such valor!" His hands flew over her hair, her face, her upper arms, gentle now, as if seeking reassurance that she had emerged unharmed.

"You were the brave one." She marveled at the courage required to face something so utterly incomprehensible and foreign to his experience.

Still holding her tightly, his tremors beginning to subside, he frowned at the retreating dune buggy. "What sort of hellish place is this? Is there no way we can escape?"

"We?" Then she understood. Of course. It was her costume. Because Elizabeth was gowned like the women of his time, he believed she too had slipped through a time warp.

Reaching, she gently framed his face between her hands and made him look at her. "I know it seems to you as if the *Black Cutter* was attacked and sunk only hours ago. But it was two hundred years ago. You must accept that. This is a different world from the one you knew." She met his eyes. "But this is my world. This is my time. What I'm wearing is a costume from an age long past. I belong here."

His arms dropped away as if her skin scalded his fingertips. "I don't understand," he whispered.

"I don't either," she said softly. "All we can do is accept. And go on from there." Her gaze flicked toward the house, but there were too many things inside that would only confuse and frighten him. It was too soon. "Look, wait here. I'll bring some toast and more coffee."

"I'll have a tankard of porter. Or rum."

"I have some rum."

He pulled a hand through his hair, still staring up the beach.

When she returned, he was standing where she had left him, facing the houses along the shore, his head tilted to watch an airplane curving out over the gulf.

"It's a flying machine," Elizabeth said helplessly. Suddenly she felt inadequate for her role.

Richard gave her a dazed nod, as if a flying machine made perfect sense, then he swallowed a long pull directly from the neck of the rum bottle.

"You must have a million questions," Elizabeth said, seating herself on the bench near the wild orchid tree. "Where do you want to begin?"

"With ye, gel," he said, surprising her. "Why are 'e alone here? Where are your elders?"

"My parents live in Seattle. That's a large city on the north west coast. I live alone."

This information appeared to shock him. "You're too young a miss to—"

"I'm twenty-eight," she said, smiling. "Three years younger than you."

"Twenty-eight?" He stared at her in disbelief. "I mistook 'e for a wench in her prime!"

Elizabeth drew herself up and scowled. "I am in my prime, thank you."

"Are ye a widow, then?"

"I've never been married."

"But ye live alone?" Shock and disapproval compressed his brow. "Your sire should be put to the lash for allowing 'e to damage your name! Ye have no male kin besides your father?"

"My uncle Cappy lives in Key West. But not with me," she added. "Captain, there's no disgrace in a woman living alone."

"Bloody hell, there isn't!"

"I have an inheritance from my grandparents, which I invested in my uncle's business. I support myself." She met his gaze. "I prefer to live alone."

Something shifted behind those stunning gray-blue eyes. Elizabeth sensed his opinion of her was undergoing a reevaluation. She didn't know whether that was good. He started to say something, changed his mind, then asked, "If this time wizardry is true, then you'll know what happened to Louie?"

"Louie?"

"When I put into Sainte Domingue last week, I learned the French king had been imprisoned."

"King Louis XVI and his wife, Marie Antoinette, were both beheaded."

"The lunatic French murdered their king?" He blinked, then swore. "That is wrong," he said flatly. "We didn't murder old George." After a moment, he turned to her again. "Did Washington build his federal city on the Potomac?"

"Yes. It's called the District of Columbia, or Washington, D.C."

"Excellent! I own some of that ground. I'll wager I see a smart profit!"

They looked into each other's eyes, then Elizabeth said softly, "I'm sorry, Richard. I know how hard this must be for you." They sat in silence for several minutes. Sunlight flashed along the rum bottle as he raised it to his lips. "Perhaps you could use a few minutes alone. And I need to change." She watched his bare toes pushing at the marl, the only indication of the turbulence he must be feeling. "I'll be back in a few minutes."

Richard studied the sway of her hips as she walked away from him, gracefully holding her hem up from her ankles. The panic he felt at seeing her go irritated and embarrassed him. He resented feeling dependent on anyone. Yet without her beside him, he felt lost and queasy inside.

It also irritated him to realize how sorely he had underestimated her. She might keep a slovenly house and serve dreck for coffee, but by God she possessed more courage than any woman he had encountered. She had faced the naked devils inside the monster and ordered them to be gone. He had never seen anything like it.

On the negative side, it was distinctly possible that she was a bawd, he thought, trying to work it out. No respectable woman lived alone. Widows and spinsters engaged a live-in companion to protect their reputation. Since he was reluctant to believe she was a whore, he chose to blame the males in her family for her unwholesome circumstances. Her father and uncle had abandoned her. It didn't excuse them, but he thought it possible they were shamed that she was still on the shelf at her age.

Frankly her age and her spinsterhood amazed him. Were the men in this age blind? Mistress Rowley was a stunning beauty, with a ready dowry. He would have supposed she'd have no dearth of offers.

That is, unless she was a bawd with a sanded reputation. If so, that might explain why she couldn't keep servants. Even servants had their standards. He frowned and rubbed a hand over his face. Thinking about Mistress Rowley merely delayed consideration of his own mystifying situation.

That he had jumped ahead in time dazzled his brain, but it seemed as good an explanation as any for the aberrations he was witnessing. Already, he had observed enough peculiarities to suspect that Mistress Rowley might be telling the truth about time jumping.

If this were true, and if he could keep his nerve steady, he would experience some astonishing novelties before he returned to his own time.

In fact, it seemed likely that finding himself hurled into the future would be the most exciting, the most enlightening experience of his life. Surely only a fool would fail to take advantage of this marvel or would fail to observe every wonder and learn all it was possible to learn.

Such thoughts calmed him and immediately he felt better.

What tales he would have to tell when he returned! A smile curved his lips as he lowered the rum bottle and pushed the base into the marl. He tried to imagine his sister, Rachel's, expression when he described the magic lantern and the metal bird. He would cause a stir, all right.

As he didn't know when he might return, and Mistress Rowley didn't know either, it occurred to him that he hadn't a moment to waste. The wind and the tunnel might snatch him up at any moment and fling him back into his own time. Therefore, it behooved him to learn all he could as swiftly as he could.

And there was Mistress Rowley to sweeten his sojourn....

IT WAS DIFFICULT TO SAY who was more surprised. Elizabeth, at finding Richard unexpectedly exploring the kitchen, or Richard, when he spied her jeans and hot pink tank top. They both gasped, as Elizabeth came around the counter into the kitchen.

"Madam!" Outrage darkened his face and stiffened his frame. "Ye will return to your chamber at once and clothe yourself decently!"

"What are you doing?" He had located the kitchen knives and had thrust one through his waistband. But it was the appliances that riveted her attention. The blender was whirring furiously. The mixer was clattering around an empty bowl. The toaster had begun to smoke. "Stop pushing buttons and levers. I'll explain everything in good time, okay?" She stepped past him, hastily shutting things off.

He caught her by the upper shoulders, turned her around and none too gently propelled her toward the door. "Consider if someone should glimpse ye clad as 'e are! Wearing undergarments above and a man's trousers below! Fie on ye, madam! I order 'e to clothe yourself proper at once, do you hear? At once!"

"Wait a minute." Placing her hands on her hips, Elizabeth leaned forward from the waist. "Did I hear you correctly? You *order* me? Nobody orders me, Captain. And nobody tells me how to dress in my own house, got that? For your information, I'm dressed perfectly respectably. Things have changed. The sooner you get used to that idea, the better."

He ran a swift disapproving scowl over her breasts, then down the length of her tight-fitting jeans. "Ye be naked for all that's left to a man's imagination! Now get 'e gone and dressed proper! We'll discuss this no further, madam."

Elizabeth sputtered. The last time someone had used that tone to her, she had been a grade schooler. "This is proper!"

"No, madam, it is not proper!" Indignation flamed in his eyes and his shoulders swelled. His pale hair stood out around a thunderous face. "I'll not be standing here chatting up a wench who looks for all the world like a cabin lad! Ye'll clad yourself decently or I'll dress 'e proper meself!"

There was not an iota of doubt that he meant what he said. Furious, Elizabeth retreated a step as he advanced toward her. She raised a hand.

"All right, Captain. You win this round. But I'm only humoring you." She hoped he understood that point. "But while we're discussing dress, you're not too properly clad yourself. Is it considered polite where you come from to wander around a lady's house dressed only in your breeches?"

He cast a quick involuntary glance at his naked chest, and a dark flush infused his face. "I apologize," he said stiffly.

"I should think so," she said, rubbing it in.

But politeness had little to do with Elizabeth's desire that he put on his shirt. The truth was, she couldn't keep her gaze away from the soft hair that covered his chest like a golden carpet. And when she looked at his naked shoulders, she mentally visualized spreading her fingers across the heavy muscle there.

They both turned to the door at the same time and entered the living room. Elizabeth thought he had continued to follow her down the hallway until she glanced over her shoulder and saw he had stopped in front of her sofa and was inspecting the crossed swords mounted above it. She retraced her steps.

"I found those swords on my second wreck dive," she explained, nodding up at them. "They belong to Cappy's museum, but Cappy lets me keep them here."

"They're ruined. No man with eyes in his head would keep swords like those. They aren't worth a tinker's sneeze."

"They're valuable artifacts. Besides, no one carries a sword anymore." She glanced at the kitchen knife stuck through his waistband. "Or a dagger or a knife."

His lip curled. "Men don't fight here?"

"I wish the world had changed that much, but it hasn't. Men still fight, but not with swords." She gave him a little push toward the guest room. "Stay put. Don't move until I come for you."

In her own room she contemplated a closet filled with clothing her guest would consider scandalous. Finally she chose a floor-length terry robe, and tied it at the waist.

"Don't say a word," she cautioned when she leaned into the guest room. "This is the best I can manage"

He stared at her. "Don't ye have underthings?" His hands stirred the air, indicating hooped petticoats.

"I assure you I am wearing underthings." This was a ludicrous conversation. "What are you doing?" He was standing inside the guest-room closet, examining a hanger and a few items of clothing. "Didn't you have closets?"

He rubbed his jaw. "I don't suppose 'e have a razor and a strap, do ye?" he asked, testing the stubble thickening on his cheeks. "I suppose not."

"I have a razor. And an extra toothbrush. Which reminds me . . ." She took his hand, her fingers disappearing within his large palm. "Come across the hall. I want to explain the bathroom."

She led him inside and waited while he inspected himself in the mirror, bending to examine the Band-Aids on his forehead. Then she directed his attention to the shower and toilet and explained their functions.

"Would you like to sample the shower?"

"Aye," he said promptly, pulling off his shirt.

As she was already aware of his lack of inhibitions, Elizabeth hastily withdrew as he reached for the loops on the fly of his breeches. "I'll fix us some breakfast. Oh, wait." Lifting his hand, she squirted shaving cream into his palm then pushed his palm against his cheek and demonstrated a safety razor. "Understand?"

"Ye made claim no man resided here." He studied the razor and shaving cream, then leveled a glare at her.

"The razor and shaving cream are mine." When he didn't look enlightened, she added, "I use them to shave my legs and underarms."

Astonishment arched his thick eyebrows. "Why would 'e do a damned fool thing like that?"

The news about hemlines staggered him.

"First women must have wigs as high as the sky, now they display shaved legs like shameless doxies."

He seemed perfectly prepared to shuck down his pants with her standing there watching, but Elizabeth wasn't. She glimpsed a flash of firm white buttocks before she hastily backed out of the bathroom door. "See you in a few minutes."

When she passed through the living room, she paused to look at the mounted swords. How many times had she studied them and thought of Richard Colter? Now he was here. The reality of it staggered her. As did the sheer physical impact of Richard Colter.

Thinking about his kiss sent a shiver down her spine. Never had she been so aware of a man's physical characteristics. Nor did she think she had ever been in the presence of such raw, unadulterated passion. After he kissed her on the beach, she had understood the word lust for the first time, a blind, unreasoning passion that depended solely on sensation and physical presence. Thought didn't enter the picture, nor did personalities. Lust was solely chemical, a deep hunger in the cells. It had very nearly overwhelmed her.

Shaking her head, Elizabeth went to brew a fresh pot of coffee, making it much stronger than she usually did. While she was rummaging in the fridge for bacon and eggs she thought she heard the front door open and close, but she decided she was mistaken as the shower was still running.

Then the front door banged open and she heard running footsteps. Half panicked, she hurried into the living room to find Richard standing on the sofa, wrenching one of the swords from its mounting.

"What—?"

"Snake!" he shouted as he dashed past her, the sword in his hand. "The biggest bloody damned snake I ever saw. Stay here!"

But of course she didn't. Jerking up the hem of her robe, she ran after him, down the steps and into the front yard, stopping near the mimosa tree.

"Damn it, woman! Don't ye ever do as you're told? Stand back!"

Raising the sword, he swung it again and again, sawing the ruined blade across the snake, then dashing forward to attack again.

"Richard." Elizabeth stepped forward. "This isn't a snake."

"Bloody hell, it isn't!" Wiping the sweat from his eyes, he hacked away. "Where's the head of this scurvy thing?" He swore. "I wouldn't believe the size of this viper if I hadn't witnessed it with me own bloody eyes!"

Elizabeth approached from the left, away from the swinging sword. Raising her hand, she held up a severed section of garden hose. "This is a tube for carrying water to the grass and flowers. Look at it. There's no blood, no meat inside. This is not a snake, Captain."

Gingerly he touched the section of hose, then held it to his eye and peered through it.

Gazing at him, Elizabeth took a deep breath then swallowed hard. Even fencers didn't wield a sword as gracefully or naturally as he did. He stood before her, large, powerful, his hair wet from the shower, looking like a magnificent figure from an historical film. Suddenly she experienced a deep bite of jealousy, thinking of the female attention he would garner. Women were going to flock all over her captain.

"Ye must think me a fool."

"No," she said, studying his pale face. "I hope I would cope as well, if I were suddenly transported two hundred years into the future." But she couldn't help it, she choked on a bubble of laughter.

His smoky eyes narrowed and he looked down at her. "Have a care, Mistress Rowley," he warned in a soft voice. "I'll not be mocked."

"I'm not laughing at you." But of course she was. She grinned up at him. "It was courageous of you to...to..." She couldn't hold it in. A great gust of laughter doubled her over. "You killed my garden hose! God, I never saw anything so funny." Even when she noticed the dark flush of embarrassment staining his cheeks, she couldn't restrain the gusts of laughter.

The flat of his sword swung hard against her bottom.

Elizabeth yelped in shock and almost toppled over. Straightening, her hands flying to her bottom, she spun and glared at him in disbelief. "You struck me!"

"Aye, madam, that I did. If 'e laugh at me again, I'll tip 'e over me knee and teach ye some manners!"

"*What?*"

Furious, Elizabeth strode over to him and grabbed a handful of his shirt. Stretching up on her tiptoes, she jerked his shirt until his nose came down almost on a level with hers.

"Listen to me, you brute," she said into his face. "Who the hell do you think you are, anyway? I'm going to tell you something and you had better listen. In this day and age, men don't smack women, don't spank them, don't discipline them. Do you understand that?"

"Are ye claiming men don't cuff a wench even when she deserves it?" He returned her furious stare. "If so, it appears a few items have not changed for the better."

"If you lift a hand to me again, I swear I'll rip your heart out and feed it to you!"

Grinning, he straightened and expanded his chest, breaking her grip on his shirt and emphasizing the difference in their size and strength. Elizabeth was petite enough that she could have walked beneath his chin, and few men could match his strength, let alone her.

But this was an issue of dominance, not of size or strength.

"Ye'll rip me heart out." His grin widened.

"You have to sleep sometime, buster," she warned, measuring him with her gaze. "If I were you, I'd keep in mind who knows the ropes here—and who doesn't!"

"You're not dealing with a thickheaded Frenchman, madam. I'll find me sea legs soon enough."

"For your sake, I hope so!" Turning on her heel, she tossed her head and strode toward the front door. "Breakfast will be ready soon. And put that sword back where you found it."

Several minutes passed before he followed her inside. And he hadn't replaced the sword. He kept it at his side.

"I fancy the food is prepared now," he said, sitting at the table. Elizabeth sat across from him and started to eat.

"Mistress Rowley!"

"Yes?" She paused, her fork halfway to her mouth.

"Haven't 'e forgotten something?"

She had poured the juice and the coffee, filled their plates. They had silverware and napkins, which she noticed he had tucked into his shirt collar. "What?" she asked, frowning.

His heavy brows came together in the expression of disapproval that was beginning to annoy her. With a small, guilty twinge of satisfaction, she noticed he had nicked himself shaving.

"Has the land reverted to paganism?"

"Make your point, Captain."

"We'll say grace, if ye please."

"For breakfast?" She blinked.

"Of course." He gave her a censorious glance, then bowed his head and folded his hands against his forehead. "Thank 'e, Lord, for sharing thy bounty and for the nourishment of our bodies, amen." At the conclusion, he frowned at her. "Are ye a scurvy papist?"

"I'm a protestant." Though not a practicing one. But she didn't think it politic to mention that right now.

"Thank heaven," he said, stirring his eggs around his plate. "I'm not a man to hold another man's faith against him, but I confess I'm relieved I haven't fallen in with a papist."

He drank a pitcher of juice, consumed half a loaf of toasted bread, ate everything on his plate and half of what was on hers. At the finish he leaned back in his chair and beamed at her.

"Mistress Rowley, me sweet, a man can face the worst on a full belly. Ye have a dismaying number of faults, but you're a fine woman to look at and 'e have a kind if overly spirited heart. I'm grateful for the bed and board, and I'll be grateful for whatever learning ye choose to share. I wager we'll rub along just fine, mark my words.''

She looked at him, recognizing a splendid, glorious optimism. He was breathtakingly handsome with the sun streaming in on his thick hair and bronzed face. "Oh, Richard," she said softly.

He had no idea what an anachronism he was. He sat there looking at her with those smoldering eyes, magnificently innocent of the shocks in store, wildly appealing with the silly Band-Aids on his wide forehead.

Already he irritated her, upset her, enchanted her, excited her, and drove her a little bit crazy. He believed she had somehow wished him here, and who was to say? Maybe she had.

" 'Tis as propitious a time as any to inquire if 'e be a whore, Mistress Rowley," he said in a pleasant and curious voice.

"What?"

"Are ye?"

"Of course not!"

"Then t'would be correct to assume 'e don't be diseased?"

"Diseased?" Elizabeth repeated, "Diseased?"

"The French pox," he explained.

Color soared in her cheeks. "Not that it's any of your business, but I most certainly do *not* have any sexually transmitted diseases!" She glared at him. "Do you?"

"Nay, praise God."

Elizabeth shook her head. Her mind was spinning at this blunt and curiously modern exchange of intimate information. Some concerns hadn't changed in two hundred years.

"And 'e don't be promised or bespoke, do that be correct?"

"I'm not engaged—betrothed—or anything like that, if that's what you're asking."

"'Tis true, then. Ye belong to me," he said happily. Immediately his gaze narrowed and she watched tiny pinpoints of desire kindle in his smoky eyes.

When he made a grab for her, Elizabeth decided it was a distinct possibility that she'd be wishing him back to his own time before this was over.

Or maybe not, she thought helplessly as his lips claimed hers and he crushed her hard against his body before she could push him away.

Chapter Four

"I'm going alone, and that's the end of it." Elizabeth glared at him.

It was mid-afternoon of his third day in the twentieth century and they were arguing. Again. Her voice was hoarse from all the disagreements and discussions they'd had in the past two days.

Richard strove mightily for patience, following her out of the kitchen and into the living room. "'Tis not proper for ye to travel unaccompanied."

She tossed back her hair, threw out her hands and rolled her eyes to the ceiling. "We don't have a choice here. I need groceries; you need clothes; we both need a break. I'm going alone and I don't want to discuss it anymore."

Richard watched as she collected her purse and something called a checkbook.

"Mistress Rowley, someone should scald your behind, then lock 'e in your chamber." His furious expression announced who that someone ought to be.

She straightened and her dark eyes turned stony. "If you try any strong-arm tactics, Captain, you'll be out of here so fast it will make your head spin. You thought your wind tunnel was upsetting? It was nothing compared to what I'll do to you if I have to."

She was such a feisty and spirited little chit, Richard thought. And so beautiful when she was angry. Her skin flushed a becoming pink, her earthy brown eyes flashed with vibrancy. She planted her hands on the curve of her hips, her shoulders squared and her breasts aimed at him like twin soldiers. He mocked her stance and clamped his brows down tight.

"Under no circumstances do ladies of quality go about unaccompanied. Fie on ye, madam. I cannot grasp your thinking. You're fair begging a blackened name. Nay, I absolutely forbid ye!"

"You *forbid* me?" She covered her eyes with one hand and leaned against the door, shaking her head. "I never realized how much the poor women of your time are to be pitied. Look, the days of requiring a chaperon are long gone, thank God."

What frustrated him to no end was that he was willing to offer his protection, willing to do what he could to salvage her tarnished name, yet she refused redemption. He was beginning to think she reveled in flaunting the rules of decency.

"Does your uncle, Mr. Haleburton, have a wife?"

"I beg your pardon?"

"A wife. An older woman to serve as your companion."

"I just told you that I don't need a companion!"

"This subject raises a delicate matter of some urgency." He tugged at his collar, trying to conceive a tactful way to broach an issue that had troubled him since his arrival. "It would be exceedingly wise, madam, to invite your aunt to stay with 'e."

"I have no aunt. Cappy was divorced years ago. Why would I want someone here anyway?"

Elizabeth Rowley continued to shock him. Civilization lay on her like a thin veneer that had failed to penetrate. To address her as a lady of quality was to flatter her, as she enjoyed but a fleeting acquaintance with respectability.

"Because," he said, patiently explaining the obvious, "ye are now sharing your quarters with a man unrelated to ye." Not a flicker of remorse for this transgression appeared in her expression. Had she no sense of decency at all? "Damn it, woman. If 'e aren't concerned for your reputation, I am! What will your neighbors think? What will your kin say when our present circumstance falls to their attention? 'Tis me obligation as a gentleman to insist that 'e engage a companion at once."

And the sooner, the better. Every time he looked at her, he wanted to crush her in his arms and devour those soft red lips. He wanted to mold her voluptuous curves against his body and savor the womanly scent and heat of her. He wanted to take her and make her his own in deed as well as thought. And he knew she wanted it too.

He read her passion when she looked at him overlong. He felt the fire in her and a momentary yielding when he caught her to him. He heard her at night, as restless in her lonely bed as he was in his.

What he did not understand was the confusing signals she threw off. That her lust throbbed as powerfully as his own, he did not doubt. But whenever he pulled her into his arms, she resisted him. Her behavior was suspiciously reminiscent of a bawd trying to act the lady. Yet gut instinct insisted she had spoken the truth. She was not a bawd. But neither was she a lady. She was some hybrid breed he did not understand.

It had become imperative that a third party be present, if he was to respect her resistance. What Mistress Rowley did not appear to grasp was that she needed protection from him. He was a man of lusty appetites, not a saint. And despite her irritating ways, she was the most beautiful, the most excitingly strange, the most powerfully desirable woman he had ever encountered. Eventually her feeble objections would not be enough to restrain him from claiming what was his. Thinking about pinning her naked body beneath his thighs was enough to bring a slick of perspiration to his forehead.

"Don't look at me like that," she protested in a faint voice. Her small pink tongue flicked out to wet her lips.

"I beg 'e, madam. Engage a companion at once." His voice was thick with desire. The denim pants she insisted on wearing hugged her thighs and curved snugly and suggestively over her ripe little buttocks. He could see every inch of her and the sight slicked his palms with moisture and dried his mouth. "Madam," he said hoarsely, "I warn ye. Your honor is in grave danger from me."

"Oh, Richard." Her sighing whisper made his groin ache with a powerful and immediate need. Her lips parted and he watched her breath quicken, her nipples hardening against the material of her shirt. But when he started toward her, she raised a shaking hand and her gaze pleaded. "Please don't. It's too soon for this kind of complication."

He stopped close enough that the pointed tips of her breasts almost brushed his chest. Such sweet torture made him groan.

"I will not force ye," he said in a low hoarse voice, raising his fingertips to stroke her cheek. She closed her eyes and gulped a breath of air. "The decision is yours."

"Richard, please. I have a thousand errands. I have to go."

He placed his hands against the door on either side of her. "Do 'e deny ye want me too, Mistress Rowley?" Her perfume reeled through his senses, filed his nostrils with the intoxication of musk and roses. The heat of her small body radiated against him, embraced him.

A tremble disturbed her lower lip. When she spoke, her voice was shaken and almost a whisper. "This isn't right, Richard. Please."

He sensed the vulnerability of the moment. It would be so easy to scoop her into his arms and carry her into the bedroom. Once there, he knew he could overcome her objections. He would caress her satiny skin and stroke the tender insides of her thighs. Experience promised that she would eventually gasp his name and beg him to claim her.

She ducked beneath his arm and darted away to stand in the middle of the living room. Her breath was rapid and shallow, her skin prettily flushed.

"Richard, stay where you are and listen to me. Sometimes when people argue, it's a form of stimulation. That's what's happening here." She ran her palms over the thighs of the denim pants. "No, please don't come any closer." A deep breath lifted her breasts beneath the thin material of her shirt. "Oh, God, I wish you wouldn't look at me like that. It makes me feel…"

"Feel what, Elizabeth?" His gaze ravaged her, plundered her secret places. In his mind's eye, he saw her spread beneath him, her dark hair thrashing across a pillow, her sweet body arching to meet his.

"You know damned well!" She spread her hands in a helpless gesture. "Richard, please. This isn't right. Don't you understand? Right now, what we're feeling is lust."

"I've felt ye tremble in my arms. I've felt your breath hot on my cheeks and mouth. I've felt ye straining against me."

"But we don't know each other yet. If we fell into bed now, all we'd be doing is scratching an itch."

"The itch grows powerful, Mistress Rowley," he said huskily, looking at her. "For the sake of your honor, engage a companion. At once. Even a gentleman can be tempted beyond his control."

"I'd feel like a fool hiring a baby-sitter for us. Surely we can handle this situation by ourselves."

"Can we?" His eyes boldly traveled up her body, pausing at the sweet cleft where her thighs joined, lingering on the breasts shaped by her shirt.

Taking a step backward she studied him for a moment, then she turned on her heel, approached a square piece of furniture in the corner of the room and twisted a tiny knob.

What happened next shocked Richard to the core. It frightened the wits out of his head and paralyzed him. He dropped into a crouch, but stood rooted to the floor staring at tiny people in a box. Speech and music swelled out of thin air.

"This is television, Richard. I'm sorry to do this to you so abruptly, but we desperately need a change of subject." With that, she walked out the door.

It took every ounce of willpower he could summon not to collapse to his knees. But he thought his pounding heart would leap from his chest.

Richard considered himself a man of courage. But never had he faced a test such as this. Sweating, he forced himself to move, not taking his eyes from the people in the box. He stepped forward on legs turned to dough. He darted a look behind the television, searching for the people he saw framed in the box front. Sweat poured from him and his hands shook violently.

"'Tis the devil's work," he whispered when he could speak. When he glanced at the magic box, his stomach rolled in long nauseous loops.

He didn't dare look away from the people in the box for fear they might jump into the room.

After a time he realized Elizabeth had gone. He discovered the rum bottle and a pitcher of iced juice on the low table in front of him. And a bowl of peanuts. He poured a tumbler of rum to fortify him while he watched the events unfolding within the box. But it was only when he pulled a sword out of the mountings on the wall that he felt a mickle better.

Finally, his eyes fixed on the box, he sank to the sofa, the sword at his side.

AFTER ELIZABETH FINISHED her shopping, she drove toward Mallory Square, cruising past the *Sante Oro*, scanning its ornate decks for Cappy. She needed to talk to someone who had heard of the Industrial Revolution and the space shuttle. Someone who didn't regard a pair of toenail clippers and a roll of toilet paper as miraculous inventions.

"Hi stranger." Cappy waved her to a canvas chair when she appeared on the sun-washed upper deck of the *Sante Oro*. He poured her a glass of lemonade. "How goes the vacation?"

She studied his wrinkled face then sat down next to him. "You look as glum as I feel."

"It's been a long time between finds." Laying back in his deck chair, he closed his eyes against the sun. "Tim and Juan took one of the boats out this morning. They're dragging off the Marquesas. It's a waste of time. Everybody and his second cousin has run a magnetometer around the Marquesas. What's left to find?" He shrugged without opening his eyes.

"Plenty. If we knew where to look."

"Don't blame yourself, honey. I know I've got the best researcher in the business." He reached out a hand and patted her knee. "It's not your fault the budget didn't stretch enough for a trip to Spain."

"I have a little nest egg. I could finance the trip myself."

"There's personal money and there's company money. It's bad business to mix the two. Hang on to your savings, honey. Until the company can afford to pay for the trip, we're stuck. All we can do is trawl in the general area."

Elizabeth frowned. "I wish I could tell you exactly where the *Madre Louisa* sank, but I can't. I've narrowed the probable site to a twenty-mile square. That's the best I can do."

Twenty square miles of ocean floor was an enormous area. Hopelessly enormous without a lot of time and a huge streak of luck.

Cappy leaned back in his chair. "I'm thinking of running a few dive excursions when the tourists return after Thanksgiving. The money isn't great, but it'll pay the bills until we break out of this dry spell. Interested?"

"Sure. I'll help out. I don't mind the tourists."

"I wouldn't ask, if our finances weren't getting pretty tense."

"I know." She drew a breath, then released it, letting the hot sun bake away her tensions. Gulls wheeled overhead, flirting with a bottomless sky. A flotilla of brightly colored sails dotted the horizon. "Cappy, do you believe in time travel?"

A laugh boomed up from his toes. "How did we get from tourists to time travel?"

"Remember the night of your party? When I called about the man on the beach?" She told him the whole story, staring at the weathered masts of the *Sante Oro* while she spoke. He didn't interrupt and he let a silence develop when she finished speaking. "So? What do you think?"

"Honestly?"

"Honestly."

"A lot of strange things have happened out there." He nodded toward the waves. "And I'm not ruling out the possibility of time leaps. But it seems unlikely."

"You don't believe me."

"Honey, it's possible you're being had. Time travel makes an interesting storybook tale, but I doubt people like you and me are going to see an example in our lifetime. No offense, but this guy has found a mark and he's playing you for all it's worth. Didn't you tell me you just bought him a whole new wardrobe? The guy's a con man. Go home and boot him out of your house before he robs you blind."

"Cappy, I believe him. He really is Capt. Richard Colter, a privateer who sailed out of Boston two hundred years ago. I know how crazy this sounds, but I believe it's true."

"Elizabeth, honey, on the outside you're this kick-butt broad who doesn't take crap off of anybody. But inside, you're a sucker, soft as putty in the noonday sun. Everybody knows you've had a fixation on the *Black Cutter* and its captain. Somebody talked too much and your guy overheard the conversation. Bingo, he sees a way to get a free place to crash and maybe some easy money. All he has to do is look surprised at any modern convenience while you run up your charge cards."

"It isn't like that," she said defensively.

Cappy studied the conviction in her dark eyes. "This guy must be good."

"Not good—genuine." For a moment she floundered. "I know it sounds impossible, but Captain Colter jumped forward in time and landed on my beach."

"I know you want to believe that, but..." Reaching, he took her hand in his. "Elizabeth, there's nothing in this for you but a lot of hurt."

"I don't need a lecture, Cappy. I need help."

He shook his balding head. "Forget it. Look, I don't know how much longer I can promise a paycheck. Before we pull out of this slump you may need whatever you've saved to live on. I'd hate like hell to see some con man sweet-talk you out of your savings. Kick him out."

"He's damned near helpless. If I showed him the door, he'd get himself killed or thrown in jail. Right now he can't function in our world."

"Suppose for a minute that's true—is it your problem?"

"Somehow I'm involved in bringing him here. Don't look at me like I've lost my mind. I don't understand it either, but I know in my heart that it's true. I'm responsible for him."

"Good God." He stared at her. "You're falling in love with this jerk."

An embarrassed blush set her cheeks on fire. "I hope not. We're about as compatible as two warring tribes." She waved a hand. "The point is, eventually he's going to need a job. He's going to need papers—a social security card, a driver's license, that kind of stuff. I'm going to need help."

"You're an adult, Elizabeth. I have no right to run your life. But I don't have to help you make a big mistake." His mouth set in a line that no amount of argument would budge. "Don't bring that bastard around here. I might take a punch at him."

The image of Cappy, who was only a couple of inches taller than Elizabeth, taking a swing at Richard made her smile. But the smile didn't override the upset she felt about arguing with him. Usually she and Cappy saw eye-to-eye on everything.

By the time Elizabeth pulled into her driveway, she had forgiven Cappy for not believing Richard's story. It was a lot to swallow.

"I'm home," she called. "Would you mind giving me a hand with these packages?" There was no answer. "Richard?"

He was watching TV exactly as she'd left him. He had one of the swords beside him and he held the rum bottle between his legs. His eyes were reddened at the rims, as if he hadn't blinked.

"Richard—"

Immediately he leaned to see around her and pointed at the screen. "There 'tis again. That gel blathering about tampons. What in bloody hell are tampons? Those people talk about things without explaining what the bloody hell the things are! 'Tis enough to drive a bloke to apoplexy." He swallowed lustily from the rum bottle, not taking his gaze from the screen. "Sit, madam. I've a thousand questions for 'e."

"Let's turn this off. I want you to try on the clothing I bought, and—"

He plunged across the room the instant she turned off the TV. Having observed her motions, he was able to turn the television back on, inadvertently sending the volume skyrocketing until she adjusted it.

"Madam," he said, scowling. "I don't know what under God's heaven I'm seeing, but I know 'tis important I see it. I'll thank 'e not to interfere. I'm learning this world."

"It's not good for you to watch hours and hours of TV. Besides, I'd like you to try on some of these—"

"I know better than 'e what's good for me and what isn't." He returned to the sofa and the rum bottle. "Did you hear that? That bloke there is relating news from Europe. And it happened *today*." A stunned look made his eyes appear silver in the glare of the TV. "*Today*, madam. Think of it. In my time we wouldn't have had news of Europe for weeks. Nay, months."

"Would you care to explain why you're so quick to insist on me doing what you think is good for me, but not vice versa?"

"I'll have me supper here, if 'e please. One of the voices announced that King Larry intends to interview the Madonna."

She stared at him. "It's Larry King, not King Larry. And he isn't a king, that's just his name." She paused. "Richard, the Madonna that Larry King plans to interview is a singer. I know it seems like this century can produce miracles, but we can't conjure up the mother of Jesus."

He looked vastly disappointed, then stubbornly disbelieving. "I'll see for meself, if 'e don't mind."

THROUGHOUT THE NEXT three weeks, Richard watched nonstop television. He ate his meals in front of the TV, snatched a few hours sleep on the sofa. The only time he left his post was to grab a quick shower and shave, and for an hour each evening, which he spent plying Elizabeth with questions.

"Hi," she said as he stepped through the balcony doors and took the patio chair next to her. She noticed that tonight he wasn't carrying the notebook she had bought for him. He looked exhausted. "No offense, Captain, but you look awful."

His eyes were swollen and red-rimmed. Shadows lay like dark half-moons beneath his lower lashes. His wheat-colored hair hung to his shoulders in tangled curls and he needed a shave. As usual of late, he smelled of rum.

"I don't think I've ever known anyone who drank as much as you," she commented, frowning at the rum bottle he placed on the table between them. Yet he never seemed intoxicated. "Would you like a cup of coffee for a change? I bought a Cuban mix strong enough to please even you."

"Coffee," he repeated in a dull voice, watching the sun spray fans of brilliant color as it began to slip beneath the waves. "Hills Brothers, Folgers, Taster's Choice."

Elizabeth studied him for a moment, admiring the classic angles of his profile. "I'll make coffee. And there's some key lime pie left. Would you like another slice?"

"Mr. Coffee, Proctor Silex, Brewmaster. Pie: Mrs. Smith, Sara Lee—"

"Richard, are you all right?"

He looked up with eyes that resembled steel ball bearings. "I want to go home." Turning back to the sea, he stared at the sunset and his fingers gripped the arms of the patio chair so tightly that his knuckles gleamed white.

Elizabeth stood in the doorway, biting her lip. "I'm sorry," she said finally, speaking in a low voice. "I know all this must be strange and difficult for you."

"I want to wake in the mornings to the crack of sail straining beneath a brisk sea breeze. I want to sleep with only the creak of the hull and the watch bells to disturb my rest. There is no silence here and no stars overhead."

"Occasionally you can see stars. But sometimes the lights from the city—"

"Your town has odd oily smells. I miss the good earthy scent of horses and the corner stables. And the sweet tang of wood smoke from kitchen ovens. I miss the quarreling of pigs and hens and the ring of a rooster's crow in the morn. I want me pipe and Crowley's pub. I want to ride me gelding over the fields outside Boston and let the autumn wind blow this dream from me head."

Elizabeth moved to stand beside him. She dropped a hand to his shoulder and felt the tension knotting the rock-hard muscles beneath her palm. "I don't know what to say."

"Ye command a legion of machines in this world. They cook for 'e, clean for 'e, work for 'e, kill enemies for ye. Machines inform ye, amuse ye, entertain ye. They carry 'e through the air, up tall buildings, over roads crowded with other machines. Machines turn night into day, winter into summer."

"Machines have made life easier, more convenient."

He shook his head and swirls of golden hair brushed the back of Elizabeth's hand. "Where are the people? In the last weeks I have seen only ye and a few strangers on the beach. In my time this house would have been noisy and alive with people. A cook, a char, maids, a stable boy, a gardener. Merchants would rap at the door, vegetable carts would rattle in the street. Voices would pass beneath the windows hawking fish and strawberries and old clothing. Ladies would call and leave their cards. Gentlemen would arrive to pay their compliments."

"You've heard me talk on the phone. I'm in constant touch with Cappy and my friend, Kelly, and a lot of people."

"There were family gatherings on Sunday afternoon. And the peal of church bells. So many bells. And the food. Jack in hot hell! The food." He buried his head in his hands. "It tasted better. After dinner there would be brandy and cigars on the back porch or in the garden. And conversation that made spirits soar. Ah, but I miss the conversation! I wish ye might have heard Mr. Woodcock discourse on the future of America. There was an orator! None of your television speakers are worth a tuppence next to Mr. Woodcock."

"I wish I could have heard him," Elizabeth said softly.

He stared up at her, his gaze narrow and intense, his rugged features bathed in the dying rays of the sun. "I'm never going back, am I?"

"I don't know."

His arms circled her waist and he pressed his head against her breasts. She held him, feeling the tremor in his shoulders.

"Give this world a chance," Elizabeth said gently, caressing his hair, trying to offer some measure of comfort and knowing she failed. "Isn't there anything here that you like and approve of?"

Gradually his grip on her waist loosened and finally his arms fell away. A look of embarrassment tightened his expression and he averted his gaze.

"I like peanut butter and me new shoes," he said finally, looking down at his Nikes. When Elizabeth couldn't hold back a laugh, he smiled up at her. "I like the shower bath and the microwave oven. I like the air conditioning too."

"And the television," Elizabeth said, hoping to tease him out of this uncharacteristic funk.

"Aye."

"Richard," she said gently, again placing her hand on his shoulder. "For the past three weeks you haven't gotten more than two or three hours of sleep a night. Go to bed. Things will look better when you're rested."

Three weeks ago her hand on his shoulder would have been interpreted as a sign of encouragement and he would have grabbed her and pulled her into his arms. He might have kissed her with a passion that left her lips swollen for hours.

Now he covered her hand with his own, that was all. Elizabeth told herself she was not disappointed . . . they were making progress.

She stood beside him in the deepening darkness, watching the night descend and listening to the hiss of waves rolling up the shore, to a symphony of crickets singing courtship songs. From somewhere nearby came the smell of grilling chicken. Someone practiced scales on a piano that was slightly out of tune.

Richard stood and covered his eyes with his hand. "Mayhaps I shall retire as ye suggest, madam. If 'e will excuse me..."

"Richard, soon you'll feel as comfortable in this world as you did in your own." Elizabeth wondered if this were true. Would he ever feel truly at home in her world?

He looked at her from tired, reddened eyes. "I have never felt so inadequate in my life. Your world humbles me." He spoke in a hoarse whisper, making no effort to conceal his dejection and bewilderment. "Good night, Mistress Rowley."

"Good night, Richard." It amazed her that his arrogance had dwindled to the point that he could admit to feelings of inadequacy. Somehow the idea of a humble Richard Colter disturbed her greatly.

In the morning he was gone.

Chapter Five

The island was small. Even so, as Richard had discovered earlier, there was too much to see and digest in a single night of exploring on foot, although tonight he managed to cover a lot of ground.

The moon was nearly full again, casting enough light to observe streets and alleyways not reached by street lamps. The salt ponds that had covered most of the island were gone. As were the mangrove swamps that had choked and stunk up the shoreline. The shoreline was also different. Two centuries of storms and landfill projects had altered the shape of the island.

In the early predawn hours, he walked along the shopping district examining storefronts and inspecting goods offered for sale. Twice a police cruiser passed and instinct warned him to conceal himself. The weeks spent staring at the television had taught that a lone man carrying a sword in the middle of the night would likely be viewed as a suspicious character.

Eventually he located the wharves. Relief and pleasure overwhelmed him as he breathed the fragrant mixture of sea, salt and fish. This was familiar; this he understood.

He chose the simplest of the boats tied along the wharf, a wooden vessel no larger than an oversized dingy, and jumped into it. The moment he seated himself and experienced the gentle rocking motion of the water, he regained a fragile control over the chaos battering his mind. Being on the water had always soothed and nourished him, and it did so now.

Here, surrounded by darkness and the comfort of familiar smells and sounds, he let the images and miracles of the twentieth century drain out of his mind until he was left with nothing but a residue of shocks, jolts and the paralyzing nightmare of what had happened to him.

His early optimism had evaporated in the glare of the TV. What he experienced now was no longer a grand adventure, but an oppressive feeling of displacement. He had seen enough and had experienced enough to know he did not belong in this century.

In his time, Richard Colter had been a man of consequence, a learned gentleman, a man of honor and respect. He was listened to and his card was welcomed at every door. He had greeted each morn with the easy confidence of a man comfortable in his own skin and certain of his place in the world.

Here he was ignorant, tentative, a misfit. He had shamed himself by displaying fear toward items a woman viewed with indifference. His convictions were an object of amusement and scorn. He saw no niche for himself in this world and thus the value he placed on himself had begun to erode.

With all his troubled soul, he craved the reappearance of the demon wind and the mysterious dark tunnel. Had the tunnel opened before him, he would have stepped inside without hesitation. And if it were possible, he would take Mistress Rowley with him. She belonged to him, of this he had no doubt, but in his own time, where the world made sense and he understood his role in it.

He must have dozed, because when he again opened his eyes the sun glowed behind a high, pearly haze and someone on the wharf was shouting in an angry voice.

"Hey, I'm talking to you. What the hell you doing in my boat? Get your butt outta there!"

Richard's head jerked up and a rush of bile soured his mouth. The man standing on the wharf was a Spaniard.

His first instinct was to leap to the wharf and run the bastard through, cut his black heart out of his thieving body.. Before he reacted, he noted the man's ragged jeans and tight fitting T-shirt. The left sleeve was rolled up around a pack of cigarettes. A livid heart tattoo spread across the Spaniard's forearm enclosing the motto; Manuel + Rosa.

Grinding his teeth, Richard forcibly reminded himself that the Spaniard on the wharf was not one of the snarling cutthroats off the *Madre Louisa.*

"Are you deaf, man? That's my boat. Get the hell out, or you got bad trouble." The Spaniard puffed himself up and his gaze narrowed menacingly. "No one messes with Manuel Ortiz."

Richard's eyes narrowed and a thin smile played at the corners of his lips. This puny dog was trying to intimidate him. He almost laughed. "If you're looking for a fight, 'e scurvy bucket of pig offal, ye've found one."

The Spaniard darted a hand into his pocket and withdrew a knife that snapped into a long blade when he whipped it down at his side. He flexed his knees and sank into a crouch, his dark eyes glittering in the morning sun. One hand brandished the knife, the other hand beckoned.

"Come on, you bastard. You calling me out? Come on."

Grinning hugely, feeling better than he had since his arrival, Richard scrambled onto the wharf, shook the weariness from his muscles and tightened his grip on the hilt of his sword. A good, hard fight was exactly what he needed.

The Spaniard froze. First he stared at Richard's sword, his expression registering disbelief. Then his eyes traveled up and up, appraising Richard's size and powerful body. Finally he leveled an uncertain frown on his opponent's unnerving grin.

Richard used the Spaniard's loss of concentration to strike. His sword flashed in the sunlight and the Spaniard's knife spun out of his hand then arched into the water. Frustration thinned Richard's lips. He was primed and eager for a challenge, but this had been too easy. He cursed between his teeth.

"Geez, man!" The Spaniard winced and gripped his hand. The sword was too dull to draw blood, but Richard knew the powerful impact of his swing had stung. The Spaniard's hand flamed red now and promised a mass of dark bruises tomorrow.

The Spaniard glanced toward the water where his knife had disappeared, then he inspected the long, tangled hair flying around Richard's head. He judged the heavy thighs straining his opponent's jeans, noted the swell of muscle rising along Richard's chest, shoulders and neck. Finally Ortiz raised his eyes to Richard's craggy face and murderous gaze.

"You and me—we got no quarrel," the Spaniard said hastily, raising his palms and moving backward. "You're out of my boat now. It's cool."

Richard gripped the sword and ground his teeth until knots pebbled his jawline. Damn it, he wanted a fight. He wanted the surge of blood and exhilaration, the ring of steel, the sweat. He wanted to experience the joy of doing something he did well.

Unfortunately he scrupled against slaughtering an unarmed man. There was no joy in dishonor. Swallowing a bitter taste of disappointment, he reluctantly lowered his sword, spat on the wharf boards, then released a long, fervent stream of curses.

Ortiz shifted from one foot to the other. He wanted to get the hell out of here, but he didn't dare turn his back on this huge, crazy gringo. He wet his lips and darted a glance toward the deserted row of shabby taverns facing the waterfront.

"Why you carrying that old sword?" Moving in slow motion so Richard could watch his hands, he unrolled his cigarettes from his T-shirt sleeve then shook one out. "Smoke?" he asked not taking his eyes from Richard's face.

"That's tobacco?"

"Marlboros."

Holding the Spaniard's gaze, Richard accepted a cigarette, recognizing it as a conciliatory gesture. The cigarette impressed him as a silly little thing, something a fancy man might select.

They stood eye-to-eye smoking, at an impasse. Pride prevented either from being the first to depart.

"How come you was on my boat?"

"I needed a place to think. I fell asleep."

"You English?"

"American. I fought in the Revolution." Pride squared Richard's shoulders. He'd been no more than a boy, but he had joined the patriots on Bunker Hill. He had stood on the ramparts beside his father and watched in grim silence as the redcoats flowed up the hill like a river of blood, their drums beating a tattoo that drove a chill deep into a man's bones.

"Nam, huh?" The Spaniard nodded and sucked on his cigarette. "Never heard it called a revolution, but I guess you could say that. My brother was there. Got the Purple Heart. Lotta good it did him—he came home in a box." He flicked a glance at the scar on Richard's forehead, then the scar that showed at the throat of his shirt. "Get those in the war?"

"At sea." He tried not to think about the bilge-rat Spaniard who had wounded him. That scurvy bastard had been dead for two centuries. It had nothing to do with this man.

"Navy." The Spaniard nodded again. "I had you figured for a marine." He looked at Richard with interest. "Look, it's early, but do you want a beer?"

"I have no money. But I thank 'e for the gesture." The admission humiliated him. His face burned and his expression hardened as he turned his face away.

The Spaniard shrugged. "Hell, man. Guess I can buy a beer for the only dude who ever took a knife off me." He swore and massaged his hand, but a glimmer of respect glowed behind his eyes.

"I accept your invitation," Richard said stiffly. The morning's encounter had left him with a powerful thirst.

They flipped their cigarettes into the water then walked toward the row of dilapidated taverns. The weathered taverns and the trash littering the street before them were a familiar sight. Every waterfront since the beginning of time had offered succor to weary seamen in dives not very different from these.

A few early patrons glanced up as Richard and Ortiz entered. Most were Cuban shrimpers, sipping frosted glasses of beer or hot *café chica,* relaxing beneath the drone of an overhead fan. They stared at Richard and his sword like he was an apparition.

"You hungry?" Ortiz asked when a tired looking waitress appeared at their table.

Richard nodded, staring at the waitress. This bruised peach was nothing like his Elizabeth. She had orange hair that stood up on her head like waxed spikes. The paint rouging her cheeks and lips had begun to melt in the morning heat.

"If I was you, I'd lean that sword out of sight. No one here is going to challenge a friend of Manuel Ortiz's, but a weapon makes 'em nervous. Know what I mean?"

The orange-haired waitress brought them huge platters of bacon and eggs fried in olive oil. There were side dishes of grits and fried potatoes and steaming Cuban bread fried on a grill. They washed it down with icy mugs of Budweiser.

"I'm obliged to 'e," Richard said when the waitress took away their platters and served them another beer.

"What's your name, man?"

"Richard Colter."

Ortiz offered another cigarette, but Richard declined. He wished he had his pipe. With his belly full and a beer in his hand, he felt reasonably content and relaxed. "How does a bloke earn his fortune here?" he asked Ortiz.

"Tourism, drug smuggling or commercial fishing. Those are the choices." Ortiz leaned back in his chair and studied Richard. "You in the wrong place, dude. If I had your looks, I'd get my butt to Hollywood." He inclined his chin toward the waitress. "Martina ain't took her eyes off you since we walked in here."

"I had an uncle who did some smuggling before the Revolution. I know the sea." He looked at Ortiz. "Tell me about drug smuggling."

Ortiz laughed, choking on a cloud of cigarette smoke. "Forget it," he said when he could speak again. "You stick out like a sore thumb. No way you're going to go slipping and sliding without ending in the slam. The cops would spot you in a minute, assuming you persuaded some boss to take you on."

Many of the words and expressions passed Richard by, but he comprehended the sense of the conversation. "How do you earn money?"

"Me?" Ortiz shrugged. "A little of this—a little of that. Sometimes I go out with the shrimp boats. During the season, I take tourists fishing. Peddle junk made out of conch shells. Deal a bit of grass now and then. My old man made cigars before the business died. There's no money in it now." He eyed Richard. "What you been doing so far?"

"I owned a ship. I ran cargo between the Caribbean and Boston." Richard didn't feel it necessary to explain that he obtained his cargo largely by plundering Spanish shipping. After a minute he added, "My ship sank."

"You got no insurance?"

"What's insurance?"

Ortiz laughed. "You dumb bastard. I have a cousin like you. Thought he could beat the odds. Minute he let his insurance lapse, an eighteen-wheeler smashed his car flatter than a tortilla. Greed don't pay, man. Next time, pay the damned premiums."

Richard glared in frustration. "I don't ken half of what 'e say."

By three that afternoon they had each consumed enough beer to float a battleship. Amazingly, neither was drunk, but they weren't far from it.

Richard focused an unsteady eye. "Ortiz, me fine friend, I thank 'e kindly for explaining the fine points of football. But the question stirring me mind is... do 'e know anything about wenches?"

"*Amigo,* you are speaking to the stud of studs. With all due modesty, I can honestly claim I know everything worth knowing about wenches. Wha' kinda problem you having?"

"I have a woman, a spirited wench as stubborn as a jack mule." He swallowed the last drops in his mug and reached for the fresh pitcher that appeared at his fingertips. Outside the window, ripples of heat rose from the street. A yellow dog panted in a scrap of shade. "She won't do as she's told."

Manuel nodded, propping his head on his hand. "Women are like that, Dick. Take my Rosa. I tell her over and over that if she flirts with Juan Hernandez I'll punch her out. And what happens? Juan comes hanging around and I end up punching him out instead. It's women's lib, Dick. Women's lib wrecked us men's lives. A man can't be a man no more and that's the truth. You try to be a man in your own damned house and the cops'll haul you away."

"So it's true. 'E can't discipline a woman, even if she needs a strong hand."

"Ain't that the truth. You ever been married, Dick?"

"I was betrothed ten years ago, but me intended died in the smallpox epidemic."

"No kidding? A smallpox epidemic? I didn't hear about that. Well, you're lucky. Take my Rosa. Before we were married, she was hot as a tamale, you know? Now it's like sex is something she never heard of."

Richard frowned and leaned forward. "That's similar to me own situation. First it's aye, then it's nay." He raised his palms. "I don't know what the wench wants."

Ortiz nodded wisely and ordered another pitcher of Bud. "You got to remember this. If a woman is saying no, but her eyes is saying maybe, then the answer is yes. Take my Rosa. Just last week she says to me..."

THE INSTANT THE PHONE rang, Elizabeth snatched it from the cradle. "Hello?" she said in a breathless voice. *Let it be him.*

"Hi, it's Kelly."

"Oh." Kelly Thayer was a neighbor and a friend, but not who Elizabeth wanted to talk to right now.

"I haven't heard from you in weeks. It's like you fell off the face of the earth."

"I'm sorry, I've been busy." Elizabeth walked to the balcony doors, straining the length of the kitchen phone cord. The beach was empty, baking in the afternoon sun.

"Yeah, I know," Kelly said in a smug voice. "I've seen who's been keeping you so busy and, God, is he gorgeous!"

"You've seen him?" Elizabeth straightened.

"Hank jogs in the morning and sometimes I get up with him. That gorgeous Viking of yours is usually standing at the edge of the water as the sun comes up."

"He is?" Elizabeth blinked. She hadn't known he did that.

"One morning I got out the binoculars to get a better look." A swooning sound came over the wire. "Wow. Is he as sexy as he looks?"

"Look, Kelly, this is important. Have you seen him lately?"

"Why?"

Elizabeth ground her teeth and passed a hand over her eyes. "As a matter of fact, I haven't seen him in two days and I'm worried out of my mind."

"Hey, arguments happen. Especially in the early stages of a relationship. He'll get over it and he'll call."

"You don't understand. He's really gone. Gone back to—" Elizabeth bit off an explanation. "Listen, Kelly, I can't talk now. I have to go."

"Well, don't let me keep you from something *important.*"

Elizabeth bit her lip. She'd make it up to Kelly later. Right now, she had to *do* something. Grabbing up her car keys, she raced through the house and out the door.

Feeling helpless and more anxious by the minute she drove up one street, then down another. Twice—feeling like an idiot—she stopped and asked pedestrians if they had seen a big blond hunk who might be carrying a sword. The people she asked stared at her as if she didn't have all her oars in the water. Even for Key West, a man walking around with a sword was unusual.

Finally she drove to the *Sante Oro*. But she should have known better than to expect comfort from Cappy. He listened, then looked up from the scuba equipment he was inspecting.

"Good riddance," was all he said.

That was exactly what Elizabeth feared. That the wind and the tunnel had reappeared and Richard was really and truly gone.

ELIZABETH AND CAPPY had Thanksgiving dinner at Alice's Restaurant, along with Tim and Juan and a few of the other divers who had no family in Key West. Everyone tried to be upbeat, talking about the return of the tourists and the beginning of the shrimping season. No one spoke about the lull in the treasure-salvaging business. But it was on everyone's mind.

"Maybe it's time to get out of treasure hunting and concentrate on the tourist business," Cappy said after dinner, when he and Elizabeth had returned to the *Sante Oro* for a snifter of brandy from Cappy's private stock.

"You'd be miserable, plus there isn't much money in it," Elizabeth commented, standing in front of a chart tacked on Cappy's office wall. The chart was covered with notations in her hand and in Cappy's.

Cappy sat on the edge of his cluttered desk and studied her. "How long has it been now?"

"Four days."

"Forget him. The guy's moved on to greener pastures. Count your blessings."

"It isn't that easy." Tears glistened in her eyes. The chart blurred in front of her. When she regained control, Elizabeth waved a hand to indicate she didn't wish to talk about Richard. "While I was working at home, I think I came a little closer to figuring where the *Madre Louisa* must have gone down."

They discussed her calculations, the conversation cheering them both a little.

"Excellent," Cappy said, contemplating the chart. "We'll work the tourists through Christmas. In January we should have enough time and money to take a serious look-see. Which reminds me. Are you still willing to take out a few dive excursions?''

Elizabeth shrugged. ''Why not? We need the money and I'm not doing anything else.''

''I'm sorry, honey,'' Cappy said as he walked her to her car. He gave her a tight hug. ''Hey, there's plenty of fish in the sea. I know you're hurt and upset right now, but believe me, you're well rid of this guy. He didn't own a thing except the clothes on his back. And you paid for those. You deserve better.''

''Oh, Cappy. I love you, and I know you mean well, but you're way off base on this one.'' She turned her face away so he wouldn't see her tears. ''I miss him so much.''

ELIZABETH HADN'T REALIZED how quickly Richard had become part of her life. The house seemed oppressively silent without the blare of the TV and without Richard shouting back at it. She missed their nightly discussions. She missed his presence and his delight in discovering new things. Most of all, she missed the way she felt when she was with him.

No man had ever made her feel as beautiful or desirable. Or so needed. When she was with Richard, the world looked new and fresh and exciting. The air was softer; colors were more vivid. Every moment was exciting. She felt alive and aware in a way she had never felt before.

''Damn!'' she said around the lump in her throat, gripping the balcony rail. She stared at the sea through a shine of tears.

With all her heart Elizabeth wished she had gone to bed with him. Like an idiot she had told herself to wait until they could come together as equals. Now she would never know what it would have been like.

Dimly she heard the doorbell ring at the front of the house and she turned back inside. As she moved through the living room, Elizabeth cast a quick glance toward the clock, embarrassed that she hadn't bothered to get dressed, that she was still wearing her robe this late in the morning.

"Bill!" she said when she opened the door.

Bill Trowbridge stood on her porch, looking crisp and cool in his dress whites, holding his uniform cap beneath his arm.

"I've just come from a navy wedding," he explained, smiling at her. "Which made me think of you."

"You're wearing a sword."

"It's tradition. The happy couple walks through an arch of crossed swords." He cleared his throat, glanced at the collar of the robe she was holding closed with one hand, then studied her face. "Have you been crying?"

"I think I've got a touch of the flu," Elizabeth said, hoping he would accept the lie as an explanation for her reddened eyes and the fact that she was still wearing her robe at this hour. "I'd invite you in, but..."

"No problem." He gave her a charming smile. "Look, I've been wondering if maybe you've had any second thoughts about our conversation last month. I've missed you and I was hoping, wondering if maybe you'd missed me?"

Elizabeth bit her lip. Why couldn't she have fallen in love with Bill Trowbridge? He didn't try to dominate her or impose his opinions on her. As far as she knew he didn't think ready-to-wear clothing was a wonderful invention, didn't flush the toilet to amuse himself. She sighed.

"I'm sorry, Bill," she said gently. "There's someone else."

"Oh." Suddenly her bathrobe and reddened eyes took on a new significance. "I've come at a bad time."

"He's not here right now." There was no point confiding that Richard would not return. It was kinder to make a clean break.

"Hey, I just stopped by to say hello..." Regret stole the warmth from his smile. "I hope the lucky stiff makes you happy."

Now that the awkward moment had passed, Elizabeth relaxed enough to accompany Bill down the steps and out to his car.

"How about a hug for old times' sake?" Bill asked, opening his arms. "If this new guy doesn't treat you right..."

"Thanks, you've—"

Elizabeth glanced over Bill's shoulder and forgot what she had been about to say.

Richard was striding up the street, the flat of his sword resting against his shoulder. He hadn't shaved in several days and a light wheat-colored beard covered his chin and jaws. The morning breeze rippled his mane of hair.

Relief buckled Elizabeth's knees and she clung to Bill for support. In a moment she knew she would be furious, but right now what she felt was sheer joy at the sight of him.

Richard saw her in Bill Trowbridge's arms a split second after Elizabeth spotted him. Instantly his expression darkened into outrage; his brows clamped together in a murderous scowl.

He broke into a run, vaulted the picket fence and dashed toward the driveway. Halting a few yards from where Bill Trowbridge held Elizabeth, Richard swung his sword down in a flourish then the blade flashed upward and steadied.

"That's my wench, ye bloody bastard. Unhand her at once and prepare to defend yourself!"

"What?" Bill Trowbridge looked over his shoulder and his jaw dropped in astonishment.

"Richard!"

"Lizzy, me love, back away from yon scurvy bloke." Richard's steely eyes didn't leave Trowbridge as he edged forward holding his sword at point. A menacing flash of sunlight glinted off the pitted blade. There was no question that he meant to use it.

Operating from a primitive survival instinct, Bill hastily fumbled with the dress sword at his side. Flushing beneath Richard's smile of contempt, he finally managed to unsheathe his sword and brandished it uncertainly in front of him.

"Call the police," he instructed Elizabeth without taking his wide eyes from Richard's face. He assumed a fencer's stance.

"Oh, my God!" Elizabeth's hands flew to cover her mouth.

There was Richard, powerful and confident, looking like a blond Captain Hook, and there was Bill, ashen-faced and hopelessly outmatched, but stepping forward to engage.

"Oh, my God," Elizabeth said again, her whisper emerging as a moan.

The duel began.

Chapter Six

Clutching the trunk of the mimosa tree to support her trembling legs, Elizabeth watched with horrified fascination as a dangerously joyous cat toyed with a very shaken mouse.

More swiftly than she would have imagined possible, Richard drew Bill away from the car and shrubbery and into the open yard. There, in a series of quick taunting strikes, Richard maneuvered Bill into a position where the sun slanted directly into Bill's glasses.

From where she stood, Elizabeth could see the sweat beading on Bill's forehead, could heard the low sounds he uttered when Richard's sword rang hard against his own. Clearly Trowbridge recognized Richard was a master swordswman and dangerously angry.

The scene was surrealistic, like something out of a Fellini film. Two men were fighting over Elizabeth, dueling in her front yard. It didn't seem real. She gave her head a sharp shake. The flashing swords and graceful postures might be horribly fascinating, horribly romantic, but the impending danger was genuine. She had to halt this craziness at once.

Pushing from the mimosa tree, she tested her shaking legs and ran forward.

"Richard! Stop this at once!"

He paid her no mind. To her dismay, Elizabeth realized he was enjoying himself immensely. His long pale hair flew around his bronzed face; he handled himself as gracefully as a dancer, hardly exerting himself. He was not sweating, was not winded. He was in his element, fully in control and maneuvering his opponent at will.

She ran around behind Bill to a position where Richard could see her face, and she shouted at him to stop this madness.

"Richard, I mean it! Stop this before someone gets hurt!" It was impossible to guess if he heard her. His thick-lashed eyes were a steely gray. His expression was more alive than she had ever seen it. His lips curled in a sensual, almost cruel half smile. Balanced on the balls of his feet, he moved with quick, agile movements, working his powerful body with ease and grace.

Wringing her hands and ignoring the pulse beat thundering in her ears, Elizabeth darted around the perimeter of the duel, shouting, demanding, begging them to halt, fighting to be heard over the clash of steel and Richard's smiling taunts.

A car squealed to a stop in the street and the driver leaned out the window, his mouth dropping open. Mrs. Callison, Elizabeth's neighbor to the south, appeared near the picket fence, her eyes as wide as pie tins.

"Stop it!" Elizabeth shouted. Neither of the men paid her any attention.

She could think of only one way to stop the duel, but it required trust and a large amount of reckless idiocy.

Before she could terrify herself by stopping to consider consequences, Elizabeth gulped a deep breath, then closed her eyes and ran straight into the middle of the flashing swords.

"Holy God!" Bill Trowbridge's horrified shout was followed by a stream of shaken whispered curses.

When Elizabeth dared open her eyes, she saw the tip of Bill's sword crossed over her shoulder and glinting in the hot sun. The blade had halted less than two inches from her throat. She closed her eyes again as a tremor ran through her body.

She gripped her shaking hands and peeked through her lashes, facing Richard. At no time had she believed herself in danger from him. She had trusted Richard's reflexes and she had been right to do so. Although she hadn't seen it happen, the instant she broke the plane of the fight, his sword arched up, around, then down. He stood before her now, obviously angered by her interference, but the point of his sword was firmly in the grass.

The flat of Bill's blade sagged against her shoulder and she felt a tremor run through it.

"I almost...I could have..." He covered his flushed face with one hand and staggered backward a step.

Although she was shaking badly, Elizabeth went to him after flinging Richard a furious accusing look over her shoulder. She dropped Bill's arm over her shoulders and led him toward his car.

"Who is that madman?" Bill whispered. Leaning both hands against the hood of the car, he dropped his head and struggled to catch his breath. "He should be locked up!"

Elizabeth glanced at the car still stopped in the street and flicked a look toward her astonished neighbor, Mrs. Callison. She opened Bill's door.

"Look, Bill, I know it's a lot to ask, but please don't report this to the police. I beg you." She cast him a beseeching look. "If you care for me at all, please do this for me."

He turned his head to stare at her. "Don't report this? You're as crazy as he is."

"Someday I'll explain what happened here, but . . . I can't right now. I'm terribly sorry about all this. But no one got hurt, so let's just forget the whole thing, okay?"

"Forget it? That crazy bastard was trying to kill me!"

Stepping forward, Elizabeth removed the sword from his limp fingers and tossed in in the back of his car. She retrieved his uniform cap from where it had fallen in the grass and put it into his hands before she gently pushed him behind the wheel.

"Please, Bill. I'm begging you. It's over. Let it go."

He flicked a glance toward Richard, then looked into Elizabeth's hot face. "Is *that* the someone else?" Incredulity tightened his voice and his expression. "That lunatic?"

"Please, I think you'd better go. I . . . I'll call you."

Bill stared up at her, then reached for the ignition. "Don't bother," he said stiffly.

The instant his car sped out of the driveway Elizabeth whirled to face Richard, as furious as she had ever been in her life.

"You crazy idiot!" she shouted. "What were you thinking of? You could have killed him!"

"Aye." Heat smoldered in his eyes. "And what were 'e thinking of, 'e crack-brained wench, to stroll into a sword battle? 'Tis a wonder that inept son of a dog didn't kill ye!"

"You...you're finding fault with *me?*" His criticism and anger staggered her, reduced her to sputtering.

She flew across the yard, her robe billowing behind a flash of bare legs, her hand upraised to strike him.

Richard caught her wrist and pulled her hard against his taut body. The raw heat of his chest and thighs scalded through layers of clothing and seared her. Passion blazed in his blue-gray eyes, flickering like dark flames.

"The bastard had no right to touch 'e. Ye belong to me!"

"I don't *belong* to anyone!" But her voice emerged breathless and scarcely audible. His body felt like steel against her soft curves.

During the previous minutes Elizabeth's emotions had run riot. First had been relief so overwhelming that she felt faint with it, then a soaring joy so consuming she had been aware of nothing but the fact that Richard was alive, still in the twentieth century and coming toward her. Next amazement had consumed her, followed by dread and finally a bone-deep fear. Now she felt another kind of fear, the fear of swaying above an abyss.

Her emotions whirled together and ignited into passion. As she registered Richard's strength and state of arousal, her stomach tightened and an electric tingle shot through her body, leaving her too weak to resist when he dropped his sword and ran his powerful hands from her shoulders to her buttocks, pressing her against him, forcing her to feel his mounting urgency. Her knees would have buckled if he hadn't been holding her.

"Oh, God," she whispered, her head falling backward as he bent to her, his tongue licking the perspiration from the hollow pulsing wildly at the base of her throat. "Please," she whispered, her mouth dry. "We can't do this."

He lifted her in his arms as if she were weightless. "Aye, gel. We can do this." His voice was rough and thick with desire.

Before Elizabeth's arms circled his neck, she saw Mrs. Callison leaning over the picket fence, both hands clasped over her breast as if she might swoon.

"No," she whispered as Richard strode up the porch steps and kicked open the door. Her heart was pounding. A light dew of perspiration covered her body. She felt as if she were on fire.

"Aye."

He carried her down the hallway, into the dim shuttered guest room and tossed her on the bed. Elizabeth lay as she had fallen, her legs slightly spread, the terry robe gaping over her breasts. Gasping for breath, she looked up at him.

Richard stood over the bed, staring down at her, his legs planted wide apart, his fingers fumbling with the buttons on his shirt. Impatient, he tore open the shirt, sending buttons flying. Elizabeth sucked in a breath and squeezed her eyes shut.

When she opened them, he was sliding his jeans over pale muscled hips, down heavy calves. He kicked out of the jeans then stood beside the bed in the dim light like a young god, powerful and perfect in form, rampant in his desire. There was nothing gentle in his narrowed gaze.

Bending, he reached for the belt on her robe, jerked it open, then flung back the edges and sucked in a sharp breath at the sight of her. His body stiffened and grew as hard as the dark heat flickering in his smoky eyes.

"Ye are so beautiful!"

Elizabeth could not move, could hardly breathe. She lay sprawled before his hungry gaze, her breasts full and hard and aching, her breath emerging in gasps.

"We're not ready for this." The protest came from some rapidly draining reservoir of resistance, a last effort to control a situation that was spinning away from her.

He leaned a knee on the bed and released the ribbon that tied her ponytail. Stretching out beside her, he plunged his hands in her tumbling dark hair.

"I've wanted to do that since I first saw 'e," he whispered hoarsely. Closing his eyes, he lifted one long strand of hair and drew it across his eyelids, his lips, his chest. "Your hair smells like wild honey."

Shafts of sunlight fell through the shutters and cast bands of dappled gold across his chest. Elizabeth watched her fingers rise as if they were not attached to her. She pushed her fingertips into the crisp golden hair burnishing his chest and made a small helpless sound as she explored the strangely silky texture. Heat and tension coiled inside her, winding tighter at the hard touch of him.

"Please," she gasped, her voice near a sob. "We have to stop while we still can."

His large rough hands stroked her sides, gliding over the full sides of her breasts, lifting her higher on the pillow. His mouth found her throat, nipping lightly at her skin, then his kisses dropped lower to circle her breasts. Pressing her firmly on the bed with his hands on her naked hips, he stroked her skin with his tongue, licking, tasting, sucking.

Elizabeth felt her nipples swell and harden and arch toward him, but he didn't sample them at once. He teased all around her nipples until she thought she would scream from wanting his mouth on her. Only then did he cover her and suck gently while he fluttered his tongue over the tiny pink buds.

The pleasure was so sharp and exquisite that Elizabeth thrashed beneath him, or would have if his strong hands hadn't pinned her down.

Still holding her hips, Richard slid his lips beneath her breasts, kissing and murmuring against her burning skin, caressing her waist, then the curve of her hips. Now his fingers trailed up the sensitive insides of her thighs, approaching and withdrawing, teasing her toward a scream.

She couldn't lie still, she couldn't. A low moan broke from Elizabeth's throat and she whispered his name in breathless urgent gasps.

When she felt the fire of his tongue on the insides of her thighs, she thought she could not bear the sweet torture without fainting. At the point that her nerves were quivering and ablaze, his mouth finally found her center and plundered her, and Elizabeth heard herself sob with pleasure. Powerful hands cupped her buttocks and raised her to his tongue and lips. Again and again he brought her to the trembling edge of orgasm only to retreat and leave her wild and sweating, twisting and turning, almost whimpering with need.

Finally he moved up beside her, tangled his hand in her hair and pulled her head back, kissing her hard on the lips, forcing her mouth open with his tongue. His kiss was hard and bruising, a kiss that shook her with its passion and heat and an urgency that surpassed need.

Not taking his lips from hers, he caught her shaking hand, guided it down between them then curved her fingers around the rigid source of his heat.

"Tell me nay," he said against her lips, his fingers buried in her damp hair. His stare smoldered down at her. "Tell me nay and I shall leave 'e."

The truth flamed in his burning eyes. He meant what he said. His control was such that he could walk away from her even now, with their naked bodies entwined, slick with sweat, with her hands on him, with their breath panting in ragged gasps.

"You win," Elizabeth whispered, her voice a sob of surrender.

He shook her. "Say it!"

He would settle for nothing less than total capitulation. But Elizabeth didn't care anymore. Electricity flashed and crackled along the surface of her skin. Her body ached and burned where he touched her. Her nerves felt exposed and raw. Reason melted in the fire of sensation and passion.

"I want you," she said, gasping for breath, her hands flying over his taut muscles.

"Say it!" His voice was hoarse.

"Take me. Richard, for God's sake—take me!"

His mouth came down hard on hers, ravaging her, plundering her, taking what was his.

His knee forced her willing legs apart and he hesitated only a moment to look down into her eyes before he plunged into her, claiming her in long, hard strokes. All the while he stared into her face, watching as she struggled to retain some small semblance of control, watching as she lost her private battle and surrendered to the transports of pure passion.

When she finally came, wildly, explosively, the world rocked around her. For an instant Elizabeth thought she had fainted. When she was again cognizant, panting and dazed, she realized Richard was still watching her, a half smile on his lips.

She gazed up at him, half in wonder, half embarrassed that he had observed her loss of control. Her lips were swollen and red. A rosy flush infused her skin.

"I never dreamed—"

He stopped her words with a long, rough kiss that took her breath away. Only now, as his body moved hard and fast over hers, did she realize he had delayed his own gratification until she was satisfied.

It was her turn to watch as perspiration slicked his body, as control faded and a low groan built in his chest. At last his magnificent body shuddered and his arms tightened convulsively around her. His damp head dropped toward her breast.

"Now ye truly belong to me!" he whispered triumphantly.

"I WAS LONELY, and I didn't even know it," Elizabeth marveled, caressing his head against her breast. "Isn't that strange?"

"'Tis not so odd, gel. I searched for 'e in a dozen port cities," he murmured against her throat. "I didn't ken what it was I sought. I only knew I never found 'e until now."

"I read everything I could find about you. I was driven to know everything about you. I even dreamed about you."

"What sort of dreams?"

She smiled and wiggled down in the bed until they lay side by side. "Romantic dreams; frustration dreams. There was an element of loss and longing, of wanting you but being unable to reach you." She framed his bearded cheeks between her hands and gazed into his eyes. The steely color had softened. Now his eyes were tender and protective.

"I know you, but I don't know you." Lightly she traced the ridges of old scars with her fingertips. "How did you get these scars? Why do you hate doctors so much? What was it like being at Bunker Hill? What do you think about? Does it hurt to remember home? Do you wonder about the people you left behind?"

Richard smiled and kissed her nose. "Why have 'e chosen not to marry? I hate doctors because their primary treatment is bleeding. 'Tis my opinion that bleeding terminated more blokes than ever it mended. Do all women work to earn money or only feisty little chits like 'e?"

She smiled and wound her arms around his neck, pressing her forehead to his. "One of my research books claimed you played the pianoforte and were partial to gambling. Is that true? Are you as thirsty as I am? Would you like a glass of lemonade?"

"Nay, not lemonade," he said, stirring against her. "Budweiser. Or strong tea with ice."

"Budweiser?" she asked, her eyebrows rising as she slipped from the bed and drew on her robe. "Now, where did you learn that? No, tell me later."

While she waited for the tea to steep, Elizabeth stepped onto the balcony off the kitchen, pitting her glow against the hot glow of the afternoon sun, smiling at nothing while she replayed their lovemaking in her mind.

Though it would have hugely embarrassed her to admit it, the orgasms she had experienced in Richard's arms were the first she'd ever had. In the past she had been unwilling or unable to relinquish control and let herself go, unable to trust her partner or herself enough to release her inhibitions and give herself entirely to the moment.

A fiery blush tinted her cheeks as she remembered. Richard had conquered her in every sense of the word.

Returning to the guest room, she gave him a large tumbler of iced tea, then sat facing him on the bed after gathering her robe around her.

"Where did you go when you disappeared?" she asked, trying to keep her voice light. "I was worried half out of my mind. You could have asked someone to phone and tell me where you were."

Sitting up, Richard propped the pillows behind his head and gave her a look that blended surprise and protest. He didn't seem at all self-conscious that his splendid body was gloriously naked and exposed to view.

The smile he gave her did not quite reach his eyes. "Ye'd have me plead your permission to venture out like a lad wheedling his nanny? Nay, madam, that I will never do."

"It isn't like that, Richard, and you know it. There's so much you still don't know. So many dangerous things that could happen. I was worried." She sipped her tea, lowered the glass to her lap. "I thought maybe the wind and the tunnel had returned and you'd... it scared me."

For a long moment he didn't speak. "I needed some time to meself, Lizzy. It didn't enter me thoughts that 'e'd be anxious. For that I do apologize. 'Twas not me intent to fuss 'e."

"Where were you? Where did you go?"

He told her about exploring the island in the darkness, about finding himself on the wharves near dawn, then how he had met Manuel Ortiz.

Elizabeth frowned. "Ortiz sounds dangerous."

Richard's smile made her heart turn over in her breast. "Lizzy, me sweet, beneath the pride and swagger Ortiz is just a man like any, trying to rub along as best he can."

He told her about staying with Ortiz and Rosa in a shotgun house built in the thirties. He told her about attending a cockfight with Ortiz and a few of his friends.

Elizabeth gasped. "Don't tell me you like or approve of cockfighting!"

"Nay. Nor bear or bull baiting either. But—meaning no disrespect to 'e—'twas good to share the company of men. To discover what interests them today, to learn what issues give rise to their gorge."

"Most men don't attend cockfights!" Elizabeth said hotly. "For one thing cockfights are illegal. For another it's a cruel and barbaric sport, if it can even be called a sport!"

"Ye won't find an argument from this mother's son," Richard said, grinning at her. "We attended a film, fished a little, and Rosa cooked a big dinner for her family and Manuel's. There was dancing." He laughed at the memory. "Lunatic dancing. Shaking and twisting and bouncing."

"Didn't you celebrate Thanksgiving in your time?"

"'Twas a church festival, a rite of harvest."

Elizabeth watched his expression, fighting a sudden bite of jealousy. His first automobile ride had been with someone else. And his first film, his first Thanksgiving, his first time on the water in a modern boat. "You enjoyed yourself, didn't you?"

"Enormously, madam."

"How did you explain not knowing so many things?"

For an instant irritation flickered across his gaze. "Perhaps me ignorance isn't as woefully apparent to others as it is to 'e, madam."

Elizabeth gazed into her glass. "Some explanation must have been necessary."

"Not so much as 'e might think," he said, swinging his legs over the side of the bed and reaching for his jeans. "Manuel and his family saw me as a man. Not as a project."

Elizabeth watched him dress. "Is that how you think I see you? As a project?"

"Do 'e truly see me as a man, Lizzy?"

After what they had just experienced together—how could she not? Something of what she was thinking must have been revealed on her expression, because suddenly he laughed.

"'Tis the wrong inquiry for the moment. If e'll excuse me, madam, I find meself in need of a shower and a shave."

Later, she made a salad and grilled salmon for dinner, then they carried their coffee outside to the balcony to watch the sunset. They sat side by side in the brilliant glow, their tennis shoes propped on the balcony railing.

"What am I doing that makes you think I don't see you as a man?" Elizabeth asked.

"'E said it yourself. I've been sharing your quarters for five weeks, yet we don't ken one another. T'is been explaining this and demonstrating that. Read this—digest that."

"There are things you have to know just to survive. Remember where you began, Richard. You were blow-ing up eggs in the microwave. You washed your socks in the toilet." The list was endless.

And, yes, stating it aloud made him sound like a student. Or a project. Elizabeth lapsed into an uncomfortable silence, watching the sun flame to orange and gold as it sank nearer the waves rippling the horizon.

Richard let the silence extend to make his point, then he cleared his throat and asked without looking at her, "Who was that bloke molesting 'e in public?"

"His name is William Trowbridge. And he wasn't trying to molest me. He was giving me a hug, saying goodbye."

"Is he courting 'e?"

"Not anymore." She bit her tongue to halt a lecture deploring the outdated concept of dueling. "The relationship never got off the ground. It was over before I met you."

"Did 'e bed Trowbridge?"

"No," she said stiffly. "Not that it's any of your business what I did before I met you. I imagine there were a few women in your life before you met me."

"Aye. But that's not the same. With men 'tis to be expected."

The urge to argue was almost overwhelming. Elizabeth longed to deliver a stinging diatribe about double standards. It damned near killed her to keep silent. But she swore she would not make him feel like a project. Not tonight.

Richard studied the struggle erupting over her features. "How does a man court a woman today?"

"I thought you didn't want any more instruction for a while." Her voice was sharp.

"Touché, madam," he said, grinning.

There was a pleasant tension between them, largely sexual, partly induced by the friction natural to two dominant personalities. But Elizabeth felt more alive, more aware of Richard, of herself, and of everything around them. The sunset was characteristically spectacular. A blooming cereus filled the warm air with a sweet, heady fragrance. The evening was too perfect to waste on verbal sparring.

"Let's start over," Elizabeth suggested, sliding one foot along the railing until it rested against his. "I know you have an older sister. Tell me about her."

Immediately the craggy lines softened beside his mouth. "Rachel is very special," he said at length. "I guess 'e know Ma died in childbirth. Of six bairns, only Rachel and meself survived to adulthood. Rachel raised us. She taught us, switched us when necessary, buried us. She was mother, friend, sister."

"Did she look like you?"

"Nay, gel. She's tiny like 'e, and just as spirited. Her hair is the color of honey and her eyes as blue as lapis. She's pretty and accomplished enough to have conquered and wed Thomas Fairbanks." He paused, remembering that Elizabeth wouldn't recognize the Fairbanks name. "Fairbanks owned the yard where the *Black Cutter* was built," he explained. "'Twas a good match."

For a while they didn't speak. Elizabeth left him with his memories as the sun sank into the waves.

"Might 'e know what happened to Rachel and her Tom?" he asked as twilight shadows gathered around them.

"History records them only as they related to you," Elizabeth said finally. "I know Rachel was widowed in her early forties and never remarried, although she lived into her seventies. She kept your house preserved exactly as you left it. She bequeathed it to the Boston Historical Society.''

Startled, Richard turned to look at her. "Me house still stands?''

Elizabeth nodded. "Rachel established a trust to maintain the property.''

"I'll be a son of a dog! She kept me house intact.'' He was quiet for several minutes. "Six years ago a British frigate mistook the *Black Cutter* for a pirate ship and bloody damned near blew us out of the water.'' Unconsciously he touched the ridge of scar that zagged through his chest hair. "We limped back to Boston harbor and Mr. Greene and Mr. Throckmorton carried me home on a canvas stretcher, more dead than alive.''

"Yes?'' Elizabeth prompted when he again fell silent.

"Rachel was waiting on the porch steps. She had summoned Dr. Culpepper and the Reverend Mr. Goodnight. She even ordered straw spread in the street to muffle the sound of hooves and wheels so as not to impede me recovery.'' He turned to look at Elizabeth. "'Twas strange. The *Black Cutter* was not due back for four months. No one had run ahead to inform her of me return or me injuries. But she knew. T'was always like that, even when we were tadpoles. Rachel knew whenever I was injured or distressed.''

"You loved her.''

"'Tis moments like this that make me head reel,'' he said in a low voice. "To me, Rachel and Tom are alive and real.''

Elizabeth drew a breath and took his hand. "I wasn't lucky enough to have a sister. I'm an only child. A conch.''

He raised his eyebrows. "A conch?"

"That's the local expression for those of us who were born and raised in Key West. I grew up in a big Queen Anne mansion on Elizabeth street. They always denied it but I think my parents named me after the street." She smiled. "My dad was career military. When the navy base closed here, he was transferred to Seattle. He retired three years ago."

"Ye lived in this Seattle?"

She nodded. "But I never forgot Key West. From the time I was a child, I was always fascinated by tales of pirates and treasure. I think I always knew I'd return here and join forces with Uncle Cappy."

She told Richard about Golden Dreams, and the trip to Seville she had taken three years ago on behalf of the company. "There are only a few hundred people who can read the wave writing the Spaniards used to keep records in the sixteenth and seventeenth centuries. I'm one of them," she said proudly.

Richard frowned, striving to understand. "You use these records to locate sunken treasure ships?"

"That's the idea. In actual fact it's like looking for one particular grain of sand in the middle of the Sahara." She sighed. "Would you like more coffee?" When Richard nodded and held out his cup, she didn't take it. Instead, she looked him in the eye and extended her own cup. "So would I. Don't forget to put cream in mine."

He looked startled and she thought he might balk. But after a brief hesitation, he accepted her cup and returned in a moment with fresh coffee for them both.

"A few years ago I invested in a salvage operation situated in Jamaica," Richard told her. "But most of the treasure ships from the Spanish Plate Fleet sank in water too deep to salvage.''

Elizabeth nodded and sipped her coffee. "Deep-water wrecks present a problem, no question." She told him about the dry spell Golden Dreams was undergoing. "It's been four years since Cappy had his last significant find. Our coffers are running low, to put it mildly."

"Are 'e looking for the *Black Cutter?* Is that how 'e came to know about me?"

"Actually I'm trying to discover the whereabouts of the *Madre Louisa*," Elizabeth explained. "I discovered you when I learned the *Madre Louisa* probably sank shortly after her battle with the *Black Cutter.*" She smiled into her coffee cup. "You were a powerful distraction, Captain. I wandered off the subject and started researching Richard Colter."

"Flattered I am to hear it, madam, and proud to learn me exploits survived into history. But pray tell, why do 'e seek the whereabouts of the scurvy *Madre Louisa?*"

Surprise filled Elizabeth's eyes. "You should know better than I. According to my resources, the *Madre Louisa* was carrying a cargo of gold and silver religious items to Mexico City. Many were jeweled. Those artifacts would be priceless today."

Richard frowned. "Nay, gel. 'E have it all wrong. The *Madre Louisa* was fresh out of port, running empty and seeking prey. I'll warrant the only treasure on board was whatever chains her scum crew wore around their bloodthirsty necks and whatever small items they skiffed from me crew. Few pirates set sail with a fat purse, madam. If ye're seeking treasure, ye're looking after the wrong prow."

Elizabeth hung on his words. "Richard, are you sure about this?"

"As sure as a bloke can be." He appeared insulted that she might doubt him. "'Tis only a few weeks since I traded cannon shot with the *Madre Louisa*. That isn't a memory one easily forgets," he added dryly. "Ye'd do better to seek after the *Black Cutter*."

Disappointment sucked the air from Elizabeth's chest. All those months of work—and she had been chasing an empty ship. It was a bitter blow.

"I'll have to tell Cappy," she said. "As for the *Black Cutter,* what's the point?"

"Aye," Richard agreed sadly. "She sank in deep water." He stood and pulled Elizabeth to her feet. "Isn't it time I exchanged how-d'ye-do's with this uncle of yours?" he asked, wrapping his arms around her waist.

It was hard to think when he touched her. Her thoughts burst into tiny flames that danced in her head.

"Ye're compromised now, me lovely Lizzy," he said, nibbling her earlobe. "'Tis time your uncle and I became acquainted."

Her eyes closed and her head fell backward, exposing her throat to his kisses. She smiled. "Shame on you, Captain, for taking advantage of me."

"Mayhaps I'll take advantage of ye again," he murmured. His powerful hands closed over her hips and molded her against him so she could feel the hard pulse of his erection. She caught a sharp breath as her body went weak and her bones turned to jelly.

"So," she said in a breathless voice. "You had me wondering, but there really was premarital sex in old New England."

His eyes widened, then he roared with laughter. "Most assuredly. Rachel used to say it required nine months to make a baby, except for firstborns who only took three months. Did 'e think me advice toward a companion were a stand against sex?''

"Hardly," she murmured, nuzzling his throat. "But your attitudes did seem contrary. One minute you were grabbing me—the next minute you were suggesting a live-in so you couldn't."

"I've a lusty nature, gel," he said, grinning down at her. "But I'm also a man of honor. T'wouldn't have been proper to abuse ye until your eyes said aye. Secondly, 'tis an outrage to trifle with a lady of quality. Despite me randy urgings, it wouldn't have been proper to bed 'e before a commitment."

Elizabeth eased back in his arms and blinked up at him. "A commitment?"

He stroked his thumb across her cheek and his gaze grew tender. "Ye called me and I came. I don't ken the how or the why of it, but I ken well enough that 'e and I are linked by forces greater than we can grasp. I believe the wind and the tunnel will not return for me alone. Ye be mine for now and evermore."

"A commitment?" Elizabeth repeated in a whisper.

She couldn't get beyond that word and concept. Her knee-jerk reaction was to pull back as she had always done before. To Elizabeth commitment meant surrender, and that wasn't what she wanted. No way.

"Richard, I think we need to talk about this commitment business," she said as he tugged at the snap and zipper of her jeans. His fingers slipped between her legs and she shivered with uncontrollable pleasure as he found her wetness and smiled at the effect his hands had on her.

"We'll talk about it later," she said in a low, breathless voice as he scooped her into his arms and carried her inside.

This time the wildness of their passion for each other built slowly as they forced themselves to delay and enjoy the pleasure of leisurely exploring each other's bodies. Elizabeth discovered Richard's crude vaccination scar and heard his pride as he explained he had been one of the first in Boston to submit to the new procedure. He kissed her appendix scar as she explained what it was. He found the ultrasensitive spot beneath her left breast; she discovered he had never made love with the woman on top and that it was wildly erotic to him.

Toward dawn, exhausted but happy, they curled into each other's arms. Before Richard dozed, he murmured against her ear. "'E know what I like best about 'e, gel?"

"What?"

He molded her into the curve of his body and closed his eyes with a contented sigh. "Aside from just about everything, 'e don't have rotten teeth and 'e don't take snuff."

"That's one of the nicest compliments I've ever received," Elizabeth said. He didn't understand when she burst out laughing.

Chapter Seven

Richard was right. Although Elizabeth dreaded the confrontation, it was time he and Cappy met. To make things easier, she had decided to host her get-acquainted dinner on neutral ground. She had made reservations at the newly renovated Papa Ernie's on the lower end of Duval Street.

Her nerves notched higher as the day wore on. By the time they were dressed and in the car she was clutching the steering wheel, her knuckles white. The closer they got to the restaurant, the more nervous she became.

"If Cappy asks what you think about the Dolphins, he's referring to the Miami football team, not fish."

"I know."

"The small fork is the salad fork."

"I'll try to recall not to blow me scurvy nose in me napkin or clean me hands on the bloody table linen."

Elizabeth parked the car, then slumped over the wheel. "I'm sorry. It's just that I want this evening to go well. I want you and Cappy to like each other."

"If 'e have so little confidence in me social graces, then perhaps 'e should have left me home, Mistress Rowley."

She heard the stiffness in his voice and knew she had offended him.

Biting her lip again, Elizabeth locked the car then accepted the arm he offered with an exaggerated gesture.

"Richard, please. I'm nervous about this meeting."

"Perhaps I should apologize beforehand for humiliating 'e." Before she could respond, he opened the restaurant door and they entered Papa Ernie's. The headwaiter rushed forward, a broad smile of welcome squeezing his sharp features. The smile slithered into a knowing smirk when he spied Richard's mane of golden hair tied back by a large black silk ribbon.

Instantly Richard's hand flashed forward. He gripped the waiter by his shirt front and lifted him off his feet.

"I'm in a black mood, ye scum slimed son of a dockside whore, and I don't fancy ye'r goat-yard grin. Either 'e wipe it off ye'r scurvy lips or I'll do it for 'e."

While Elizabeth watched in speechless horror, the headwaiter made a gurgling sound and stared wide-eyed into Richard's murderous gaze.

When she could speak, she hissed, "Put that man down this instant! What in God's name are you thinking of?"

When Richard released the white-faced man, Elizabeth squared her shoulders and tried to ignore the embarrassment flushing her cheeks. She addressed the waiter in a pleasant voice, as if he had not just been mauled by her escort. "We're meeting Cappy Haleburton. Has he arrived?"

The waiter coughed, smoothed his shirt and jacket without taking his eyes from Richard's menacing face.

"Cappy Haleburton," Elizabeth repeated firmly.

"This way," he snapped. He led them to Cappy, threw Richard a poisonous glance, then hastily retreated.

Elizabeth drew an uncertain breath. "Cappy, this is Richard Colter. Richard, this is my uncle."

The two men scowled at each other, then Cappy extended his hand. They shook with obvious reluctance. Cappy wore white slacks, a red-and-blue print shirt and a white jacket. His face and balding head were darkly tanned. It occurred to Elizabeth that Cappy resembled a still handsome but aging hawk. Richard loomed over him, a foot taller and seventy pounds heavier.

To Elizabeth's relief, a waitress appeared to take their drink orders the instant they sat down. Elizabeth ordered a piña colada and Richard followed her lead, even though Elizabeth knew he would have preferred rum.

"Expensive tastes," Cappy commented, flicking a glance at Elizabeth. He ordered a beer for himself, then sat back in his chair and folded his arms across his chest. Any conversation would have to originate from their side of the table.

Elizabeth twisted her hands in her lap. "Well," she said brightly, nodding at the hurricane lamps that glowed across the restaurant. "Do you approve of the renovations? Have you met the new proprietors yet?"

Cappy continued to stare at Richard. "The tourists will like the place. There's a lot of ferns and atmosphere. So, Colter. What do you do for a living when you're working?"

Richard's gaze didn't waver. "I'm a sea captain. Before my ship sank, I ran cargo from the Caribbean to Boston. If a Spaniard or an occasional Frenchman crossed by prow, I captured him if I could."

Cappy's lip curled in a half smile. "Captured them. Ah, yes, you claim you were some kind of pirate in the eighteenth century, right?" He said it with a straight face, but his voice dripped sarcasm.

"A privateer, sir. I'm proud to say that Capt. Richard Colter never failed to return a handsome profit to his investors."

"Uncle Cappy, you know Richard's story." And right now, Elizabeth deeply regretted having told him.

"Do you really expect anyone to believe you blipped through some kind of time warp and just happened to land on my niece's beach?"

Neither man had taken his eyes from the other's face. "I don't ken what happened and I don't expect ye to. But I was born in 1760 and now I'm here, and that's the scurvy truth."

Elizabeth raised her menu. "The salmon looks good tonight," she said desperately. "Or maybe lobster. I'm in the mood for lobster. Is anyone else?"

"That's crap," Cappy snapped, his dark eyes sending off sparks. "Tell it to the *Enquirer*, pal. Maybe they'll buy this cock-and-bull scam. I sure as hell don't."

Richard's jaw set and his eyes flickered dangerously in the glow of the lamp. "All ye need to accept, *sir*, is that me intentions toward your niece, Mistress Rowley, be honorable."

"Is that so?" Cappy said, draining his beer. He signaled the bar waitress and pointed to his empty glass. Richard did the same. Both seemed to have forgotten Elizabeth whose glass was also empty. "I got news for you, buddy. In this century no man worth the name lives off a woman's labor."

"Maybe grilled chicken," Elizabeth suggested in a small voice. "Does grilled chicken sound good?"

"I've got news for 'e, buddy. No gentleman worthy of the name lived off a woman's labors in *any* century." Richard's shoulders squared and his eyes hardened. "I give ye me vow that as soon as I find me way, I shall repay Mistress Rowley every pence she has expended on me behalf!"

Cappy leaned forward. "If you don't start repaying her pretty damned fast, you'll answer to me. You got that?"

Elizabeth choked. It was like watching an aging bantam rooster threaten a young condor.

"Set ye'r gorge to rest, sir. I'll not abuse ye'r niece's hospitality without repayment in kind. 'Tis a debt which has troubled me sorely since me arrival."

Elizabeth lowered the menu and stared. "I didn't know that. Look, I don't mind—"

He ignored her. "To me vast regret I'm a man without a trade in this world. A sea dog without a ship. How does a man in such sore circumstance earn his fortune?"

"Richard," Elizabeth interjected, "it's too soon to worry about this. There's still so much you don't know. You can't drive a car, you can't—"

"Before I'd let a woman support me I'd wash dishes in a barroom dive," Cappy interrupted. "I'd wait tables, I'd drive a garbage truck or pump gas. I'd dig ditches."

Richard answered coldly. "I am a gentleman, sir. I have dined with Mr. Washington, have discoursed with Mr. Franklin, have entertained the governor in me own snug parlor. I hold no distaste for honest labor and pride meself that I can labor longer and harder than any man ye care to put agin me. But I'll not dishonor me-self or me lady by accepting less than a gentleman's trade. I'll not indenture meself to servant's work.''

"Ha!" Cappy cast Elizabeth a look of triumph. "That's a rich one. Let's see if I understand the gist of this. You're willing, even eager to work, except there's no job good enough for you. Is that right? If someone would just offer a position worthy of you, say, the presidency of General Motors, then you'd graciously condescend to get off your butt and show up?''

Richard placed both hands on the table and leaned forward. The cords rose on his neck. "The only reason I'm not tearing ye'r head off ye'r scrawny neck is due to me high regard for Mistress Rowley.''

"It's her I'm looking out for, buster. And believe me, she can do a lot better than taking up with some pretty-boy, fancy-talking con man.''

Engaged in their verbal battle, neither Cappy nor Richard noticed the waitress approach their table. As she smiled down at them expectantly, Elizabeth ordered. "The gentlemen, and I use the term loosely, will share a set of dueling pistols. And I,'' she said in a calm voice, "will have a cup of hemlock.''

THEY WATCHED HER RUN out of the restaurant.

"Jack in hot hell!" Richard rose from his chair. "I'll fetch after her.''

"Might as well sit down and relax. There's nothing either of us can say or do right now that will calm her feathers.'' They sat in silence, watching the door of the restaurant. Elizabeth did not return. "Here's the thing, Colter. I'm just trying to look after Elizabeth's best in-terests. I have nothing against you personally, I just think you're scum as far as Elizabeth is concerned. If you were in my shoes, you'd feel the same way."

"I ken ye perfectly. If we're speaking frankly, I might mention that ye should be lashed and branded for ignoring your obligations in regard to your niece. I fault ye greatly for not insisting on us meeting earlier. As Mistress Rowley's sole male protector, 'tis ye'r duty to monitor the company she keeps."

"I considered instigating a confrontation, but it would have made her mad."

"Ye allowed a woman's opinion to hold 'e from your duty?" Richard made a snorting noise.

Cappy narrowed his eyes into slits. "Are you a drinking man, Colter?"

"Are 'e seeking to test me elbow?"

"Could be. Right now I feel like tying one on and I don't want to do it alone. There's a bar near the *Sante Oro* where there's no damned ferns or chichi decorations and a man can take off his jacket and roll up his sleeves."

At once Richard understood why Cappy preferred the No-Name Bar to Papa Ernie's. The No-Name was a local joint tucked on a side street out of the path of tourists. A jukebox blared country and salsa tunes at the side of a tiny crowded dance floor. The air was thick with smoke and laughter; most of the patrons appeared to know one another. The women wore shorts or slacks and none of the men wore jackets.

Richard and Cappy settled into a booth, within easy shouting distance of the bar. They removed their jackets, opened their collars and made themselves comfortable for a lengthy stay.

"Okay, Colter," Cappy said, after a bottle of Bacardi and two glasses appeared on the table. "Cut the crap. What's the real story with you?'' Cappy leaned back in the booth and studied him. ''Either you're some new-age breed of scam artist or you're crazier than a fruitcake. I'm beginning to lean toward the fruitcake theory. Do me a favor, will you? Take off that stupid hair ribbon.''

Richard had already realized his error.

''That's better.'' Cappy jutted his chin at Richard's empty glass. ''Don't be shy just because I'm paying. We're here to drink, so feel free.''

Richard pushed a hand through his hair and frowned. ''Once I was a rich man, Haleburton. I even had funds invested in a salvage operation in Jamaica.''

''Oh, yeah? A salvage operation? Treasure hunting?''

''Some. 'Twas mostly cargo salvage.''

''Did you make any money at it?''

Richard shrugged. ''Truth is, I lost me arse. Most of the wrecks sank in water too deep to salvage. Even with the bell and the best divers from Margarita Island, we couldn't bring up enough booty to justify the expense.''

Cappy leaned forward with interest. ''I read about salvage bells. They used to drop a huge bell on the surface of a calm sea. When the bell was lowered it trapped a pocket of air inside. The divers used the bell to stay down longer by coming up inside it for a gulp of air.''

''The divers still couldn't stay down long enough,'' Richard said.

Cappy ordered another bottle. ''I imagine Elizabeth has mentioned that we're in a funk right now. We've got an interim job salvaging a World War II tanker, but it won't pay much.'' He flexed his shoulders. ''And it's not treasure diving. There's no thrill. The thrill is in the hunt, that moment of discovery, not knowing if you're going to find rotting timbers or if you'll find the sand littered with gold doubloons.''

''Have 'e ever seen the bottom littered with gold doubloons?''

''Once.'' Warming to the subject, Cappy refilled their glasses and launched into a series of anecdotes from his early glory days. Cappy's memories drew an audience and a half dozen men pulled up their chairs and interrupted with related stories.

Caught up in the camaraderie and tales of the sea, Richard contributed a few recollections of his own. He told about the time Mr. Groggins was keelhauled, then related the sea battle with Peg Leg Baldoon, one of the last genuine pirates to operate out of Tortuga.

''There was another time...'' he continued at his audience's urging. ''Envision this, lads. There I was, snuggled 'tween the pillows of the prettiest little whore in Port-au-Prince when the door flies open and there stands Morgan L'Grande, the most bloodthirsty dog ever to sail the Caribbean and that's a fact. There I was, buck naked with L'Grande's favorite filly and her uttering squeals of delight, if I do say so.'' He grinned.

''What happened?''

''Well, lad, it was some fight. L'Grande was heavier, more ruthless and more experienced with a rapier, but I was younger and quicker and had no clothes to slow me movements. We fought up and downstairs, out into the street and all the way down to the wharf. Crowds gathered and money changed hands. Pretty women lined the boards to clap and cheer me nakedness. We fought like men possessed. L'Grande's sword broke. Mine broke. We went at each other with daggers, then with teeth and claws.''

"Who won?"

"L'Grande lost an ear and I still bear his mark on me thigh. Only one of us crawled away with our manhood intact." He laughed out loud, remembering, then winked. "A man hates to be interrupted at his pleasuring."

The men crowding around the booth laughed and applauded. "That's a good yarn, man, You had me believing every word. Are you a writer?"

Cappy chose that moment to stretch and cover an elaborate yawn. "Hell, boys, don't you have homes? It's almost two o'clock. Time to call it a night." After Cappy settled the tab, a process Richard could hardly bear to witness, his shame was so great, Cappy reached up and clapped him on the back. "The *Sante Oro* is a couple of blocks from here. Come on, I'll show you my operation."

They staggered through the warm darkness, singing sea chanteys and pretending they were less in their cups than they were.

Once on board the *Sante Oro,* a bastardized version of a Spanish treasure galleon, Cappy showed Richard the equipment for snorkeling, scuba diving, salvage and scavenging. The various items were fascinating but incomprehensible. They ran together in his mind. The dive boats made sense, but the engines were a mystery.

They ended in deck chairs on the upper deck, holding snifters of brandy on their stomachs and gazing up at a canopy of stars.

"I know what you're thinking," Cappy said, breaking a pleasant interval of silence. "I should offer you a job."

"Are 'e seeking a ship's captain?"

Cappy smiled. "I might have known you'd want to start at the top. No, there's only one captain in this outfit, and that's me. Even if you'd condescend to take a lesser position, I don't have one for you. I was watching while you examined the dive equipment. You didn't recognize a damned thing. You don't know crap about diving. When I showed you the boats, you looked at the instrument panels like you'd never seen one before."

"I can learn."

"Not on my time, you can't. Hell, Colter, I can hardly pay my people now. I can't afford the time or the money to hire on a novice who can't tell a regulator from a gas cap. Besides, I haven't made up my mind about you."

Richard stared at the stars and wondered if Elizabeth was asleep or if she was sitting up still angry.

"When the wind and the tunnel return, I mean to take your niece back with me."

Cappy lifted up on a elbow. "You are one crazy bastard, do you know that? I'm starting to think you really believe this crap about being a time traveler. I'll give you this much, you sure talk a good story. If I didn't know it was impossible..." Cappy fell back in his chair. "As soon as you can afford it, Colter, you need a shrink."

Richard continued looking up at the stars. "'Tis important to Elizabeth that you and I get on together."

A long silence stretched before Cappy said, "There's no way I'm buying your story. But for Elizabeth's sake, I'll say no more about it. But if you hurt her, Colter, I'll come after you."

"Agreed."

ELIZABETH SAT IN THE kitchen, tapping her toe against a chair leg and drinking her morning coffee, watching the telephone and willing it to ring. Ten minutes passed, then another ten. As usual, the awful thought crept into her mind that maybe Richard was gone. Maybe the wind and the tunnel had returned. Finally she swore under her breath, slammed down her coffee mug and went to find him. There weren't that many places he could be. If he was in the twentieth century.

When Elizabeth arrived at the docks, the *Scavenger II* was easing out of her slip, on her way to the site of the sunken tanker. Cappy waved to Elizabeth from the afterdeck. He looked apologetic, hung over and a bit sheepish.

But that description didn't apply to Richard. She found him on the upper deck of the *Sante Oro*. For a moment they regarded each other warily, uncertain how to begin. Richard's clothing was rumpled and he needed a shave, otherwise he looked as fresh as if he'd slept in his own bed after an evening of drinking nothing stronger than Diet Coke.

Returning anger overpowered the relief Elizabeth felt at finding him. She planted her fists on her hips and scowled. "Last night you and Cappy were—"

She didn't have a chance to finish. Richard crossed the deck in three strides, caught her by the forearms and smothered her words with deep kisses. When he released her, Elizabeth was breathless and at a loss to recall what she had been saying.

He gazed into her dark eyes. "I extend me profound apologies, in the sincere hope that 'e can find it in ye'r generous heart to forgive my unforgivable actions. Otherwise, honor requires me to fall on me sword and do away with me worthless self."

Elizabeth rolled her eyes, then laughed and wound her arms around his neck. His hands on her waist were large and warm and possessive. "It occurs to me that modern men don't know the first thing about apologizing."

"I'm truly sorry. Will ye forgive me bad behavior?"

"Did you and Cappy patch things up?"

"Aye. I approve of your uncle, gel. I see where your feistiness comes from."

She gazed up into his blue-gray eyes and remembered how much she had missed him in her bed. She longed for him. "Let's go home," she said in a throaty voice.

He kissed her again, his mouth hard and eager, promising private delights. "There's nothing I'd like better," he said, his voice a rumbling growl. "But first, take a minute and teach me how to use that equipment."

She followed where he pointed. "The diving equipment?"

"Aye, gel" He kept his arm around her waist.

"Right now? Richard, it requires more than a minute to learn diving."

Indecision flickered in his eyes. "I might not be here tomorrow." He swept the horizon with a searching glance, which Elizabeth realized she had seen before. He was looking for the reappearance of his demon wind and whirling tunnel.

Slowly the realization dawned on her that the wind and the tunnel would always be in their minds if not existing in fact. No matter what the future held, the threat of the wind and the tunnel would continue to haunt them like an invisible menace. The time anomaly had occurred once; it could occur again. The possibility that Richard could vanish as unexpectedly as he had appeared affected everything they did.

She met Richard's steady gaze and knew she was reading his thoughts as clearly as if they were written on his shirtfront.

"You believe your time here is limited, don't you? That the wind and the tunnel could reappear at any second." He wanted to experience everything he could before he was snatched away.

"Aye, gel." He stared down into her eyes.

Where did that leave her?

Richard stepped forward and caught her by the shoulders. "When the moment comes, I mean to take 'e with me."

Elizabeth wet her lips and searched his gaze. "But what if I don't want to go?"

"'E don't wish to return home with me?" His hands tightened on her arms.

"I don't know." They stared into each other's eyes.

Elizabeth suspected she would be helpless in a world lacking electricity and running water. She hadn't the vaguest idea how to sew a dress from scratch, or how to make fried chicken when the recipe started with a live chicken. The sanitary conditions of Richard's era horrified her; the state of medical knowledge scared her to death. Her independence and attitudes would doom her as an outcast.

"Richard, I'm a researcher, a scholar. I don't have the faintest clue how to make soap or candles."

"'E can learn."

But did she want to? "I can't sew or embroider or quilt. I don't know the first thing about cooking on a wood stove or a coal stove. I'd look stupid in a powdered wig. I like a hot shower every day. I don't think I'd have a prayer of fitting into your time."

It was great fun to fantasize about stepping back into history, but to actually leave the good old twentieth century with it's birth-control pills and Big Macs?

"I'd miss 'Northern Exposure' and my book clubs," Elizabeth said, trying to lighten the seriousness of the discussion. But she cast an anxious glance over Richard's shoulder, suddenly worried that the wind and tunnel might snatch her up before she had thought this through.

"It isn't that I don't want to be with you. It's just that... well, it would be different if I could come back if things didn't work out, but..." She knew it wounded him that she didn't immediately agree to his suggestion. She tried to make a joke. "Boy when you talk commitment, you really want a commitment."

"'E don't have to decide this minute."

Until now, Elizabeth hadn't realized she had to decide at all. She pressed her hands together and drew a breath. "How about you staying here? You don't have to step into the time tunnel, do you?"

They stared at each other, feeling a tug between them, each wanting the other to offer concessions. And suddenly Elizabeth realized they had no tomorrow. No future. None.

Theirs was not a relationship that could ripen and develop over time. They had no time of their own, only his time and hers. Whatever they shared together was solely in the present and could end within the next minute.

"Oh, my God," she whispered. "The wind could return at any second." Her fingers trembled on his shoulders. Panic rose in her throat.

Richard stared into her eyes, then his arms tightened and he crushed her against him in a fierce embrace. "Forget the bloody dive equipment. Let's get the hell out of here. I need 'e, Lizzy."

"Yes," she said wildly, grabbing his hand. "Hurry. Richard, hurry!"

Chapter Eight

Richard was a natural athlete and a quick study. Snorkeling delighted him but didn't provide a real challenge. Immediately Elizabeth moved him into scuba gear. Aside from a spurt of initial panic at breathing under water, Richard took to scuba diving like, well, like a duck to water. When Elizabeth knew in advance that the tourists on her tourist excursions planned to dive, she took Richard along. For Christmas, she gave him a regulator and vest and Richard gave her a necklace made out of shells he had collected from the coral reef that tracked the Keys.

The tourist trade diminished considerably during the week before Christmas and the week after. All the dive boats were moored in their slips, which Elizabeth saw as an opportunity for a break from the tourists and some private diving.

She ducked her head inside Cappy's office door, her dark ponytail swinging. "Hi, stranger. Haven't seen much of you lately. Is it alright with you if I take the *Scavenger III* out tomorrow? I want to show Richard Grecian Rocks."

"You know it irritates me when you ask things like that," Cappy said, not looking up from the ledgers opened across his desk. "The dive boats are as much yours as mine."

"In a bad mood, are we?"

He looked up and ran a hand over his forehead. "Come in and sit down for a minute, will you? And close the door."

Elizabeth's smile faded. The last time she remembered Cappy closing his office door, a hurricane had been ravaging the island. Taking the chair in front of his desk, she searched his expression. Exhaustion tugged his sun-darkened cheeks. Deep worry lines creased his brow. Missing was the buoyant optimism that was so much a part of Cappy's nature.

"It's bad news, isn't it?"

Cappy nodded and let is pencil drop on the ledgers. He leaned back in his chair and rubbed at the weariness in his eyes. "I've been working these figures since yesterday afternoon, but the answer always comes out the same."

"Bad."

"Very bad. Elizabeth, honey, it's time to take a look at some hard choices."

"The money from the tanker salvage is spent?"

"It went in a heartbeat." He turned the expense ledger to face her and indicated a column of figures. "Fuel bills, slip fees, license fees, maintenance, a new engine for *Scavenger II,* payroll." He pinched the bridge of his nose. "We've spent the tanker fee and then some."

"Maybe the bank—"

"We're mortgaged to the hilt right now."

"Juan and Tim might find something with the magnetometer."

"They did, a barge that sank about eight years ago. Nothing of value on board." A large sigh collapsed his chest. "If the *Madre Louisa* sank in that quadrant, the cannon is so silted over they don't register even a faint blip."

"Wait a minute." Elizabeth frowned at him. "I told you what Richard said. It's a waste of time and money to search for the *Madre Louisa*. She was running empty, except for whatever personal items the crew might have been carrying."

Cappy laced his fingers on top of the ledgers and spoke in an expressionless voice. "Is Colter our primary research source?"

A blush heated Elizabeth's cheeks. "Of course not. But I was able to verify what he claimed. The *Madre Louisa* wasn't carrying treasure like we hoped."

"Okay, I needed to hear it verified by more conventional means than Colter." Bending, Cappy opened a bottom drawer and removed an antique bottle of sherry. "I don't know how this will taste," he said as he poured them each a glass. "I brought it up three years ago from a wreck off Haiti. It's from the Napoleonic era. I was saving this bottle for an occasion."

"I'm not sure I want to know what the occasion is."

He touched his glass to hers. "To the end of Golden Dreams. We enjoyed a longer run than most. But like most treasure hunters we finished broke and discouraged."

Elizabeth stared. "You're serious? This is really the end?"

"You don't know how sorry I am, honey. I never should have let you invest in the company. I thought we could turn things around, but . . ."

Elizabeth thought about Tim and Juan and Frank and all the others. A lot of people would lose jobs they loved, if Golden Dreams folded.

"Cappy, there must be something we can do."

"That brings us back to hard choices. First, we could forget about treasure hunting, pare the crew, and concentrate on jobs like the tanker salvage. None of us would get rich, but we'd probably squeak by."

"If we accept that choice, we'll have to fire a lot of people and sell off the dive boats to create some breathing room with the bank. Then we'd have to hope like hell that some other salvage company didn't undercut our prices and steal the jobs." Elizabeth tasted the sherry. It might have been wonderful, but right now it tasted like liquid ashes. "If we went longer than thirty days without a job, we'd be out of business."

"Another possibility is to sell the *Sante Oro* and the treasure-hunting equipment and concentrate on the tourist trade."

"Sell the *Sante Oro?*" It was unthinkable. The *Sante Oro* was practically a Key West landmark. "And depend on a seasonal business?" Elizabeth shook her head. "The competition is fierce and we aren't set up to compete. Our dive boats don't offer luxury accommodations. Plus there isn't enough money in it to support more than one or two people."

"The last option is to give the keys to the bank and walk into the sunset." Cappy looked away from her stricken face. "Honey, I don't know what else to suggest."

"What about the items in the museum? Couldn't we sell some of the pieces?"

Cappy looked embarrassed. "I did that a long time ago. What's left is either fake or on loan from the state."

Elizabeth dropped her head and spoke in a whisper. "Have you told the crew yet?"

"I wanted to talk to you first. Assuming we catch our fair share of tourist excursions, we can hang on another four, maybe five weeks. That gives you and me time to decide how we want to wrap things up and we can still give the crew a couple of weeks notice before the paychecks run out."

The only thing that kept Elizabeth from bursting into tears was the knowledge that her tears would have hurt Cappy more than he was already hurting.

When she could speak in a steady voice, she said, "You've always come through before. Maybe something positive will turn up at the eleventh hour."

"Honey, this *is* the eleventh hour." Cappy refilled his sherry glass then leaned back in his chair and shook his head. "I wish I could be optimistic, but it's not going to happen that way this time. In the past I always had something going. Back in '81 we found the ship's bell from the *Annunciata* two days before the bank was scheduled to foreclose." He smiled, remembering. "It kept this company fat for almost eight years."

"Maybe we'll find another *Annunciata,*" Elizabeth said. The hopelessness in her voice was obvious even to her.

"You can't find something when you're not even looking. It's expensive and pointless to send Tim and Juan out with the magnetometer. We have no leads. Nothing."

"If only I—"

Cappy spoke sharply. "Stop it. You did your job. It's not your fault that we couldn't afford to send you to Seville to verify and follow up the leads you generated. If you want to talk about blame, how about me throwing the Pirates' Ball? What I spent on that party—"

"You're right," Elizabeth interrupted. "There's no sense looking backward." She walked around the desk and hugged him. "What will you do?" she whispered, fighting back tears. "What happens to old treasure hunters?"

"I'll get by. It's you I'm worried about. You've got a mortgage, a car payment… Good-paying jobs are hard to come by in these parts."

Suddenly it struck Elizabeth that no area of her life was solid or secure. Golden Dreams was heading toward a nightmare ending. She was about to lose her investment and lose her job. It was possible—maybe likely—that she would lose her beach house before she found another good-paying position. Which probably would not be in the field she loved.

Then there was her personal life. She was crazy about a man who could vanish like smoke at any second. That was the first awful scenario. The second awful scenario was that he wanted to take her with him into a past century for which she was wildly unsuited. She was about as confused as she had ever been.

Her spirits plummeted. There was nothing to hang on to, no safe place.

"Honey? Are you all right?"

"Don't worry about me," Elizabeth murmured. She gave Cappy a wobbly smile. "For all I know, this time next week I'll be sitting in eighteenth-century Boston trying to figure out how to churn butter."

SHE FOUND RICHARD on the balcony off the kitchen inspecting the parts from her electric coffeemaker. Screws and coils and wire and bits of metal were strewn across the picnic table.

"The bloody thing wouldn't operate," he explained after he kissed her. "I'm trying to repair it."

The possibility of Richard fixing the coffeemaker impressed Elizabeth as about as likely as her lassoing a whale for dinner.

"Are you sure it was plugged in?"

He gave her a blank look then slapped his forehead and groaned. He sat down and stared at the parts. "I'll reassemble it." When she didn't tease him or make a comment, he gave her a hard look. "Have you been weeping, madam?"

His question was all it took to open the floodgates. Tears poured from Elizabeth's eyes. While Richard held her, she explained the collapse of Golden Dreams.

"Treasure hunting and salvage work are all that Cappy knows. And the others...I don't know what will happen to them."

Richard tilted her face up to his. "What about 'e, gel?"

"I'll probably lose my house," she said without thinking. "I've got to find another job." She blew her nose in his handkerchief. "But I don't know where I'll find something that pays as much as I'm used to. Frankly, there isn't much of a demand for my specialty." She stopped speaking for a moment, fighting the lump in her throat. "Right now I'm too upset to think about what to do next. I can't get past the idea of Golden Dreams shutting its doors. Somehow I thought we'd make it."

While she pressed the handkerchief to her eyes, Richard strode across the balcony and gripped the railing. His stormy gaze swept the sea. "'E shouldn't have to fuss yourself with things like seeking employment, paying for a house or putting bread on the table. 'E shouldn't be anxious about saving a business. Those are men's concerns."

"Richard, please. I don't have the energy to deal with your insecurities right now. I have too many of my own."

"'Tis the very thing that blackens me bile! Ye shouldn't be worrying about anything. I should be taking care of 'e."

"You don't understand. I don't want anyone to take care of me! I don't want to depend on you or anyone." Her dark eyes flashed. "When you're dependent on someone, that someone has the power and the control. I learned that while I was growing up. My father had the job and the money, and he never let my mother and me forget it! You know what his favorite phrase was? 'As long as I'm paying the bills, you'll do it my way.' I wish I had a dollar for every time I heard my father say that. When I grew up, I told myself I'd never be in that position again. *I'd* be in control. No man was going to lord it over me ever again!"

They stared at each other.

"This tale about your father explains much," Richard said softly.

"What are you talking about?"

"You're correct, Lizzy. When one person is dependent upon another, the other exercises power and control." His gaze held hers. "'Tis a seductive position, is it not?"

A rush of heat filled her cheeks. "I see the point you're trying to make, but our situation is different."

"Is it? Every time I've spoken of seeking employment, you've listed a dozen reasons why I should not. I have swallowed me frustrations and allowed 'e to persuade me that me limitations be too severe to go in search of income. Is that true? Or does it please ye to keep me dependent and under your thumb?"

"Don't be ridiculous!" She turned away from him, uncomfortable with what he was saying, unsure anymore what the truth was. "You're hardly under my thumb."

"Nay, I'm not. But 'tisn't for your lack of trying."

Only Kelly Thayer's appearance saved the conversation from escalating into an argument. Elizabeth's neighbor bounded up the steps from the beach and gave Richard a grin and a high-five.

"You two have met?" Elizabeth asked, surprised.

"Didn't Richie tell you? We met when he went jogging with Hank. They're out there at the ungodly hour of five-thirty." Kelly made a mock shudder and smiled flirtatiously at Richard. "I found some chicory coffee strong enough that even you will like it."

Richard grinned, running an appreciative eye over the long, shapely legs extending below Kelly's cutoffs. "Now if we can do something about yer biscuits..."

Kelly laughed and tossed back a wave of shining blond curls. "That was a disaster, wasn't it?" Turning to Elizabeth, she explained, "I thought I'd have a nice breakfast waiting when Hank and Richie got back from their run, but I actually dozed standing at the sink. When they arrived the biscuits were burning and there was smoke pouring out of the oven. They thought the house was on fire. Hank went for the fire extinguisher and Richie carried me outside, rescuing me. It was so funny.''

''I'll bet it was,'' Elizabeth said in an acid voice.

She looked at Richard, seeing him in a new light. It made her feel funny inside to realize he had made friends independent of her and was building relationships that did not include her.

There was something else. Watching Kelly flirt with him, seeing him through Kelly's eyes, Elizabeth realized how incredibly sexy Richard was. He stood wide legged, his pelvis thrust slightly forward, his muscled arms crossed over his chest. There was power in that stance, an aggressive masculinity that made women acutely conscious of their own sexual nature. No woman could look at Richard's self-assured posture or look into those smoldering blue-gray eyes without... wondering. Without experiencing a secret thrill of speculation.

''What's all this?'' Kelly asked, looking down at the bits and pieces strewn across the picnic table.

''I'm attempting to repair the coffeemaker,'' Richard said. He made a face that deepened the bronzed lines down his cheeks then smiled at her. '''Tis a puzzle.''

''There was nothing wrong with it in the first place,'' Elizabeth commented sharply. ''He forgot to plug it in.''

The remark was petty and mean spirited. All three of them knew it. A blush of embarrassment heated Elizabeth's cheeks and she bit her lips, wondering what had come over her. But of course she knew. Hot, nasty jealousy; the need to seize control of the moment and whittle it down to more comfortable proportions.

"Well," Kelly said when the silence had grown uncomfortable. "Look, guys, we're having a few people for dinner and we'd like you two to join us. It's nothing fancy, we'll just throw some steaks on the grill. Come as you are."

Richard smiled and said, "Thank 'e kindly." At the same moment Elizabeth said, "Maybe some other time."

Kelly looked from one to the other. "That sounds like a resounding maybe. What's it going to be?"

The unspoken question was: Who's in control here?

"I'd be pleased to accept your invitation," Richard said softly. He spoke to Kelly, but he continued looking at Elizabeth. Elizabeth understood there was more at stake than a simple dinner invitation. They were jockeying for command.

"I'm sorry, Kelly, but I'll take a rain check." She held Richard's steady gaze. "I've had a lousy day. I'm afraid I wouldn't be good company."

The statement was blatantly manipulative. She was reminding Richard that her desires should come first.

"I thought an evening apart from your troubles would be beneficial to 'e."

"It's too bad you didn't think to ask what I thought."

"Beguiling, isn't it, Lizzy," he said softly, his voice almost a caress, repeating what he had said earlier.

Heaven knew what Kelly made of this exchange, but Elizabeth understood it perfectly. She stiffened.

Control is seductive. It was a need, an opiate.

Kelly coughed into her hand. "Guess I'll be running along. See you in about an hour, Richie." She ran down the steps and called from the bottom. "If you change your mind, Elizabeth, come along. It's been awhile since we've seen you."

Elizabeth waited until Kelly was out of earshot, then she stared hard at Richard. When she spoke, her voice was tight and choked. *"Richie?"*

He watched her with an unreadable expression.

"Kelly and Hank have been living together for two years. They plan to marry this summer. You know that, don't you, *Richie?* Kelly isn't up for grabs."

Oh, God. She sounded sarcastic and transparent. Jealous and possessive. Controlling. That was exactly how she was feeling.

He didn't speak, didn't justify, didn't argue. Richard crossed the balcony in three steps, lifted her in his arms and held her against his chest until she stopped struggling, then he carried her inside to her bedroom.

When he placed her on the bed, Elizabeth stared up at him and clenched her fists at her sides. "If you're thinking about making love, forget it." She knew she was being small and nasty, but she couldn't stop herself. "You think that making love washes away any problem. Well, it doesn't!"

When it occurred to her that he might believe her, turn and walk away, she curled into her pillow and burst into tears. She didn't know why she was behaving like this.

Richard lay beside her and gently pulled her against his body. He cradled her in his arms and kissed her tears and the trembling corners of her lips.

"Richard please. Just stop, I—"

He touched his forefingers to her lips. "Shh. Don't speak."

Being cuddled and soothed felt good, but it also made her angry. Never mind what she said she wanted. Richard believed he knew her needs better than she did.

Control is seductive. And he was in control, she thought, despairing, wanting to resist him but unable to.

Slowly he undressed her, kissing each inch of flesh as he bared it, moving over her rigid body with infinite tenderness as if he had never observed her naked before. His fingertips caressed her skin as if she were fragile and unknown, a precious and beautiful blossom to be appreciated and viewed with wonder.

Heaven help her, Elizabeth responded. She wanted to be alone to sort through the confusing tangle of problems and emotions. She wanted to retain control of herself and, yes, of him. But it was impossible to resist. Useless and self-defeating to try.

They shared a chemistry so volatile that a single touch could kindle an inferno. What ignited between them was more than desire, it was a powerful and instantaneous passion. And Elizabeth had learned that passion was as different from desire as a cyclone from a summer breeze. True passion could not be resisted. Its explosive nature swept everything in its path.

Her emotional turmoil melted and fell away in the wake of hot waves of sensation. Tiny fingers of flame traveled beneath her skin, following his fingertips. Elizabeth could no more have rejected his teasing lips and hands than she could have held back the wind. His tongue touched her skin and caused a series of tiny chemical explosions. She went weak inside, then hot and tense and every nerve ending, every hidden cell awakened and wanted more. Their bodies drew each other like powerful magnets. A low groan of surrender broke from Elizabeth's throat and she reached for him, but he pressed her back on the bed.

"Nay, gel. Lie quiet."

Sliding to the end of the bed, he placed one of her bare feet against the crotch of his jeans where she could feel the hard pulse of his arousal. Then he lifted her other foot to his lips and sucked her toes into his mouth.

"Oh, my God," Elizabeth groaned. She couldn't believe that such an act could be so wildly erotic, but it was. She writhed under his attentions as he made love to her with his tongue. Strange, exotic sensations shuddered through her body.

When he finally kicked off his jeans and came to her, she met him with a passion that she feared would tear them both apart.

LATER, WHEN ELIZABETH awoke from a doze, it was dark outside and Richard had gone. Without turning on the lights, she found her terry robe and tied it around her waist, then padded through the house to the kitchen. She poured a large tumbler of orange juice and carried it onto the balcony.

By leaning far out over the railing she could glimpse Kelly and Hank's back deck. Several couples sat around a charcoal grill. Their voices and an occasional outburst of laughter floated on the evening air, a counterpoint to the Van Halen arrangements throbbing from outdoor speakers.

She spotted Richard at once. He was the tallest man at the party. The deck lights shone on his hair, turning it almost white. He was holding a glass, grinning down at a red-haired woman who looked as if she were trying to coax him into dancing.

A huge hole of loneliness burned through Elizabeth's heart. Suddenly she felt like a friendless waif pressing her face to a window beyond which the rest of the world partied. She had never experienced this feeling before and it was awful.

For one frantic moment she considered throwing on her clothes and running down the beach to join the party.

"But that's not what you want to do," she said aloud, stepping back from the railing. Raising the iced glass of orange juice, she pressed it against the frown marks between her eyes.

She'd had a rotten day. The last thing she wanted was to sit around a smoking grill making small talk while she worried if Richard was going to casually mention that he'd been present at the American Revolution.

Was that fair? Surely Richard couldn't be making friends of his own if he spoke like a lunatic. Clearly he had found ways to cope, ways to circumvent awkward questions. He was carving a place for himself. And he was doing it without Elizabeth's help. His need for her was lessening.

While her own need seemed to be increasing.

Frowning, feeling the sting of tears behind her eyelids, she sat in one of the deck chairs and propped her bare feet on the railing, trying to swallow the lump clogging her throat.

The Richard Colter whose portrait had infatuated her—that Richard Colter would not have instructed her what to wear or what to do or how to live. He wouldn't have been quick to take offense, swift to argue. She was sure of it. That Richard Colter would not have transformed everything—even sex, even going to a neighborhood barbecue—into an issue of control.

The Richard Colter for whom she had fallen, and to whom she had called across the centuries, was considerate, sensitive and selfless. At the same time he was bold, reckless and daring. He anticipated a woman's every wish, yet answered to no man. He was a man of strong opinions, but not domineering or dogmatic.

Elizabeth made a sound midway between a sob and a laugh.

The personality she had constructed for the man in the portrait was so shot full of contradictions that he couldn't possibly exist. She saw that now. No flesh-and-blood man could possibly live up to the fantasy creature she had created. What stunned her most was the realization that she would not have liked her fantasy man. She would have lost respect for him the instant she discovered she could manipulate him.

There was the rub. Elizabeth would fight like a tiger to be the dominant partner in any relationship. But in her heart, she couldn't respect a man who would let her dominate him. And she sure as hell didn't intend to allow any man to dominate her.

She turned to glance at the bright lights shining over Kelly and Hank's deck and she bit her lip.

What possible future could she and Richard have? He had made it plain that he would not permit her to make decisions for him. And she would never allow him to make her decisions. They both insisted on being captain of the ship.

THE TEMPERATURE WAS IN the mid-eighties, the sky clear. The sea presented a calm jade surface. It was a perfect day for diving, Richard thought as he clasped his vest and pulled on his flippers while Elizabeth ran up the red-striped flag to warn any passing craft that divers were in the area.

For a moment he paused, captivated by Elizabeth's beauty. Although she thought her hips were too large,

in his eyes she was perfection. Today she wore a neon
pink bikini that glowed in tiny strips across her golden
tan. She might as well have been naked.

To a man who had not glimpsed a strange woman's
ankle until he was twelve, who had not seen a fully
naked woman until he was eighteen and who had never
dreamed of, let alone actually seen, a partially naked
woman standing in daylight sunshine, the sight of
Elizabeth in her bikini was a powerfully erotic image.

Unaware that he watched, she slid into her vest, adjusted her air tanks, then pulled down her goggles.
"Ready?"

"Are 'e sure ye wouldn't like to talk first?" She had
barely spoken two words during the sail to the reef.

She touched his shoulder then climbed onto the dive
platform. "We came to dive. Let's do it."

He studied her a moment. But before he could speak,
she entered the water.

He followed her, splashing backward into the warm
blue sea. Immediately the sound of his own breathing
filled his ears. For a moment Richard's throat closed,
then he forcibly reminded himself to breathe and with
that first hesitant inhalation came a joy so intense it
seared him.

Each time he dived, the miracle unfolded afresh. The
stunning ability to breathe underwater opened strange
new vistas of breathtaking beauty. Each time it dazzled
him.

Sunlight filtered past the surface in watery streams
that illuminated high coral archways and canyons and
made of them an otherworldly cathedral. Color ex-
ploded from a background of opaque blues and mossy
browns. Rusty yellow sponges, purple sea fans, fire
coral. Green lacy formations, the red-and-yellow flash

of parrot fish, the iridescent glow of a queen angel, the powdery white of the sandy floor.

A school of demoiselle fish surrounded him, moving as if guided by one mind, made fearless by the superiority of their numbers. He watched them in awe, lifted his hand to touch and found them gone in an instant.

There were shapes and creatures a few feet below the surface that Richard had never suspected the existence of. Below him lizard fish and sea robbins peeked out of the sand bottom. Scorpion fish and four-eyed butterfly fish. Rose pink images and silver flashes. Steep canyon walls formed of living coral, giant arches and beckoning tunnels.

In the midst of this brilliantly ornamented otherworld was Elizabeth. She hung suspended and almost motionless in the middle of the demoiselles, a delighted smile curving her lips. Her long hair floated around her face like a mermaid's halo attracting the demoiselles that wove through her floating tresses like blue-and-yellow flowers.

Richard stared in wonder and believed he had never witnessed anything so beautiful. She was a sea nymph, a Lorelei, a mermaid queen of majestic form and beauty.

When he approached her the demoiselles flashed away, then surrounded them again. Richard caught her ankles and ran his hands up her legs, shaping her calves and thighs under his palms. The water was warm, but her skin was warmer. Her legs wrapped around him as he glided up her body and clasped her to him. He pressed the side of his head to her flat naked stomach, his cheek against the silky texture of her belly. He held her, letting the current wrap them in a lovers' embrace.

She stroked his cheek, then slid upward, out of his arms. Her body arched, then cut downward. Before she glided through a coral arch, she darted a mischievous glance over her shoulder, her hair flowing behind her like rich, dark seaweed.

He followed her and they played and explored, staying within sight of one another. Elizabeth showed him a stunning spray of staghorn coral; he showed her an eel with razor rows of gleaming teeth. They found a rusted wheelbarrow half buried in the sand, an inexplicable artifact they would laugh about later. They collected shells in the nets tied at their waists.

The next time Richard looked up, Elizabeth was nowhere in sight. He caught up to her in a richly colored cavernlike room that opened at the top to shafts of watery sunlight. His mermaid had folded her arms around her, her face lifted to the opaque filtered light. She spun slowly in the center of the room, surrounded by tiny bubbles.

Richard came up behind her and pulled her tightly against his body, pressing her against his powerful arousal. He smoothed his hands down her waist, peeling off the pink bikini bottom, guiding it down her legs before he released it. The scrap of pink spiraled up and up, riding the bubbles from their air tanks.

Turning her in his arms, feeling her legs wrap around his waist, he opened her vest and then her bikini top exposing her lush pink-tipped breasts to his hands. As she tugged at his trunks and finally sent them spiraling after her bikini bottom, he rubbed his thumbs over her nipples.

The only sound in their underwater cathedral was the sound of his labored breathing. She would hear only her own quickening.

His hands slid over her splendid body. One hand clasped her by the waist, the other slipped between her legs and found the deeper heat within. Her throat arched and her hair floated like a fan behind her. Her nipples nested in the hair on his chest.

Then she clasped his rigidity between her thighs, holding him thus as they drifted upward in a slow spiral. As they passed out of the coral room, he spread her legs with his fingers then gripped her by the waist and guided her down on him, gasping as her inner heat enveloped him.

Locked within her, holding her clasped against his body, he rode the current in her arms, listening to the roar of his breath like distant thunder in his ears. If he lived to reach ninety, Richard knew he would never forget this moment, this strange, weightless, ethereal moment when, locked together, they flowed one into the other, becoming one being, one mind, a single entity.

When they surfaced, a few yards from the dive boat, they released each other and swam for the platform. Once on board the dive boat, they hastily divested themselves of now-cumbersome gear and, glistening in the afternoon sun, kissed the seawater from each other's faces and throats.

Richard took her on the deck of the dive boat. No other boats were nearby, but he was unmindful of that fact. His passion was so urgent, so overpowering that he would have taken her in the midst of a flotilla. He couldn't get enough of her, nor she of him. Her fingernails raked his back and shoulders and he felt nothing except the wild excitement of her body arching to meet his thrust. Dimly he registered that they rolled against things, banged against things, but he was barely cognizant of this.

Once he opened his eyes and she sat astride him, her head thrown back, her lips parted, sunlight blazing on her eyelids and on her magnificent glistening breasts. The next time he looked, she thrashed on the deck beneath him, gasping his name, lost down a path he hastened to follow.

Finally, panting and exhausted, they lay side by side on the deck, holding hands, letting the sun and sea breeze dry their wet bodies.

"Never in my life . . . have I experienced anything remotely like that," Elizabeth whispered, fighting for breath. She rolled her head on the deck to look at him, her eyes almost black, soft and glowing from within.

"Nor I, madam." He shifted to his side and placed his hand on her belly, opening his fingers until his thumb brushed the underswell of her breast and the tip of his little finger rested atop the dark arrow that pointed to her mystery.

"I've never known another like 'e, Elizabeth Rowley." He had believed nothing in his life could surpass the experience of the wind and the tunnel. Then he had found her.

"To say I've never known anyone like you would be the understatement of a lifetime," she said, smiling up at him. "You make me feel things I've never felt before."

A moment ago she had been a wanton, wild and demanding in her passion. Now she lay before him, as naked as a newborn babe, and there was innocence in her nakedness, a vulnerability that made him ache with loving her.

She was a confusing, exciting collection of contrasts. At times she was so unconsciously erotic that sweat popped over his brow and his groin ached at the sight of her. Other times she seemed so fragile and vulnerable that he wanted to clasp her protectively in one arm and slay dragons for her with the other. She was strong and crackling with her version of tough-guy vitality in one instance; soft and vulnerable to pain in the next moment. She would give and give, then take in a challenging manner, as if she expected him to protest her right to grasp anything for herself. Unlike any woman he had known she met him head-on, with a spirit that refused to bow or be conquered.

He drew his fingertip along her jawline and down her throat.

"There are things I would say to ye, Mistress Rowley, but I haven't that right yet," he said in a low voice. He had no worldly goods to offer, no future to promise. God help him, but he wanted her again. He would never have his fill of this woman.

"You can say whatever you like."

"Not if I dare call meself a man of honor. Prepare yourself, madam. When my situation improves I shall have things to say to ye." He cupped her chin and tilted her head back until he could gaze into her eyes. "I swear this by all I hold dear. I shall make my way in this world. I shall repay my debt to ye. Set your mind at ease. I shall provide for us very soon."

She sat up abruptly and reached for her cutoffs and shirt. "It's been a fabulous day, Captain. Let's not spoil it by discussing problems."

He narrowed his eyes as her sun-pinked body disappeared into her clothing. She wrapped her wet hair into a loose knot on top of her head. "Ye don't believe me. Ye think me incapable of paying me own way, let alone providing as a man for us both."

"Please don't assume you know what I'm thinking. It's annoying."

"Then I've erred, madam?"

Their gaze locked before she looked away and turned to the horizon. "It's getting late. I think we'll use the engine instead of sailing back. Want to give me a hand?"

She knew damned well that he didn't know anything about engines or motors. And her silence made it plain that she didn't believe he could contribute to the household coffers. Suddenly they were in the midst of a familiar struggle, battling the swift undertow that ran below their passion for each other.

"Teach me about engines," he demanded, speaking between his teeth.

"Some other time," she said over her shoulder, walking away from him. He wasn't certain, but he thought he'd spied tears in her eyes before she turned away. "If you'll stow the diving gear, I'll start the engine."

RICHARD PAUSED WITH his hand on the handle of the car door. After a moment's thought, he leaned to the window.

"You go ahead. I'll come along later."

Elizabeth leaned past the steering wheel to look at him. Surprise flickered in her dark eyes. "Where are you going?"

"To visit a friend."

"A friend? When will you be home? In time for dinner?"

"I don't know."

Before she could ask more questions, Richard turned away from the car and set off on foot for the wharves fronting the Bight.

IT WAS STARTING to get dark before he found the address he sought. Finally he found the right house on a narrow street crowded with other houses exactly like it. A sagging picket fence defined a minuscule yard enclosing a lemon tree and a scattering of children's toys. The pulsing beat of a salsa tune pounded through a torn screen door.

Richard shouted into the dim interior. The fragrant scent of roasted chilies and baking tortillas wafted toward him. From the back of the narrow house came the shriek of children's laughter.

After a minute or two Manuel Ortiz appeared at the door wearing a pair of cutoff jeans and a loose shirt, holding a sweating can of Budweiser. He grinned and opened the screen door.

"*Holà*. Long time no see. Come in." He shouted over his shoulder. "Rosa! Turn down that radio. Dick's here. Set another place at the table."

After dinner, Richard and Ortiz sat on the back porch steps, drinking beer and watching Ortiz's children chase fireflies across the grass.

Richard swallowed a long pull from the beer can, then he swallowed his pride. "Ortiz, me friend, I need yer help."

"You got it, dude. Wha' you need? Money?"

"I need a job."

"Legal or illegal?"

Richard smiled. "What I don't need is trouble. Legal."

"I can get you on with the shrimp fleet. But you won' like it, man. You was a captain—you owned your own ship. On the fleet, all you gonna be is a strong back and a pair of hands."

"What does the job pay?"

Ortiz named a figure that meant nothing to Richard. He didn't know if the sum represented a lot or a little. It occurred to him that he hadn't a notion of the value of things.

Ortiz slid him a sideways look. "Somethin' 'bout you, Dick, makes me think you don' got no papers."

"What kind of papers?"

"A Social Security card, for one. A driver's license for another. Any employer gonna ask for those things."

"I don't have any papers."

Ortiz nodded. "I know someone who can solve this problem. He'll get the papers you need. But it's gonna cost, man." He watched Richard crush the Budweiser can between his fingers. "I'll take care of it. You pay me back when you can."

A ferocious expression tightened Richard's features. "Thank you, *amigo*. I have to prove to meself—and to someone else—that I can make it in yer world."

Ortiz stared at him. "Someday," he said softly, "I would like to hear your story, my friend."

Chapter Nine

Elizabeth was tired and out of sorts. She'd spent the day on the reef catering to two demanding couples who criticized the utilitarian accommodations on the dive boat, scorned the lunch Elizabeth and Tim served and appeared to blame Elizabeth for the rainstorm that blew up mid-afternoon.

After returning to the docks, she worked in her office for an hour boxing a few files, rolling up charts she would not need again. She paid some personal bills and brooded over her dwindling bank balance.

Although she and Cappy had not decided which option they would select, the final countdown had begun. Golden Dreams was moving through its final days. A month from now, the company in its present form would be only a memory.

Frowning, Elizabeth gazed around her office trying to estimate how many boxes she would need for her mini-library and her personal items. A glisten of tears moistened her eyes. This was the only job she had ever wanted. She had dreamed of hunting treasure all her life. The inheritance that allowed her to buy in as Cappy's partner had been the fulfillment of a lifelong dream.

Standing, she rubbed her eyes, then glanced at the date circled in red on her calendar. Three weeks from tonight she and Cappy would meet and decide how to dismantle Golden Dreams.

Elizabeth intended to argue in favor of concentrating solely on small salvage jobs. Cappy, Tim and Juan could handle the operation. If a big job happened along, Cappy could hire part-time divers.

Accepting this plan would mean laying off twenty-five people, plus Elizabeth. But at least Cappy would emerge from the debacle with a way to make a living. As for herself . . .

Elizabeth closed her office door and walked to her car. Next week she would compose a resumé and start sending it out. Maybe there was a company out there that was dying to hire a research assistant whose specialty was ancient Spanish wave writing.

Right.

As she pulled into her driveway she noticed the red vines crawling along her picket fence looking straggly and badly in need of a trim. Hibiscus was taking over her yard. Maybe after Richard left for work she'd dig out her yard clippers and release some frustrations by attacking the vines.

She found him in the kitchen making peanut-butter sandwiches to pack in his black lunchbox. Earlier on Elizabeth had decided no one on the face of the earth loved peanut butter as devotedly as Capt. Richard Colter. Once Elizabeth had asked what Richard would take back to the eighteenth century if he could take only one thing. Without a second's pause he had answered, peanut butter!

Richard kissed her and ran his hands over her buttocks before Elizabeth ducked out of reach, opening the fridge for a glass of tea. The joy she always felt when she first saw him was diminished by the stress of mounting problems. She felt his speculative gaze before he returned to wrapping his sandwiches.

"Did you dive today?" he asked.

"It was an aggravating day." Briefly she described the excursion, then sat at the kitchen table and rubbed the back of her neck. "I didn't feel like diving." She stared out the balcony doors at the sea. "Does rain effect shrimping?"

"I haven't been at the job long enough to guess."

Neither of them spoke while Richard filled his coffee Thermos. He clipped the Thermos inside his lunchbox, then closed the lid and snapped the latches. Elizabeth tried to decide if the noise he was making was an accusation, a protest against making his own sandwiches. She had an idea Richard believed anything to do with food was women's work.

"I recognize that expression," he commented, glancing at her from the counter. He poured himself a cup of coffee from the new coffeemaker Elizabeth had bought. "If you have a burr in your back teeth, madam, spit it out."

"I don't like feeling guilty about not making your lunch."

He was silent a moment before he said, "I regret 'e had an unpleasant day."

Elizabeth ground her teeth. She was looking for a fight; it was that kind of a day. But he didn't deserve this kind of greeting.

"I'm taking it out on you. I'm sorry."

"The problem brewing betwixt us is not your unpleasant day, nor who makes me sandwiches. 'Tis me—my—employment." Taking a seat across from her at the kitchen table, Richard frowned at the protest forming on her expression. "I don't ken your objection. Given the unfortunate circumstance with Golden Dreams, my earnings should be welcome. Certainly it will salve me pride to make a contribution."

"I don't object to your taking a job," Elizabeth said after a pause. "All things considered, shrimping seems a natural choice. But that night in the restaurant, it was you who said you wouldn't settle for less than a gentleman's trade."

The objection sounded paltry even to her. But it would have sounded even worse to admit that she resented being alone at night, that she resented Richard for wasting a single moment of their precious time together by being away from her.

Richard dropped his head and gazed into his coffee cup. "I've learned a bit since that night," he said finally, speaking in a low voice. "Me skills aren't worth a pig dropping in this era. I've been forced to lower me sights."

A humble Capt. Richard Colter startled Elizabeth and made her feel peculiar inside, as if an invisible hand squeezed her heart. Richard had been a wealthy man. He had sailed the Caribbean as a captain of his own rig. He had called no man master. Manning a shrimp net must seem an appalling comedown. "Richard, do you enjoy going out with the shrimp fleet?"

While he considered his response, Elizabeth studied him, her heart in her eyes. She had trimmed his mane of wheat-colored hair, but it was still long, a style that suited him. He wore it neatly pulled back and tied with a piece of twine. Although the late afternoon was warm, it would be cool on the water at night so he wore a T-shirt he would later cover with a heavy sweater. Beneath the form-fitting T-shirt were the jeans he loved and a pair of white waterproofed shrimping boots.

Although she thought she identified new lines in his craggy face, he was as heart-stoppingly handsome as the night she had pulled him from the water. His smoldering eyes still had the power to turn her breathless and shivery inside. His touch thrilled her and ignited fires in her stomach.

A helpless feeling stole over her as she realized how much he meant to her. There were times when she looked at Richard and felt overcome, awestruck, by the fact that he was here. With her. The sheer miracle of it paralyzed her with joy.

And the things he said, the compliments he paid, indicated Richard held strong feelings for her. But he hadn't told her that he loved her, therefore she didn't say the words either.

The omission had begun to trouble her. A lot.

Richard continued to gaze into his coffee cup and did not see her expression. "'Tis difficult working alongside so many Spaniards," he said at length. A humorless smile twitched the corner of his lips. "'Tis a continual struggle to remind meself these are not the same scurvy Spaniards who plundered and fired me ship. And it rankles to labor at night. I miss you. But 'tis good to be on the water. 'Tis good to feel a freshening wind on me face and smell the sea and the weather."

"You can smell the weather?" She managed a smile.

"Aye. The sea is what I know, gel. It's where I want to be. If I can't labor aboard me own ship, the next best is to labor aboard another man's."

Elizabeth doubted there was a next-best in this instant. If pride had allowed Richard to be entirely truthful, she suspected he would have admitted he wanted his own command. Anything less was a personal affront.

Usually Richard rode Elizabeth's bicycle to the docks, but tonight she drove him to Land's End and parked as near the Bight as she could. Nearly four hundred boats trawled for Key West pinks during the season, which ran from November to July. Not all the boats were in port at the same time. Some stayed out for longer periods, working the Mexican coast. Others, like the boat Richard was assigned, returned each morning.

Richard collected his lunchbox, his sweater and his cap, then kissed her and held her tightly. "I detest arguing with 'e, Lizzy. Even small arguments."

Elizabeth wrapped her arms around his waist and gazed up at him. "I hate it too. But I hate it worse that you're gone at night. Richard, you don't have to do this. We'll get by."

Anger turned his eyes a stormy gray and his arms dropped from her waist. "Damn it, madam! Can 'e not accept a man's need to be a man?"

They stared into each other's eyes as whistles blew, signaling the departure of the fleet. Without another word, Richard spun and ran toward a boat that had already slipped its mooring. He vaulted into it and disappeared into the wheelhouse without turning to wave as he usually did.

Elizabeth remained on the pier until the ship's boom looked like a distant twig bobbing in the twilight haze. Silently she castigated herself for saying all the wrong things. She didn't understand all the stresses pulling at her, but lately her emotions had been zigzagging on an erratic course. She felt a strange tension gathering inside, a prickly feeling as if a storm were coming.

"WAKE UP, MADAM!"

Elizabeth opened one eye. "What time is it?" she protested, burrowing deeper into her pillow. A persistent hand tugged at her shoulder. "I hope that's coffee I'm smelling."

Richard sat on the bed beside her. He lifted her up and mounded the pillows at her back. "'Tis seven o'clock. Take this. It's coffee with a generous helping of rum."

"Rum? At seven in the morning?" Elizabeth pushed back a wave of tangled hair and laughed. "Before I've even brushed my teeth?"

"We're celebrating."

"Whatever we're celebrating must be important."

She could see that it was. Generally Richard didn't wake her until he had showered and shaved. And he was home an hour earlier than usual. She took a closer look. His eyes seemed more blue than gray and sparkled in the morning light. He couldn't sit still, he was almost electric with excitement.

"Did you walk home?"

"Martinez gave me a ride." Taking her hand, he raised it and made her sip her coffee. "Are you awake yet?"

"Aaargh." Elizabeth made a face. "This isn't coffee with rum. it's rum with a splash of coffee. But I'm definitely awake. What's the occasion?"

"Do I smell like fish, madam?" Suddenly his impatience transformed to anxiety. "Mayhaps I should shower and shave first. Change me clothing into something more appropriate for a speech."

Elizabeth's smile widened. Whatever else Richard was, he was not predictable. "You intend to make a speech?"

"Aye. I've been rehearsing in me head all night."

"Well, then." Elizabeth straightened her nightgown and settled herself comfortably against the mounded pillows. She raised her rum and coffee in a salute.

Composing his features into a solemn expression, Richard pulled off his cap, spit on his palms and smoothed back his hair then tugged at his T-shirt, tucking it firmly into his jeans. Apparently the speech could not be delivered sitting on the side of a bed because he stood and chose a spot before the bureau, cleared his throat then squared his broad shoulders.

"A mickle more than three months ago the most extraordinary astonishment occurred. While facing certain death, this mother's son was plucked from me burning ship, sucked through a tunnel and coughed out on a midnight beach. If that weren't amazement enough, I found myself thrown forward two hundred years in time."

Elizabeth met his eyes and smiled encouragement.

"'Tis impossible to describe the frights and terrors of a man in a position such as I found meself. Penniless and ignorant, confused and disbelieving. Surrounded by mechanical beasts and terrifying miracles. 'Tis enough to addle a man's wits and push him insane. Surely this would have been my fate had I not enjoyed the enormous good fortune to have an angel as me guide."

"An angel?" Elizabeth asked with a grin.

"This angel has an irritating habit of interrupting important speeches," Richard said with a mock glare, "otherwise she is very nearly without fault."

Elizabeth rolled her eyes.

"The angel under discussion dragged a stranger from the night sea and offered him the hospitality of her home, though he was bleeding and blathering at the time. She tended him and soothed his confusion. She devoted tireless effort and untold weeks to educating this traveler in a strange land.''

"Richard—"

"I confess I worried for your pagan ways when first I arrived, Mistress Rowley. But I have warmed meself in the glow of your spirit, and I now ken that goodness is not gained in a Sunday pew but in the generosity of one's heart. There is no heart kinder than yours. You have fed and sheltered me, clothed and cosseted me, ye have done so without complaint or hope of repayment. You have given unstintingly of your knowledge and have displayed enormous patience in the face of enormous ignorance. Ye have forgiven all manner of unwitting insult and offense. Ye have shared your thoughts and your woman's warmth and comfort."

Not once did he take his eyes from her face.

"Words fail when I attempt to describe all I hold in me heart toward ye, Mistress Rowley. Gratitude becomes a paltry word, as does any word I could choose to express me appreciation and thankfulness for all ye have given. I can say without reservation that ye are brave and honorable and good. Ye are truly a lady of quality and I am proud to have been given this time with ye."

He drew a breath. "I have thought long on this. When the wind and the tunnel return, I wish ye to accompany me home. I cannot conceive a worthwhile life without ye at me side. If the wind and the tunnel appear when I am alone, or if ye decide ye cannot in good conscience leave this time, I shall grieve yer loss the rest of me days. I shall never—never!—forget ye. If ye remain behind, the best part of me will remain here with ye."

"Oh, Richard." Tears sprang to her eyes. He had said everything but the three small words she most longed to hear. "That's the loveliest speech I've ever heard."

"I have decided upon me epitaph and will instruct my solicitor to this effect. When I die, me epitaph shall read: Here lies Capt. Richard C. Colter. He had the privilege to know Elizabeth Rowley."

Blindly Elizabeth lifted her arms and threw herself against him when he came to her.

"Now for the best part, the surprise," he said, easing her back on the mound of pillows. His eyes danced with excitement and a proud smile spread from ear to ear. He made a flourish with his hand and bowed to her. "This is for you."

After wiping her eyes, Elizabeth peered at the envelope he placed on her lap. "What is it?"

"This is me earnings. The sum won't begin to repay all yer many kindnesses, but at least yer house is saved, thank God!"

"It is? Oh, Richard, thank you, thank you!" If she hadn't been so caught in the emotion of the moment...if she had paused even a few seconds to think... Instead, fingers trembling with anticipation and eagerness, Elizabeth ripped open the envelope and removed the check inside. She stared at it, blinked hard and felt the excitement drain from her expression.

Richard's smile wavered. "What is it?"

The sum was ridiculously small. But of course it would be. A week's pay for a laborer on a shrimp boat was hardly more than a pittance. Elizabeth lowered the check and battled to swallow her disappointment. For one crazy instant her mind had failed to function; she had believed in miracles.

Richard caught her chin and forced her to look at him. His voice was harsh. "It isn't a substantial sum," he said flatly. "I see it in your face."

The last thing she wanted was to hurt him. He had rushed home from the docks to offer her all he owned in this world. He had believed he was rescuing her. Elizabeth fingered the check and searched for the energy to lie.

"Nay, gel. The truth," he demanded.

"It isn't enough money to save the house," she whispered, feeling miserable.

The final residue of hope and pride rushed away, leaving Richard's face pale and his eyes a dull gray. A sudden and devastating onslaught of embarrassment made it impossible for him to meet her eyes. When he spoke, Elizabeth had to lean forward to hear. "Will this scurvy sum repay most of the debt on your house?" She tried, but she couldn't answer. "Some of it?"

"Richard... I'm sorry."

Abruptly he stood and strode to the door. "If 'e will excuse me, madam, I stink. I'll have me shower now."

"Richard!" But he was gone.

Elizabeth held the check in her hands, staring at it. She had believed the sole purpose behind Richard's hiring on with the shrimp fleet had been some macho need to prove his worth as a man. But he had done it for her, to save the house he knew she loved. And all she had done was complain about his hours, about him being gone. Embarrassment and regret overwhelmed her.

She dropped her head into her hands, positive she heard a sharp crack as her heart broke.

RICHARD STILL FELT foolish three days later.

He waited at the boat's stern as Martinez threw out the try net and the engine throttled forward. If the try net came up empty of shrimp, they would move further south seeking more fertile grounds. Richard stared into the darkness beyond the brightness cast by the shrimp boat's strong spotlights.

As he had a hundred times before, he berated himself for insisting on delivering his caw-handed speech. Why had he been so bloody arrogant as to announce that his earnings would save Elizabeth's house? He couldn't just give her the envelope and judge by her reaction whether the sum was adequate. No, he had to make a flourish, he was hell-bent on making a fool of himself.

He helped Martinez haul in the try net, then waited as the boat moved farther south. The low rumble of the engine was a sound Richard wondered if he would ever grow accustomed to. Right now he longed for his own ship, for sounds with which he was familiar. There was nothing to ease a troubled mind like the comfortable creak of a familiar hull or the sight of a noble mast rocking against a star-studded night sky.

Usually he didn't allow himself to think about the people from his own time. Knowing they were gone and forgotten was too painful to contemplate. But tonight he missed Rachel so strongly that his chest ached. His sister would have laughed at the tale of his speech and his arrogance. Then, when she finished teasing, Rachel would have found a way to lessen his humiliation. Perhaps she would have excused his vanity by way of his ignorance.

Ignorant he certainly was. Moreover, he had always been ignorant of spending. In England a true gentleman did not engage in trade, did not soil his hands or his honor by handling money. In colonial America gentlemen engaged in trade, but in a holdover from their English heritage few gentlemen dispersed money.

In Richard's situation, his solicitor and banker managed his warehouses and land holdings. His housekeeper retired his household expenses. When at sea, Mr. Greene, Richard's first officer, paid anchor fees, port duty, customs fees and tavern lists. Months might elapse without Richard opening his purse.

Small wonder that he had given little thought to the cost of items in the twentieth century. His obligation as a man of honor was to earn the fortune that others dispersed in his behalf. The price of butter did not interest him or engage his intellect.

Now he saw that it should have. Only by comprehending the costs of living—knowledge he once had known instinctively or through familiarity—could he understand what constituted a fortune in this age.

Martinez shouted at him. "Stand clear."

He helped Martinez haul in the try net, then watched as the trawling booms lowered the huge, cone-shaped nets. The three big nets were made of mesh woven with holes of decreasing size so the smaller shrimp fell back into the sea and only the larger shrimp remained in the nets.

The engine rumbled louder and the boat picked up speed. The rim of the nets cast a wake that gleamed silver in the light of a crescent moon. In the lull before the nets filled and were hauled on board, Richard and Martinez leaned against the housing and smoked cigars that Martinez offered from his lunch pail.

"I miss my pipe," Richard mentioned absently. Tonight he missed many things. Rachel, his friends, his ship, his pipe. His own place in the world. "What does a house cost?"

"What kind of house? A big house, a little house, a rented house, a trailer house?"

He described Elizabeth's house.

"A house on the beach? In Manhattan Cove?" Martinez made a sound deep in his throat. "A house like that cost at least two hundred thousand. Maybe more."

Richard stared in shock. "It's a small house."

"It's on the beach, man." Martinez shrugged.

Richard's home in Boston was three or four times the size of Elizabeth's beach house. He had a stables, a carriage house, gardens and a fine view of the harbor. He had built it for eight hundred dollars, an enormous sum at the time.

He didn't speak another dozen words. Whenever he thought about his weekly earnings, his face burned with shame.

Chapter Ten

Barefoot, dressed in shorts and T-shirts, Richard and Elizabeth walked along the beach, leaving footprints in the wet verge. It was a beautiful morning. An overnight rain had left the trees and shrubs lining the shore bright and freshly laundered.

They didn't touch.

When they approached a piece of ancient wood tossed up on the beach during the night they stopped and Richard picked up the piece, turning it between his large hands. A light breeze teased Elizabeth's ponytail over her shoulder, rattled the palm fronds a few yards away.

"'Tis part of a ship," he said. "See the wormholes? It's been in the water a long time."

"Richard...what are you really trying to say?" Elizabeth struggled to keep her voice level. She lowered her head and stared unseeing at the piece of rotted oak.

"I told 'e." Richard broke the board between his hands, then flung the pieces back into the sea. He frowned at the spot where the pieces of wood had disappeared. Hard muscle swelled over his shoulders as he crossed his arms over his chest.

Elizabeth glanced at his unyielding profile. Her mind still reeled from his announcement. "Tell me again."

"I need to be on me own."

It wasn't a hot day but Elizabeth could have sworn the sun pounded the top of her head, giving her a painful headache. The air was so thick and humid she felt as if she were choking.

"You never mentioned wanting to live alone before."

"I didn't know 'twas necessary."

"It isn't necessary. We can accomplish whatever you're trying to prove some other way."

God, she was practically begging him not to leave her. Shock and a hint of panic hovered beneath her tone. Elizabeth raised her fingertips to her temples and closed her eyes. Richard was preparing to leave her and she didn't know how to stop him.

"Nay, gel." He spoke softly but in a firm voice. "I must do it this way."

Turning, her ponytail swinging, she lashed out at him. "You don't have to rent an apartment to discover what things cost!"

"Elizabeth, listen to me." He gripped her upper arms so strongly that she winced. "'Tis painfully obvious I don't ken the sums required to be a man in your world. This I must learn."

"Why bother?" She hated the tears threatening behind her eyes, hated this outburst of uncharacteristic weakness. "You're just marking time, waiting for your precious wind and tunnel to come and take you home!"

He was so unswervingly positive that the wind and the tunnel would return that his conviction persuaded Elizabeth that every day with him could be her last. If he was correct, then what he was suggesting would cut short their precious time together. She loathed losing the hours she spent with the tourists and he spent with the shrimp fleet. That Richard wanted to extend their time apart by renting his own apartment left Elizabeth feeling as if she had received a physical blow.

Didn't he know that she loved him? That she cherished every moment with him? He must. How could he not know how much she loved the look of him and the touch of him? She loved the deep, rich sound of his voice and the way he approached the world. She loved his protective instincts and even his stubborn insistence on independence. She loved his delight in ordinary things and the joy and wonder he brought into her life. She loved the way he made her feel about herself.

Elizabeth resented every moment spent apart from him. She had let herself believe he felt the same way. But he seemed to be saying that he needed to put some distance between them.

She hadn't known rejection could hurt this much. In past relationships, it had been she who eased away. The process had been unpleasant but not painful. This was agony.

"'Tis the source of me greatest anxiety that the wind and the tunnel will return whilst I'm apart from ye," Richard said, staring into her eyes.

"If that's true, then don't leave!"

Until now it had not occurred to Elizabeth that men from past eras had lines. She had been naive. Men had been stringing women along since time began. And that's what Richard was doing. He said one thing, but did another. He paid her extravagant compliments and said all the pretty words short of I love you. Then he did what he damned well pleased, with precious little thought for how she felt about it.

The thing was, she had believed Richard loved her but for some reason couldn't say the words. Now she began to believe she'd been wrong. The realization was like a knife blade in her heart. Richard didn't love her. He was grateful to her.

He gave her a shake hard enough that the tears brimming in her eyes spilled onto her cheeks.

"If I knew for certain that the wind and the tunnel would return tomorrow or the day after or next week, no force could wrest me from your side, madam."

If he truly meant what he was saying, then he meant it because he felt grateful to her, or because he read the love in her eyes and he pitied her.

"But I don't know when the sorcery will return! I may be here another week or another three months, maybe longer." It was the first time he had admitted aloud the possibility that the return of the wind and the tunnel might not be imminent. "If I am to remain for a lengthy sojourn, honor demands I pay me way."

"Richard—don't go." She had no shame. Where was her pride? Richard wanted to leave her. She should spit in his eye and shout good riddance.

Frustration deepened the lines framing his mouth. "Madam, I beg your understanding."

Elizabeth stepped backward. She was surprised that she didn't hear pieces of herself rattling around inside. "There's nothing I can say to make you change your mind about moving out, is there?" Her voice was a whisper. "You've made up your mind."

"'Tis for the best."

"Why don't you just admit the truth?" She clenched her hands at her sides and fought desperately not to say the next words. But they poured out in a torrent of hurt and anger. "Why don't you just say that you're tired of this relationship? That it's over for you."

"What?" He frowned at her.

"Don't give me that innocent look, like you don't understand what I'm saying. Why can't you at least be honest? You're grateful to me for taking you in and helping you cope with all that's happened to you. But you don't like me trying to tell you what to do. You think I'm too controlling. It's been a struggle from the first. You think I should be some kind of handmaiden who does your bidding. If that's what you're looking for, then go on and leave!"

"Lizzy—"

She dashed a hand across her eyes. "I don't want your damned gratitude! I did the best I could, Richard. If that's not good enough for you, then to hell with you! It doesn't make any difference to me, I don't care. If you want to go, then go! And take your paycheck, I don't want that either! But if you go, don't come back! You aren't going to play me for a sucker again. No more talk about empty commitments, no more pretty talk about you not wanting a life without me. Liar!"

Spinning on her heel, Elizabeth ran down the beach angrily wiping tears from her eyes, furious that she'd lost control and allowed him to see how badly she was hurting. She flew through the house, pausing only to snatch up her car keys. As she jumped into her car she heard Richard shouting behind her, but she ignored him and stepped on the gas, spraying gravel behind her.

Three hours later she returned home. Her eyes were reddened and hot and she couldn't remember where she had been. But she remembered the speech he had made, the pretty words that she had fallen for.

Moving like a sleepwalker she walked through the house, then out to the balcony looking for him. But Richard was gone. She told herself that she was glad. If their relationship had been what she had believed and what she wanted it to be, then he wouldn't have left her.

Finally she entered the guest room where Richard kept his clothing and she opened his closet. He had taken the clothes he arrived in and he had taken his shrimp boots and work clothes. He had left behind everything else she had bought for him.

For one heart-thumping moment Elizabeth thought this meant he would be coming back. Then her shoulders slumped and she covered her face with her hands. It was pride, not his intention to return, that made him leave her purchases behind.

Their relationship was over.

IT WAS GOOD THAT ORTIZ offered to help him obtain an apartment, because Richard was too distracted to focus his attention on the process.

Elizabeth's reaction had stunned and confused him. Naively he had assumed she would support his need to make it on his own. But no matter how patiently and logically he had explained, nothing he said cut past her objections. She wanted him to remain dependent; then suddenly she didn't. After arguing that he should remain with her, she spun a hundred and eighty degrees and ordered him to leave and never return. She had called him a liar.

"She don' mean it, dude."

He glanced at Ortiz as they inspected the third apartment they had looked at so far.

"Ain't that what this is about?" Ortiz spread his hands in a gesture of sympathy. "We looking for a place 'cause your woman kicked you out?"

"Leaving was me own desire." And not a good one, as things had turned out. It appeared he had acted under a set of assumptions that no longer applied. Maybe they never had. He had assumed Elizabeth cared for him. He had dared hope she loved him.

After a cursory glance around an apartment about the size of a mousetrap, Richard shrugged and said it would do.

The monthly rent shocked him. A third of his wages would go for the apartment, this before he fed or clothed himself. The apartment was close enough to the Bight that he could walk to work, thank heaven.

After he signed a month-to-month lease, he fanned out his remaining money and counted it with a moody expression. "At least do I have enough to buy us some beers?"

Ortiz grinned. "You got that much."

They walked to the tavern near where they had first met. Richard slapped half of his bills on the table and told Martina, the orange-haired waitress, to bring pitchers of Bud until the money was gone.

He turned his head to the window. He could see the waters of the Bight from here. Suddenly he wished he were on one of the dive boats with his beautiful Elizabeth, about to tip backwards into that solitary otherworld beneath the waves. In that underwater world nothing at all was familiar. And total unfamiliarity was more comfortable than being on land where some things were just familiar enough to lull him into thinking he knew what the hell he was doing.

"Do you scuba dive?" he asked Ortiz.

"I've got a bad ear." When Richard looked puzzled, Ortiz explained, "When I was a kid, I got in a fight and my left ear got screwed up. Anything below thirty feet and the pressure is like a knife in my ear, man." He shrugged. "Sometimes if I get some extra money Rosa don' know about, I rent some equipment and go out on the reef. But nothing deep."

An important implication resonated through Ortiz's words, something elusive and just out of reach. Too many distractions occurred before Richard could isolate what it was. Martina interrupted with another pitcher of Bud; one of the men in the tavern snapped on the television over the bar. The conversation moved to other topics. By the time Richard and Ortiz left the bar, he had forgotten the moment.

ELIZABETH TRIED TO KEEP busy. She cleaned her house from top to bottom, symbolically washing away Richard's memory.

The effort wasn't successful. Everywhere she looked, she found reminders of him.

She scheduled lunch with friends, ran daily tourist excursions, rented movies at night. And told herself she didn't miss Richard, told herself she was fine.

It was a lie. She missed him every minute of every day.

And she wasn't fine. Her emotions were running amuck; she had lost control of both her professional and personal future. She who had prided herself on running a tight ship was now adrift in a rudderless boat. She had never felt as helpless in her life.

Midweek she met Cappy at the *Sante Oro* to discuss dismantling Golden Dreams. She dreaded the meeting, knew it was the end.

Cappy ran a hand over his bald head and leaned back in his desk chair. "Well, honey, this is it." He laced his fingers together and blew out a deep breath. "I've considered your argument for paring down the equipment and crew and concentrating on small salvage jobs. That's just prolonging the agony, don't you think? A couple of months of bad luck and no jobs and we'd be right back where we are now. Staring bankruptcy in the face."

Elizabeth tried to focus on what he was saying. "What, then? Are you suggesting that we just shut the doors and walk away? Let the bank take everything you've worked a lifetime to build?"

Cappy tilted back in his chair and stared at the ceiling. "I started this business to look for treasure, not to salvage scrap iron. Maybe treasure hunters get one big strike and that's all. If so, I had mine. There isn't going to be another *Annunciata.*" Finally he looked at her and Elizabeth read the pain in his eyes. "Honey, it's time to cut our losses and move on down the road."

"I can't believe it," Elizabeth said in a dull voice, twisting her hands in her lap. "It's really over, isn't it? Golden Dreams and…" She bit her lip against the tears forming in her eyes.

"And what, honey?"

"Richard's gone." The words blurted out before she could stop them. "This time for good."

"I'm sorry to hear that," Cappy said, surprising her. "The guy's nuts, but he was likable enough. I know you cared for him."

Cappy's use of the past tense sounded so final that Elizabeth embarrassed herself by bursting into tears. Between sobs, she told Cappy the whole story.

At the end, he leaned over his desk and offered his handkerchief. "Believe me, I hate to say this, but you're wrong on this one, honey. Colter's doing what he has to do. Assume for a minute that he really is from another century." Cappy grimaced, irritated to hear himself saying such a stupid thing. "If we assume that's true, then he knows nothing about current finances. And he isn't going to learn if you're paying his expenses. I'll tell you something else. Sure Colter is grateful for everything you've done for him. But he's also crazy about you. Anyone who's seen the two of you together knows that."

Elizabeth blew her nose. "It's gratitude, that's all."

"I don't want to sound like a cornball here, but Colter seems to believe the two of you share a passion that transcends time." Cappy actually blushed.

"He's never even said he loved me!"

Cappy leaned back in his desk chair and watched her dab her eyes. "You're the historian—why do you think that is?"

She stared at Cappy, suddenly realizing how muddled her thinking had been. The answer was right under her nose, so close that she hadn't seen it. She spoke slowly, working it out. "In Richard's time a man didn't tell a woman he loved her until he was prepared to follow his declaration with a marriage proposal."

"And?"

"And he didn't make a marriage proposal until he was financially able to provide a home, furnishings and so on."

Cappy beamed at her. "Whether or not Colter dropped out of another time zone, the point is he believes he did. Doesn't it follow that he would adopt the attitudes of the time period he claims to hail from? He's out there trying to make a fortune so he can declare himself. He isn't going to put together any real money working for the shrimp fleet, but he doesn't know that."

"He does now."

"That he's out there trying to learn how to make his fortune tells me he's plenty serious about you. Why else do you think he's living in a fleabag apartment? Because he likes it?"

"Oh, God." Elizabeth stared at him. Everything he said made perfect sense. It was a classic case of being too close to the forest to see the trees. "Cappy, I called Richard a liar and told him never to come back! I've been an idiot! What am I going to do?"

Cappy laughed. "Colter isn't a man to let any woman tell him what to do, not even you. You might persuade him of something or manipulate him without his knowing it. But flat out telling him..." Cappy shook his head, grinning. "That won't work. Colter is as stubborn as you are. Trust me—when he's ready, he'll show up on your doorstep." He rubbed his jaw. "He's probably steamed about being called a liar though."

A blaze of hope illuminated Elizabeth's eyes. She felt happier than she'd felt in four days, but apprehensive too. What if Cappy was wrong? Maybe she was grasping at straws.

"You said Richard was living in a fleabag apartment. Do you know that for a fact?" She ached inside with wanting to see him.

"Everybody on the wharf knows what everybody else is doing. You know that. Oh. You want his address."

"I have an apology to make." Her glance darted to the ship's clock behind Cappy and her face fell when she realized Richard was out with the fleet. "I'll have to wait until morning," she said, wishing the night away.

Impatience burned a hole in her heart. She wanted to tell him what a blind fool she had been, wanted to smother him with support. And she wanted—needed— to do it *now*.

RICHARD LEANED AGAINST the railing, smoking his pipe. He and Martinez watched the try net, hoping their next attempt would yield more than an earlier one. Their catch had been a collection of debris, a life preserver and bits of a wrecked dingy.

"My ship is out there somewhere," Richard remarked, studying the debris. His new pipe didn't draw as well as the pipe he'd lost aboard the *Black Cutter*, but it pleased him. A good pipe and the sea went hand in hand. "She went down fast. There wouldn't have been much debris."

"You salvage anything?"

"Nay."

"Not worth salvaging?"

"Her cargo would more than compensate any salvage attempt," Richard said with a humorless smile. "Unfortunately me ship sank in water too deep to salvage."

"How deep?"

Martinez kept his gaze on the net, not really interested in Richard's reply. They were making idle conversation while they waited to see if shrimp showed up in the area.

"Me ship sank in about thirteen fathoms." The scene would live forever in his mind. The fire, the screams, the hissing water.

Martinez flipped his cigar over the rail, yawned and stretched. "What's a fathom, man? What's that in feet?"

"It's..." Richard stiffened. "Jack in hot hell!" For an instant his mind was as startled and rigid as his body. Then his thoughts leaped forward at a furious pace, pausing only to castigate himself and release a torrent of swearing.

Fathoms. Feet.

He hadn't calculated the conversion before, had not even thought about it.

"Net's up," Martinez announced, moving toward the stern. "Back to work."

Richard had performed the routine often enough that he could work without thought. Fortunate, because his mind raced and darted, recalling scraps of conversation that only now began to take shape and knit together.

He had asked if Ortiz scuba dived. Ortiz had answered that his ear ached at a depth below thirty feet.

He remembered Elizabeth clipping a depth gauge to his vest and although they had not dived much below fifteen feet, the indicator on the depth gauge displayed a range of one hundred and twenty feet.

Finally he remembered Cappy showing him the equipment aboard the *Sante Oro,* remembered wondering why Cappy required lights that worked underwater. Now he remembered Cappy attempting to explain something he called a "mailbox," a device that directed the prop wash below the surface to blow sand away from the ocean floor. The air blast from Cappy's mailbox could reach more than sixty feet to clear layers of bottom sediment down to bedrock.

Always the depth was measured in feet, not fathoms.

But feet were measurements on a gauge, that's all. Feet were small units that did not represent a depth

Richard automatically understood. All his life he had thought in terms of fathoms.

"I've been a crack-brained gudgeon!" he swore, staring at nothing.

Feet. Fathoms.

The possible implications were so stunning they dazzled him. If he was right . . .

Impatient, he asked Martinez what time it was and groaned when he heard the answer. Elizabeth's face rose before his eyes, angry and hurting as he had last seen her. Feeling wild inside, he cast a glance back toward Key West. Right now she was meeting with Cappy to dissolve Golden Dreams. He would have moved the earth to be with her right now, to catch her up in his arms and stop that meeting.

But time held him prisoner on the water. This was going to be the longest night of his life.

As soon as the sun popped over the horizon, Elizabeth knew it was going to be a scorcher of a day. The sun blazed white, sucking the color from the landscape and energy from those below.

She stood beside her car, wringing her hands and watching the shrimp boats return to the pier, suddenly unsure of herself. If Richard wanted to see her, wouldn't he have made the first move? Was seeking him out a good idea or was it an unconscious effort to regain control? Maybe coming here had been a big, big mistake.

She was still hanging back, feeling crazy inside and biting her lip in uncertainty, when she saw his boat come in. Before she could decide whether to step forward, she saw Richard leap from the boat to the wharf and start running.

This surprised her so much that she involuntarily shouted his name and bolted forward. He halted and looked around, spotted her, then ran to meet her.

"Lizzy!" They flew into each other's arms. He caught her on the run, swinging her up in a circle until she was breathless and her ponytail flew out behind her. He set her on her feet and crushed her in his arms. "Lord God Almighty, gel, but I've missed 'e! Were ye this beautiful a week ago?"

The speech Elizabeth had rehearsed evaporated from her mind. Her fingers flew over his face, his hair, his muscled shoulders, reassuring herself that he was solid and real and still here. His thighs were rock hard against hers; his hands felt like a circle of flame around her waist.

"I've missed you every minute of every day," she started to say, but his mouth covered hers and drowned the words. He kissed her roughly, passionately, with a hard hunger that told her his need was as great as hers.

Whistles and catcalls sounded from the shrimp boats, and a round of applause erupted when Richard released her. Richard waved and grinned; Elizabeth blushed bright red and prayed her knees would not collapse. His kiss, the pressure of his hot, hard body against hers, had left her shaken and wanting him with a desire she felt certain was obvious to anyone who saw her.

"I have so much to say to you," she said, looking up at him. His blue-gray eyes smoldered down at her, passionate and alive, and Elizabeth's stomach tensed into a series of flip-flops.

"And I have things to say to 'e, gel."

"Where were you running off to?"

"To you."

"Oh, Richard." Now that she had seen him again, now that she was standing beside him, thrilling to the chemistry that flashed and crackled between them, she didn't doubt what he was saying. She didn't know how it was possible that she ever had. She had only to gaze into his blazing eyes to know he spoke the truth.

But there was more than truth and desire in his intensity. He was electric today, vibrating with an excitement so hot and fierce that he seemed to throw off sparks. He resonated with an inner heat, radiated it. A strange joy and tension gripped his expression, kindled embers in his eyes.

"We have to talk, gel. Now." His fingers clasped her shoulders with the power she'd come to associate with Capt. Richard Colter.

"I know." Even if talking had not been her intention, she could not have resisted. His electric intensity was like a cyclone sweeping away any obstacle in its path.

He stared into her eyes with a look so penetrating that Elizabeth forgot they were standing in a parking lot surrounded by people. The world narrowed to Richard's eyes, blazing into hers like twin suns. His fingers tightened on her shoulders.

"How many feet make a fathom?"

"What?"

It was a question she could not have anticipated in a million years. If he had asked if she loved him, that she was prepared for, that she would have understood. Dumbfounded, she stared up at him until he gave her an impatient shake and repeated the question.

"If I live to be a hundred, I'll never understand you."

"Lizzy." The impatience in his voice emerged as a cry of near anguish. "Tell me I haven't erred, gel. Tell me how many feet are in a fathom!"

"Six feet to a fathom, give or take an inch or so," she said finally.

"Aye!" Turning from her, he raised his fists in the air, then struck the hood of her car hard enough to leave a dent. Elizabeth stared in astonishment.

"Aye, aye! I've been a bloody fool!"

Oddly, his physical outburst was more an expression of excitement than anger. Elizabeth blinked at the dent, then stared at him.

He grabbed her hand. "Come on, gel, run."

"Run? Run where?" None of this was unfolding as Elizabeth had anticipated. She was totally confused.

"To the *Santa Oro*. Is Cappy there?"

"I suppose so, he—"

But Richard pulled her forward into a run. Holding hands, they pelted along the wharves, running as if the devil nipped their heels, running until the *Sante Oro* came into view, until Elizabeth was gasping for breath and sure her heart would burst.

When they reached the ramp leading aboard the old galleon, she stopped and refused to take another step until she caught her breath. Bending, Elizabeth placed her hands on her knees and panted, gulping air and feeling the blood pulse in her head.

"What . . . is this . . . all about?"

Richard wasn't even winded. Impatient, he scooped Elizabeth into his arms and dashed up the ramp onto the lower deck of the *Sante Oro*, shouting Cappy's name.

"Haleburton! Haleburton, where are ye, man?"

Cappy emerged from his office, shading his eyes from the sun. When he saw Elizabeth laying limp against Richard's chest, he halted and the blood drained from his sunburned face.

"What's happened? Is she hurt?"

Grinning, Richard set Elizabeth on her feet. He stood with legs planted wide apart, fists on hips, the sun blazing in his mane of golden hair.

"How much would three tons of gold bullion be worth on today's market?"

Elizabeth and Cappy exchanged a puzzled glance then Elizabeth returned to Richard. "Gold is worth approximately three hundred and fifty dollars an ounce. That would be—wait a minute—thirty-two thousand ounces in a ton, times three tons, multiplied by three hundred and fifty dollars an ounce," frowning, she calculated the figures. "Okay, three tons of gold bullion would be worth approximately thirty-three and a half million dollars."

Richard's grin widened. "Do I be correct, madam, in thinking thirty-three million dollars t'would be a bloody fortune in any damned century?"

"It sure as hell would," Cappy confirmed.

Elizabeth wet her lips. "Richard, why are you asking this?"

"Because I know where to find three tons of gold bullion." He tossed back his mane of golden hair and laughed with sheer joy. "Would Golden Dreams be interested in salvaging it?"

Chapter Eleven

They moved into Cappy's office out of the hot sun. Without saying a word, Cappy opened three icy cans of beer and handed them around before he settled behind his desk and propped his sandals on the desktop.

"You're full of crap, Colter. But I'll say this for you, you know how to make an entrance."

"Richard, what are you talking about?"

They gazed at him as if he had suffered a sunstroke. Richard smiled, excited by the heat burning inside him.

"A fathom equals six feet," he explained, grinning broadly and talking too fast. When they didn't react, he spread his hands. "Don't 'e understand? Me ship sank in thirteen fathoms—seventy-eight feet. I know where it is!"

Elizabeth spoke slowly. Her legs looked as long as a main mast, tanned and golden beneath her shorts. "Are you suggesting we salvage the *Black Cutter?*"

"Aye!" The word burst from his chest.

"I don't get it," Cappy said, frowning at Elizabeth. "Didn't you say the *Black Cutter* was carrying perishables?"

Elizabeth nodded. "I have a copy of the cargo manifest in my office. The *Black Cutter* was carrying bananas and raw sugar. That makes her empty, as far as we're concerned."

Richard slapped his forehead and excitement leaped in his eyes. "Now I understand! I thought ye weren't interested in the *Black Cutter* because she sank too deep to salvage. But 'e weren't interested because 'e thought she were carrying sugar!"

"That's all that's listed on the manifest."

"Do 'e think I'd list three tons of bullion on the manifest, gel? If I'd done something that crack-brained, I wouldn't have cleared the harbor before being over-run by the French or by pirates! T'would be like painting a target on me stern!"

They stared at him.

"Okay, Colter, for the sake of discussion—you claim you were shipping three tons of gold bullion. How did you get it?"

" 'Tis a long tale."

Cappy sipped his beer. "I'm not doing anything for the rest of my life. Just sitting here waiting for some damned fool to come along and dangle three tons worth of treasure."

Richard laughed. "Have you heard of a black slave named Pierre Dominque Toussaint L'Ouverture?"

"The leader of the 1794 Haitian slave uprising?" When Richard didn't register recognition, Elizabeth added, "Sainte Domingue is now Haiti, remember?"

He nodded. "Aye, then that would be the same man. To make a long tale brief, Toussaint stole the gold from the French. He intended to use it to finance his revolution. But he feared keeping the gold on the island, lest the French retake it or one of his own people betray him. Toussaint hired me to ship the gold to Boston and place it in a bank vault until the revolution began."

"You're saying you had Toussaint's gold on the *Black Cutter* when it sank?" Cappy asked.

"That would explain why the *Madre Louisa* attacked you," Elizabeth said, thinking out loud. "I couldn't understand why the Spaniards attacked a ship carrying sugar. I guessed the history was skewed. I figured *you* must have attacked the *Madre Louisa*."

"Nay, gel. I was running flat out for Boston. But some scurvy dog betrayed us to the Spaniards. They were on the chase from the minute we cleared the Port-au-Prince harbor."

"So why didn't you mention this before now?" Cappy asked. His face remained carefully expressionless.

"In my day 'twas impossible to salvage a ship that sank in thirteen fathoms. Five fathoms, six—anything deeper was a total loss. I assumed we all meant the same when we spoke of a deep-water wreck." Excitement leaped in his eyes. "But we don't! Lord knows what you people consider a deep-water wreck, but it sure as bloody hell isn't what I assumed."

"With the proper equipment, a two-thousand-foot wreck can be salvaged. I'm not saying it would be easy, only that it could be done," Cappy said, staring at him. "An eighty-foot wreck is a relatively simple undertaking."

Elizabeth closed her eyes, then opened them. "Richard, where is the *Black Cutter?*"

A silence descended as Richard approached the wall chart and studied it. "Here," he said finally, jabbing a finger against the chart. "I can't be as precise as ye are today, me instruments weren't as accurate. Plus some drift occurred during the battle with the *Madre Louisa*, but me ship must have gone down—here."

Elizabeth's perfume rose in his nostrils as she and Cappy stepped up beside him. He wanted to tear off her T-shirt and shorts and make love to her until she thrashed like a wild thing beneath him. It required excessive willpower not to pull her into his arms right now.

"I don't understand how that location can be possible," she said finally. Raising her hand, she penciled an X on the chart. "Every scrap of research I've turned up says this is where the *Madre Louisa* sank, and, Richard, we know she sank less than an hour after the *Black Cutter*. At least one survivor was picked up by a Cuban trawler. I've read his account of the battle and the sinking of the *Madre Louisa*. That account—and all other evidence—places the battle site a good hundred miles from where you claim it happened."

He blinked. "Are ye calling me a liar, madam?"

"There's certainly a big discrepancy," Cappy interrupted. He ran a sun-browned finger from Richard's indicated site to the X on the chart. "If you're right," he said, "then the *Madre Louisa*, ablaze and taking on water, drifted nearly a hundred miles in an hour." He shook his head. "It's not possible. Elizabeth can show you half a dozen historical references which state that both ships sank in this area." His finger jabbed the X.

"I'm telling 'e, that's not where it happened! 'Twas my ship, man! I was *there!* The battle took place *here.* Your research is bloody damned wrong!"

In the silence that followed, Richard understood he had stated the core of the problem. For Elizabeth Rowley and Cappy Haleburton to believe the *Black Cutter* sank a hundred miles from the site indicated by surviving documents...they had to believe Richard Colter was who and what he claimed to be.

The droning hum of the overhead fan was the only sound in Cappy's small office.

Finally Cappy stepped away from the wall chart and returned to his desk chair. It squeaked as he sat down and leaned back.

"You had me going for a minute or two," he said in a voice flat with disappointment.

"Elizabeth?" When she didn't answer, Richard turned to Cappy, his shoulders stiff and squared. "I'm asking ye to believe me, Haleburton." He drew a breath and laid his pride on the line. "I've pondered lengthy and hard on me situation, and I see a future for meself in salvage."

Leaning forward, Richard placed both palms on Cappy's desk. "Think on it, man." He nodded to one of the wall charts. "Ye'r looking for the Spanish Plate Fleet. Yer chasing clues obscured by two hundred and fifty-nine years. But for me, that fleet sank only fifty-nine years ago. The stories—and the clues—are fresh. It's all up here." He tapped a finger against his temple. "I can find those galleons."

"I've heard some crazy ideas in my time, but this one takes the cake."

Richard's chin jutted stubbornly. "I'm willing to offer a partnership. Our new company can be funded by the salvage from the *Black Cutter*. Help me find me ship, Haleburton; discover for yourself if I know what I'm saying. What do 'e have to lose?"

Cappy ran a tired hand over his face. "Do you know what it would cost to mag an area as large as you're indicating?"

Elizabeth finally spoke, but she didn't meet Richard's eyes. "We could delay obtaining the exploration license and the security bond until we actually hit something. That would save a bundle.''

"You know the law," Cappy said.

"I know that particular law is broken all the time. And we could use the sonar sled instead of magging. That way we could save the cost of towing out the platform buoys and extra men to do the triangulation and gridding."

"The sonar sled isn't a good choice for an area this big, and it only works if part of the wreck is above the sand. In this particular case, surviving timber seems unlikely. Plus, you still need triangulation if you want a hope in hell of covering everything." Cappy jerked his head toward the chart. "You heard Colter. He can't give us a precise location, plus he admits there was a drift factor." He shrugged. "Hell, that ship could be anywhere." He looked up at them. "We're out of time and money."

Richard threw out his hands in frustration. "What exactly is a bloody magnetometer? What are you speaking of when you refer to magging?''

"A magnetometer registers the presence of metal." Elizabeth's large dark eyes lifted to him. "That's a ridiculously simplified explanation, but the magnetometer will identify the presence of cannon, a ship's bell, an anchor.''

"I'm sorry, Colter, forget it. If I were thirty years younger I'd probably beg, borrow or steal enough money to follow up a lead even as crazy as this one." Cappy ran a hand over his balding head. "But not now. The few dollars left in the company account are earmarked for wrap-up expenses. Believe it or not, it costs a lot to go out of business."

Richard dropped into a chair and stared at them in disbelief. "I'm telling 'e where to find thirty-three million dollars worth of gold bullion . . . and ye aren't interested."

It wasn't only their future at stake but his own. If Cappy and Elizabeth wouldn't believe he knew what he was talking about, no other salvage company would either. Richard smashed his fist on the arm of the chair and swore through his teeth.

Elizabeth observed his frustration and his anger, watched defeat replace his energy and excitement.

She understood why Cappy had to reject Richard's request. Refusal was her first instinct too. Richard was a student in this world, an authority on nothing. Everything he stated as fact was suspect, because his knowledge was limited and his opinions were founded in ignorance or based on outdated assumptions.

For a moment she tried to imagine what it would feel like never to be taken seriously, to have one's opinions and beliefs dismissed with amusement or indifference. She tried to imagine Richard's frustration at believing he could glimpse a future for himself when no one would offer the help he had to have.

She drew a long, deep breath and looked at him.

"I believe you," she said quietly.

Richard's head snapped up and he gave her a look of such gratitude, such smoldering intensity that Elizabeth was glad she was seated. That particular look made her knees go weak.

She drew another long breath. "I'll fund the search. I have enough money in my savings account to pay for—" she performed a swift calculation "—four days." then she would be dead broke. "We'll have to do it on the cheap, without the buoy platforms. And we'll be absolutely dependent on a hell of a lot of luck."

"Have you lost your mind?" Cappy bolted forward over his desk. "You know the company policy about using personal funds for business goals. If we were willing to break that rule, we would have used personal money to send you to the archives in Spain."

"I'm going to do this, Cappy."

"It's crazy! You know damned well you can't begin to cover an area this large in four days!"

"We can try. We could get lucky."

"Elizabeth, let me remind you that you won't recover your investment in Golden Dreams. Whatever you have in savings is all you have in the world. You'll come out of this insanity with flat nothing. You'll lose your house. Hell, you won't have enough money left to buy a postage stamp to send out your resumé."

"Is that true?" Richard did not take his eyes from her face.

Now that the decision was made, Elizabeth felt a strange sense of calm. Life was totally out of control, but it didn't feel as terrible or as devastating as she had always imagined it would. In fact, there was something exhilarating and freeing about throwing herself into the midst of the chaos instead of fighting the inevitable and battling to regain control.

And there was something else. Even stronger than her own instinct for self-preservation was the need to save Richard. All that he was and all that he might become depended on whether they believed that he knew where his ship had sunk. If they couldn't believe this—then he would never be believed about anything. Such an outcome would destroy Richard Colter. For such a man, death was a preferable fate to life without honor.

"I believe you," she repeated softly. "I'm willing to stake everything I own on that belief."

This, then, was commitment. To fly in the face of logic and hard evidence. To risk all. To irreversibly link one's fate and future to that of another. And to believe in her heart that what she was doing was utterly and absolutely right.

Richard sprang from his chair and knelt before her, taking her hands in his. His craggy face was hard and determined.

"'Tis not proper for a woman to enter business. Ye should accept your uncle's advice."

Elizabeth looked into his eyes and read what this statement cost him. She touched his cheek. "I'm a woman of my times, Captain. I'll make my own decisions, but thank you. Here's the deal. I'll pay all expenses for a four-day search. If we find anything, half is mine. We're equal partners."

"Equal partners with a woman." For an instant the thought shocked him, then he grinned. "I shall not fail ye, madam. Ye will not regret this decision."

"I know," she whispered. They would triumph or fail together. That was all that mattered.

"You're insane! Both of you!" Cappy slammed his beer can down on his desk. "Elizabeth, there isn't a shred of evidence to support Colter's claim. Hell, even *he* doesn't know for sure where the damned thing sank! He measured latitude by the stars and longitude was in its infancy in his time." Cappy's eyes widened and he looked startled. "Good God, what am I saying? I sound like I accept this lunatic's story." A shudder of distaste ran down his spine. "Elizabeth, I beg you not to throw away what little you have left on a man who has a screw loose. Colter is *not* from some other century! He doesn't know, couldn't possibly know, where the *Black Cutter* sank. Be reasonable—you read the cargo manifest, you know damned well there was no gold aboard that ship! Listen to me. Colter recognizes the difference between a prow and a stern, but this man is not a sailor and never was!''

Richard straightened and swung around. A dangerous flicker blazed in his eyes. ''Believe what ye might about me past and me beginnings, Haleburton. But I'll not bear your insults regarding me professional calling. Another offense of that nature and I'll feed ye to the bloody fishes!''

Cappy leaned over his desk and glared. ''If you're a seaman, pal, I'll eat my shorts!''

''Stop it.'' Elizabeth moved between them. ''The decision is made,'' she said, speaking in a firm voice. After rummaging through the papers on Cappy's desk, she found a notepad and began a list. ''I'll need the *Scavenger II,* is that all right?''

''Hell no, it isn't all right!'' When she stared up at him Cappy ran a hand over his head, then sighed and dropped back into his chair. He swore. ''All right. This is the stupidest mistake you ever made, but if you won't listen to reason... I won't stand in your way. Take the *Scavenger II.*''

''Okay, next item. Tim is the best there is on the earphones...''

''I give up.'' Cappy gave her a helpless shrug. ''Pull Tim off tourist duty. You can have him.''

''Excellent. I'll dive, Tim will man the earphones and Richard, you drive the boat. You've been out on the *Scavenger II.* You can handle it.''

''Hold it!'' Cappy lifted a hand. ''I don't want some fruitcake landlubber driving an expensive dive boat! He doesn't know anything about the instruments, let alone the engines."

"I can learn." Richard still wore a hard challenge in his eyes. Knots rose along his jawline.

Elizabeth interrupted the beginning of what promised to be a furious argument. "If that's a condition, then I'll drive and Richard can dive. He's qualified. This isn't a problem."

Cappy rose behind his desk and slapped his palms on the desk top. His face was thunderous. "You are absolutely hell-bent on doing this? There's nothing I can say to talk sense into you?"

"We're going after the *Black Cutter,* Cappy. And we're going to find it."

"I'm telling 'e, 'e mangy bag of bones, I know where she is!"

Cappy shook his head and swore for two solid minutes. "Count me in for half," he said finally, staring at them. His expression indicated he couldn't believe what he was saying. "Half the expenses and half of whatever you find."

"You'd never forgive yourself if we found the *Black Cutter* and you weren't in on it," Elizabeth said, smiling. She felt a rush of affection for her small, fiesty uncle. She'd figured Cappy would come around. The only surprise was how quickly he'd done it.

"Bloody hell, Haleburton! You're in for half the expenses and a third of the prize less one percent off the top." Richard was grinning, but his eyes were hard and closed to negotiation.

"You pirate! That's robbery! And what's this one percent off the top?"

"The one percent is for a man named Manuel Ortiz. Ortiz gets one percent before the partnership split or the deal's off. I owe the man." Richard lifted an eyebrow in Elizabeth's direction and she smiled and nodded. "Take it or leave it, Haleburton." He slipped an arm around Elizabeth's waist.

Cappy swore. "Like as not I'm being held up for half the expenses and a third of nothing." He threw out his hands. "All right, I'm in. I'll match Elizabeth's four days, bringing us up to eight. But eight days is all we've got."

Elizabeth's pencil flew over her notebook listing provisions and necessary errands. "If we get cracking on this, we can get everything we need before the stores close and begin the search tomorrow."

But when she glanced up and saw the burning look in Richard's gaze, Elizabeth knew there would be a delay. A blush flamed on her cheeks and her fingers trembled in a sudden rush of heat and anticipation.

"I can't believe I'm doing this," Cappy said, shaking his bald head.

Elizabeth laughed. "I knew you wouldn't be able to resist," she said. "Old treasure hunters never die."

Cappy gave them both a weak smile. "They just go crazy and start backing lunatic time travelers."

THEY LEFT CAPPY'S office and ran down the ramp, halting at the bottom because they could not wait another second to touch each other. Richard pulled her roughly into his arms and caught her mouth in a hungry kiss. His kiss was hot and possessive, eager and demanding. If he hadn't been holding her, Elizabeth's trembling body would have melted and collapsed.

"Your place or mine?" he murmured hoarsely near her ear.

She laughed. "Where did you learn that line?"

"I heard it on a TV movie," he said, grinning down at her.

WHILE RICHARD THREW OPEN the love seat hide-a-bed, Elizabeth tore off her clothing. When Richard turned to her and sucked in a hard breath, she gazed at him with melting eyes, feeling a tremor of desire that began in her calves and swept through her naked curves. A deep hunger consumed her. It was lust and love and passion rolled into a single blazing imperative.

Running forward, wild in her need for him, she grabbed at his clothes. When he was finally, gloriously naked, she threw herself against his hot skin, gasping as he caught her and molded her against his rock-hard body. His lips bruised hers and his tongue plundered the sweetness within.

"Oh, God, I missed you!" she moaned when she could speak.

They fell on the bed, rolling in each other's arms, straining to press closer, closer, to blend into each other, to become one. Richard's urgent knee opened her legs and she arched upward, releasing a tiny scream of joy when he thrust into her.

There was nothing soft in their lovemaking, the passion between them was too titanic, too wild, too ardent and consuming to permit the subtleties of tenderness. Tenderness would come later. They took each other selfishly, greedily. Theirs was a timeless passion born of obsession and defined by untamed urgency. It was a contest fought to a draw over who would conquer and who would surrender, who would take more by giving more. Each groan, each sigh, each tiny scream of unbearable pleasure was a victory for both, a surrender for both.

They climaxed together, soaring, riding a cyclone of pleasure while wrapped in each other's arms.

"Sometimes I can believe I brought you here," Elizabeth whispered as they lay exhausted and sated. She kissed his shoulder. "Sometimes I think my need for you is powerful enough to reach through time."

Realizing she needed him was as stunning as having said it aloud. To admit needing another person was the ultimate loss of control, the final surrender of domination and power. But she forced herself to remain relaxed. She had cast her lot; she had made a commitment. She had to trust her heart and believe two strong personalities could find a way to live together.

"Lizzy, gel, look at me."

Rousing herself, Elizabeth turned in his arms and moved up so she could gaze into his eyes. Their hips and legs pressed together, still needing the closeness.

Richard stroked wet hair away away from her forehead and cheeks, then framed her face between his large calloused hands.

"It wounds me to think I hurt you by leaving. 'Twas the only way."

"I know that now." Lifting a fingertip, she traced the firm, broad contours of his lips. "I behaved badly and I'm sorry."

"I have never lied to 'e, gel."

She read the urgency in his gaze, knew it was important to him that she believe. She did.

"I know." She closed her eyes for a moment, relishing the pleasure of their intertwined legs, the silky brush of his chest hair against her breasts. "You and I are from very different backgrounds and experiences. Our assumptions and attitudes are going to clash on occasion. We'll have misunderstandings. That's inevitable. It's something we have to accept.''

He smiled and kissed her nose. "Does that mean I can come home?''

"Do you want to? Are you ready?'' It pleased her inordinately that Richard referred to her beach house as home. But she didn't want to think about how close she was to losing it.

"I've learned what I sought, Lizzy. I know how much money I need and I know how to obtain it. A third of thirty-three million surely will secure me a position as a man of means.'' His gray eyes darkened suddenly. "And more important, I learned that I can't live without ye at my side.''

She smiled at his words. "The final split won't amount to a full third. The state of Florida will claim twenty-five percent and we'll have to pay all kinds of taxes. Plus, we'll have expenses after we locate the *Black Cutter*. A full-scale salvage operation is not inexpensive.''

A flicker of anxiety returned to Richard's gaze. "Thirty three million dollars isn't enough?''

She laughed. "My dearest Richard. If we do indeed find your gold, the three of us will each bank about six million dollars after expenses. Believe me, that's enough to make you a man of means by anyone's definition. You can have your salvage company, if that's what you want.''

"And ye won't be dependent on anyone ever again.'' he smiled and ran his hand over her shoulder, down her waist to her hip.

"There's something I learned while we were apart,'' Elizabeth said in a low voice. She closed her eyes. "I don't want to be totally independent. I learned that I'm dependent on you in a thousand ways. And, Richard, none of them has to do with money." She opened her eyes and looked up at him. "You know what else? It's all right. I think I like it."

He bent over and kissed her long and deeply. When he spoke, his voice was hoarse with emotion. "Ye can't ken how I longed to hear ye say that, Lizzy, me gel."

THE SUN TIPPED THE horizon and tinted the sea foam pink as the *Scavenger II* slipped its mooring.

With Elizabeth at the wheel, they passed over the mud flats, ridges of golden sandbanks, then past the false reef alive with clumps of turtle and eel grass. Finally they cut into the delft blue of deep water. It was a beautiful morning. A light froth of clouds scudded overhead. The sea slid around them like liquid glass.

When they left Key West—and Cappy—behind, Elizabeth offered the wheel to Richard.

"You might as well get the feel of an engine," she said, ignoring Tim's silent disapproval.

Tim, a thin, wiry, sun-blackened man who had been with Cappy for twenty years, was Cappy's emissary on the expedition. Cappy refused to participate in the madness himself, but it was clear he had appointed Tim to act as his ears and eyes.

While Tim smoked and watched with a frown, Elizabeth passed the next hour explaining the instrument panels. The gadgetry and readouts amazed and delighted Richard. They also disappointed him.

"With all this," he said, waving a hand at the dials and digital readings, "anyone can captain a ship."

"You got that right, buckaroo," Tim said under his breath, as if Richard's presence at the wheel did indeed prove that.

Elizabeth threw him a sharp look, but she didn't say anything. She couldn't force Tim to respect Richard. Richard would have to earn it.

When they approached the site, Elizabeth stood beside Richard as he throttled down, pressing her lips together to halt an urge to jump in with reminders and instructions. He was a bit clumsy, irritated by his unfamiliarity with the instruments. When he glanced at her afterward, his gaze warned her not to offer unearned praise. Elizabeth bit her tongue and said nothing.

Tim dropped the magnetometer off the stern, checked the control box and his earphones. Then he gave Elizabeth a steady look. "It's going to be stop-and-start work. I'd prefer you at the wheel."

"Richard will drive," Elizabeth said quietly but firmly, holding Tim's gaze. "I'll watch the mag line and when we get a hit I'll check it out."

Tim shrugged and placed the earphones over his ears. "It's your money, your show."

Elizabeth turned to Richard. "Hold to the perimeters the best you can." It wouldn't be easy. There was nothing on the watery horizon on which to fix a point of reference. "Maintain a steady speed between three and five knots. Stop when Tim calls hit."

Richard nodded and returned to the wheel, his mouth set in a grim line.

The *Scavenger II* shot forward like a rocket.

The unexpected burst threw Elizabeth to the deck. She pulled herself upright in time to be flung down again as the engine cut out and the *Scavenger II* did the equivalent of a sidelong skid. Both Tim and Richard released a stream of horrendous curses.

When the *Scavenger II* moved forward again, the start was still too fast, but not rocket speed. Elizabeth clung to the railing and squeezed her eyes shut, listening as Richard throttled down, easing the engine into a low, steady rumble.

There was nothing to do now but wait.

Thirty minutes later Richard turned and started back the way they had come. Without the platform buoys and triangulation, there was no way to guess if Richard positioned them over new ocean floor or across territory they had already magged. Elizabeth dropped a buoy at the turn, knowing it was better than nothing.

Fifteen minutes later Tim shouted: "Hit!"

Richard's stop was choppy and allowed too much drift, but his response was instantaneous. He and Tim silently watched as Elizabeth donned her scuba gear.

"Strong or weak hit?" she asked as he clasped her vest over the top of a lightweight wet suit.

"About what I'd expect if a cannon was sitting down there."

Elizabeth met Richard's eyes and saw a leap of excitement darken his intent gaze.

"After two hundred years, I doubt we're going to find any cannons that aren't under several feet of sediment," she said.

Tim shrugged. "Maybe. Maybe not. As stormy as this section is, those cannons have probably been covered and uncovered more times than a Miami whore." He looked at Elizabeth's startled expression and mumbled, "sorry. You know what I mean."

She glanced at Richard before she lowered her mask, wanting to warn against letting his hopes soar too high. Most hits resulted in disappointment.

But she said nothing because she too felt a burst of excitement pumping through her veins. The hunt was on and they were all caught up in it. Even Tim.

Elizabeth waved, then fell backward off the dive platform. The water on the surface was warm but cooled considerably as she kicked down, down, listening to the sound of her breathing.

When her depth gauge registered thirty feet she halted her downward plunge and moved in place, turning on a powerful spotlight. At this depth the only colors were an opaque blue, green and brown. The spotlight sliced through twenty feet of murky blue and played over the bottom sand. She swam forward slowly, guiding the light back and forth over the bottom. Eventually she found what she was looking for and snapped off the spot before kicking upward.

"It's a metal storage drum," she said after she climbed aboard the dive platform and removed her regulator.

"Okay." Tim lowered his earphones. "Let's go."

The disappointment in Richard's eyes was painful to observe. He stared at Elizabeth as if he had failed her, then turned on his heel and strode to the wheelhouse.

During the next ten hours they found four more metal drums, an iron wheel, a pile of scrap and the ship's bell from a World War II navy vessel. But no *Black Cutter.*

On the return trip, Elizabeth took the wheel as they approached port. She maneuvered the *Scavenger II* into its slip.

"We'll try again tomorrow," she said, dredging a note of cheerfulness out of sheer exhaustion. Tim smiled and waved and walked up the ramp of the *Sante Oro* toward Cappy's office. To report to him, no doubt.

Cappy was in the deal, but hanging back. She couldn't really blame him. No one knew better than he how tedious this part of the search was, or how greatly the odds were stacked against them.

On the way home she and Richard bought burgers. But they were both so fatigued from the day's exertion and the strain of constant emotional ups and downs that neither had the energy to eat them.

For the first time since they had become lovers, they lay quietly in the same bed but didn't make love. Finally Richard's voice split the silence.

"I was so sure we'd find her." He sounded as bone weary as she.

"On the first day? That would have been a miracle."

"How long did Cappy search for the *Annunciata?*"

"After he pinned down the general wreck site?"

"Aye."

"Three years." A long silence ensued before Elizabeth, trying to offer encouragement, said, "It was a different type of wreck. The *Annunciata* didn't go down in one piece, she broke up in a hurricane. The scatter pattern covered almost four miles." Another silence opened. "The *Black Cutter* won't have much scatter. Once we find anything, even a single item, we'll have it all. It'll be a much easier wreck to find and deal with."

They lay side by side, holding hands in the warm darkness, listening to night creaks and cricket symphonies, listening to the deepening hush of wavering hope.

They had seven more days, seven more chances.

For the first time Richard truly grasped the magnitude of Elizabeth's act of faith. She had staked everything on a wild possibility, which he now understood was so remote as to approach miraculous proportions. No. That wasn't correct. Elizabeth hadn't staked everything on the possibility of a miracle. She had staked everything on him. He was the one who needed a miracle.

He would never forgive himself if Elizabeth's belief in him ended in her ruin.

The *Black Cutter* was out there. And by God, he would find it. He had to.

"*Hit!*"

Knowing she was dulled by exhaustion, Elizabeth carefully checked her air tanks and equipment before she tipped backward into the water. On an earlier dive she had forgotten her spotlight and had caused further delay by having to return to the boat to get it.

On this dive she really didn't need the light. The bottom rose upward in a series of dunes, most of which she could see unaided. Almost immediately she spotted the lead-bottomed hull of an old pleasure boat.

"Nothing," she shouted when she climbed back onto the drive platform.

Even as the boat moved forward again, she remained on the platform so she wouldn't have to observe Richard's bitter disappointment.

This was the sixth day. They were all aware that if Cappy hadn't joined forces with them, the search would have ended two days ago.

A long hour later Tim yelled "hit!" again.

Each hit was a new ball game, not necessarily a repetition of previous failures. But each failure nibbled away at their hope. A grim sense of urgency had replaced their initial excitement. Time was running out.

Elizabeth drew a deep breath and reached inside for the energy she needed, then tipped into the water.

A few minutes later she resurfaced. "It was another one of those damned iron drums!" Her body felt like deadweight as she pulled herself onto the dive platform. "Some idiot must have dumped a couple hundred of them out here!"

Before Richard returned to the wheelhouse their eyes met and Elizabeth's heart cracked.

She wanted to tell him it was all right if they failed to find the *Black Cutter*.

He wanted to tell her that he loved her.

But neither spoke the words.

THE DAYS SPED BY. A double line of buoys marked the area they had searched, a larger area than Elizabeth had believed they could cover in the time allotted.

Then suddenly it was the eighth day. Then noon on the last day. Then five o'clock on the last day. Then darkness.

No one spoke as Tim reeled in the magnetometer for the last time and packed away his earphones.

Elizabeth stood in the wheelhouse beside Richard as they returned to Key West. Tears blurred the lights along the wharves. She longed to wrap her arms around his waist and offer whatever comfort she could. But his rigid body and hard eyes rejected comfort.

It was over. They had failed.

Chapter Twelve

"Haleburton, I need to talk to 'e."

"Forget it, Colter. It's finished." Cappy looked his age today, older, distracted, a smudge of defeat darkening his eyes. His desk was surrounded with packing boxes. Most of the charts were gone from the walls.

"I want to borrow a sailboat."

"Elizabeth's down at the employment agency, I'm bleeding all over the floor and you want to go sailing. Terrific."

Richard ground his teeth and reminded himself that it wasn't wise to strangle a man when you needed a favor from him.

"I need to go out to the site one more time."

"Colter...there is no site. You found nothing. Nada. Zip. Get it? There's no ship out there. Let it go."

"I need to feel the sea," Richard insisted stubbornly. He jabbed a hand through his hair and clenched his teeth. "A man can't feel the sea in a motorized vessel. I need sail."

"You need a job. You need a shrink. You need to get drunk and beat up a few people. You don't need a sailboat."

"The *Black Cutter* is out there, Haleburton."

"I agree. Except it's about a hundred miles from where you're looking for it. Forget it."

"Do 'e want me to beg, is that it?"

Cappy swore. "You didn't find anything in eight days when you had the best equipment money can buy. What on earth makes you think you can find anything with a sailboat and no equipment?"

"Come with me and find out."

"By God, I'm tempted. I wouldn't mind watching you make a fool of yourself. Maybe that would put an end to this craziness."

Richard's smile didn't reach his eyes. "Fine. We'll go the day after tomorrow, after the storm."

Cappy's brows rose. "There's no storm predicted."

"There's a storm coming. I feel it."

"Now you know more than the weather service." Cappy shook his head. "If you're hell-bent on making an arrogant fool of yourself, then I want to be there to see it. We'll go out tomorrow, storm or no storm. I don't know how long I've got before the bank sweeps in here and padlocks everything."

Richard released a long breath. "I'll meet ye at dawn tomorrow. Thank you, Cappy. You won't regret this."

"I regret it already. And, Colter—this is the end. After tomorrow, it's finished. Understand?"

ELIZABETH LEANED AGAINST the stern railing, frowning at a swiftly advancing bank of black clouds. The temperature had dropped noticeably and a light chop tossed the waves. The sensible thing would be to head in. She suspected that's what Cappy would insist on if he weren't napping below.

Every few minutes she glanced toward Richard, who stood at the wheel running the *Starbird* through a series of peculiar maneuvers. Rising wind whipped his long hair around his face, but he didn't appear to notice. His features were drawn in an expression of intensely focused concentration.

Biting her lip Elizabeth continued to watch, struggling to comprehend the strange erratic pattern he wove across the sea's disturbed surface.

Suddenly she understood. She leaned forward, staring at nothing, then she smiled. Yes. Richard was re-creating the *Black Cutter*'s last battle. He was attempting to discover how far the battle had driven him off course, how much drift had occurred.

"Lizzy!"

When she approached the wheel, she saw a strange exultation blazing in his eyes. "I've found it!"

Then he noticed the squall rapidly bearing down on them and his expression instantly altered. Recognition narrowed his gaze to stony pinpoints and his mouth clamped into a line.

Elizabeth gasped and her hands flew to her throat. "Oh, no! You don't think..." She spun to face the wind and flying darkness. "Is that...?"

"I don't know." Richard's eyes swept over her, memorizing her, claiming her. She knew he would have caught her in his arms in a fierce embrace if he had dared take his hands from the wheel. He shot a glance toward the approaching squall, then quickly away—forcing himself to concentrate. "You can't dive," he said flatly, stating the obvious.

Elizabeth refused to look at the gathering storm. It looked ominous, threatening—in more ways than one. Its fierce power would destroy the boat, plunge her to a watery grave.... But all Elizabeth could think of was that it might be the wind that would pull Richard away from her for all time. With her shaking hands she grasped his and her eyes fastened to his face. "There are so many things we haven't said to each other."

"Aye, gel." He spoke so softly that she almost didn't hear. Then he gave his head a shake, as if to clear it of the same thoughts. And fears as hers. "Quickly, there are things to be done and we may not have much time. Can we mark the site somehow?"

"We can mark it with a UBT. An Underwater Beacon Transformer. It's a homing device."

"Can it direct us back to this exact site?" When Elizabeth nodded, trying to tame the hair that flew around her face, he glanced at the black sky, then nodded sharply. "Place the beacon, gel." He studied the storm. "And tell Cappy. Make sure he knows we found it."

Because Richard wouldn't be here to tell Cappy himself? So he believed this was the end, too. Elizabeth gazed up at him and her heart lurched.

"Storms erupt out here all the time. That's all it is," she shouted through the rising wind. She wouldn't allow herself to believe the squall was anything but natural, as if the force of her belief would make it so. "Maybe we can outrun it."

They stared at each other. Mere seconds passed, but it felt like eons before Richard touched her cheek, then returned to the wheel, and Elizabeth raced to search for the UBT.

The first fat raindrops splatted on the deck and she stared at them with mounting fear. No. She absolutely would not accept that the storm overtaking them was Richard's wind and tunnel. No. It couldn't be. Not yet. Please God, not yet. She wasn't ready.

Richard shouted at her over his shoulder. "Can you take the wheel while I bring in the sail?"

Elizabeth shot a glance toward the menacing sky and felt the pitch of the deck beneath her tennis shoes. "I'll bring in the sail. You stay at the wheel." The waves were higher now, hissing angrily.

The storm was going to be bad. Very bad.

CAPPY COULDN'T BELIEVE it. One minute he was napping in his bunk, the next minute he found himself roughly flung to the floor. Worse, the *Starbird* was pitching violently, tossing as if she'd been dropped into a blender.

While he fought to regain his feet, he heard a crack of lightning and a crashing roll of thunder. Rain pounded the decks like tiny hammers.

Cursing, he threw on a slicker and ran up the steps. The minute he opened the door, the wind flung it away from him and sucked the breath from his body. A huge wave roared over his head, then slammed over the railing. He clung to the staircase railing as a ton of water roiled past his knees and rushed down the steps.

He cursed again, horrified to think a lunatic who didn't know a sailboat from a surfboard was manning the wheel. And in the worst squall he'd seen in fifteen years. If the *Starbird* survived without swamping or capsizing, it would be a damned miracle. Fighting every step, Cappy ducked his head and battled the wind and driving rain toward the wheel. Their only hope was that he remembered enough about sailing to save them.

Before he reached the wheel, hands reached out and grabbed him. Elizabeth lashed a tether around his waist and jerked it tight, then she reeled him next to her beneath the overhang and secured the rope to a safety ring. She was drenched. Her long, wet hair flew in the wind.

"Untie this, for God's sake! I've got to get to the wheel," he shouted, scrabbling furiously at the tether. "Why in the name of God didn't you wake me?"

"No need," she shouted back.

When he stared at her in disbelief, he saw tears running from her eyes. She trembled violently, racked with an emotion that stemmed from something greater than being lashed to a bulkhead in the midst of a killer squall. She was chanting, "Not yet, not yet, not yet," in a steady stream of words that flowed together like a frightened mantra.

He followed the direction of her riveted eyes and sucked in a breath.

A shuddering crack of lightning split the sky and Cappy saw Colter. He stood at the wheel, his legs planted wide apart, his hair whipping around a face transfixed by sheer joy. A mountain of roaring water reared up before him and he laughed. He threw back his head and laughed! Cappy couldn't believe it. Instinctively he hunched his shoulders and tightened his body, tensing against the wall of water about to slam over them.

It didn't.

When Cappy dared to breathe and look up again, he wiped the rain from his eyes in amazement. The mountain of raging water had fallen away without swamping them. All they suffered was a stinging spray. He stared at Colter in disbelief. Colter was maneuvering the *Starbird* with the skill and finesse of an Olympic skier dodging moguls. And he was loving every minute, shouting at the storm, challenging it.

"I thought I'd seen everything." Cappy breathed. "But in all my years on the water, I've never seen anything like this!" He looked at Elizabeth who was white-faced and watching Colter as if he were a ghost, as if she absolutely expected him to vanish at any moment. She was as deranged as the maniac at the wheel.

And that maniac was the best damned seaman, bar none, that Cappy Haleburton had ever seen.

It was a hair-raising three hours, and Cappy hoped to hell he never experienced anything like it again. He felt weak with relief when he spotted the wharf through the raindrops.

He also knew he wouldn't have missed this experience for the world. Few men were given the opportunity to witness such a feat of seamanship. It happened once in a lifetime.

As they tacked into the harbor, Cappy went forward to stand beside Richard. Colter was soaked to the skin. A wild light still burned in his eyes.

Cappy clasped his hands behind his back and faced the harbor. "Nice job...Captain."

Richard waited to answer until he brought the *Starbird* home to her slip. "Thank 'e...Captain." He cast Cappy a sidelong glance. "How would 'e like your shorts? Boiled or roasted?"

"Any damned way you want to serve 'em up. I owe you an apology."

Richard smiled. "Accepted. Did Lizzy tell you? I found the *Black Cutter*. We marked the site with a UBT."

It was impossible. The *Black Cutter* simply could not be where Colter claimed. And with the weather as it was, Colter and Elizabeth could not have verified anything by diving.

"You really believe that?"

"Aye."

Frowning, Cappy cursed himself for an idiot and a fool. He released a long breath through his teeth. "If you say it's there, Captain, that's good enough for me. I've seen what you can do. I'll hold off the bank. And I'll find the money for one more day. But one day is all we've got. We'll take the *Scavenger II* out the day after tomorrow. Give the surface twenty-four hours to settle."

It was going to be the longest twenty-four hours any of them ever spent. But they had another chance.

Richard sought Elizabeth in the darkness of the harbor. He found her sagged against the bulkhead, her face buried in her hands. Tremors racked her body, but when he lifted her face, joy blazed in her eyes.

"You're here…you're still here…" she cried out on a sob.

Richard crushed her to his chest, exhausted and yet exhilarated.

"I thought your wind had come for you," Elizabeth whispered against his chest. Her voice was still raw. Tears sluiced down her face, mingling with the raindrops.

He wiped her cheeks and framed them with his hands.

"For a time I thought so too, gel."

"I was so afraid I was going to lose you. I thought…" The tears choked her voice. "I wondered what you would do if…"

Richard didn't answer. He wrapped his arms around her and stared silently into the darkness.

THE *SCAVENGER II* LOCKED on the Underwater Beacon Transformer and guided them back to the site. It was clear and hot overhead, but the water was still choppy. No one mentioned it was not an ideal day for diving as they donned rubber suits, vests and flippers.

They wouldn't use scuba equipment today. Proceeding under the assumption that Richard had not erred, they used the Desco system, a full face mask connected by a rubber hose to a surface air compressor. The Desco system allowed divers to remain underwater for an unlimited length of time.

"All right," Cappy said after he had inspected the equipment. "Here's the plan. Tim, you stay on the *Scavenger II* and make sure we maintain a constant air supply." He turned to Richard and Elizabeth. "The storm will have stirred things up, visibility will be limited. Don't wander off—stay in visual contact. What kind of cannon were you carrying, Captain?" For a moment Cappy looked slightly dazed that he could ask such a question, then his expression steadied and he waited for Richard's answer.

"Twenty-four bronze Demiculverins with an eight-foot chase and weighing over a ton each, plus four six-pounders—two Minions and two Falcons, also bronze."

"If they were bronze, they'll still be there. If anyone finds one, mark it with a buoy. I guess I don't need to mention that what we really need is a gold bar. Give me a gold bar and we're back in business in spades. I'll have the bank eating out my hand by this time tomorrow." He grinned at them.

Richard didn't smile. Cappy had come full circle, spinning from utter disbelief to full faith, based on nothing but Richard's performance during the storm and his gut feeling that this was the site. He looked at

Cappy's valiant effort to grin and at Elizabeth's clear-eyed confidence. His heart swelled to painful dimensions.

"There's something I wish to say to 'e," he said, swallowing heavily.

Elizabeth squeezed his shoulder. "There's no need."

Cappy took his hand and pumped it. "Let's go, Captain. The *Cutter*'s waiting for us. Let's find those gold bars."

Before he tipped backward into the chop, Richard paused and whispered a small prayer. *These are good people, Lord. Don't let me have misled them. Give us a bloody gold bar.*

Pulse thudding in his ears, his stomach suddenly queasy, he dropped into the water and tested his Desco unit. The air was clean and dry. He drew a deep breath, then opened his eyes and kicked downward, praying to see evidence that he had not erred, dreading that he might see nothing but sand and seaweed.

The water was dark and murky, awash with suspended particles and storm debris. As he went down, he switched on an underwater flash, noticed the glow of Elizabeth and Cappy's lights.

Twenty hope-devouring minutes elapsed before Richard spotted a pile of round stones. Another pile rose ten feet away from the first. Richard's breath hitched and he felt his heart skip. Ballast stones. Through the murk he saw Elizabeth and Cappy wave their lights. They too had spotted the stones.

Richard pointed, directing them to follow the ballast. The gold had been in the stern castle. The problem was locating where the stern had sunk. The gold might have scattered as the ship sank; over the centuries it would have sunk to bedrock.

As for himself, the gold no longer interested him. He played his light over the encrusted ballast stones and shards of rotted timber, feeling numb. This had been his ship; his life. His ambitions and dreams, his honor and sense of self, all that he was or had hoped to be reposed in what was now wreckage and rot.

Moving slowly in the deep currents, his mind chilled, he glided above the ballast stones, moving his flash in a slow arc.

Here and there he spotted pieces of timber, but most of the *Black Cutter*'s hull had long ago succumbed to teredo worms. Eventually he came upon two cannons, a Falcon and one of the Demiculverins. There was incrustation, but not much, not like there would have been if his cannons had been iron. The Demiculverin looked as if it had dropped into the sea yesterday. Richard forgot to tag them with buoys and he didn't bother verifying the markings. He knew they were his.

Here and there, embedded in the sand, he saw pieces of his crew's crockery. Once he glided over a heavily encrusted object whose shape indicated a sword. He deliberately kept his mind blank, refusing to speculate whose sword it might have been.

In the murky opaque silence, time lost meaning. He watched Cappy tag a cannon bore and release a buoy. Once Elizabeth came to him and showed him a gold coin that must have belonged to one of his crew. He had no idea how long they had been down.

Then unexpectedly a small heavily corroded iron chest loomed out of the murk in front of him. A hot jolt stabbed through Richard's body as he steadied his light. The chest sat upright on the sand as if the storm had rearranged the bottom and placed it there for him to find.

Carefully he settled in front of the chest and reached one trembling finger to the lid. The iron crumbled in a burst of orange that gradually floated away. Richard knew he should place the chest inside the net he carried, the net the others referred to as a "goodie bag." But he didn't.

With shaking fingers, he opened the chest that bore his initials and carefully laid the items inside upon the sand. His leather money pouch had disintegrated, but the coins survived. The silver pieces had corroded and melted together, but the gold pieces were as bright as the day he placed them in the chest. Another encrusted lump had been his best silver buckles. He turned the clump in his hands, then laid it aside. The oilskin flap that had held his papers fell apart in his fingers. Next he removed an ivory case that contained a delicate gold chain supporting a small diamond-studded garnet that he had commissioned for his sister Rachel. He stared at it for a long, long time before he reached for his pewter drinking cup. The pewter was coated by a black film but he could still make out his name engraved along the handle.

Finally he found what was left of his pipe. The carved stem was broken and a piece had cracked out of the bowl. The delicate silver filigree crumbled at his touch and floated away.

Richard held the broken pipe in his hand and dropped his head. For the first time since childhood he felt like weeping. It would have devastated him to know that Elizabeth watched.

"You found the wreck!" Tim shouted excitedly when they surfaced. "Every time I saw a buoy bob up I thought I was going to have a heart attack!" The sea was clustered with marking buoys that identified an item of interest. Tim darted about the deck, helping them off with their gear. "I can't stand it. Tell me! Did you find the gold?"

Elizabeth shook her head. "No bars, but I found a gold coin and a clump of silver." She opened her goodie bag. "Look at this beautiful pewter pitcher. It must have belonged to an officer. A bit of polishing and it will look as good as new."

Silently Richard opened his goodie bag and laid his personal possessions on the deck. Something in his expression made the others fall silent as well. "I want ye to have this," he said quietly, offering Elizabeth the case containing Rachel's garnet.

Elizabeth gasped when she looked inside the case. Sadness softened her gaze when she lifted her head. "I wish I could keep it, but I can't. Everything we bring up has to be catalogued and accounted for. Once we've salvaged the entire site, we'll meet with the state officials and decide how to split the spoils." A look of discomfort pinched her expression as she realized she had referred to Richard's personal belongings as spoils. After a moment he nodded and turned his face away.

"The gold," Tim said with a groan. "Did anyone find the gold?"

Cappy passed a hand over his head. "We've found the wreck. It's a small scatter pattern. The bullion ought to be simple to locate. All we need is time to grid the area and conduct an organized search." He looked at them and frustration smudged his eyes. "Unfortunately, we don't have any more time." He swore and pressed the heels of his palms against his eyes. "Damn it. We were this close. This close!"

Shock wiped the expression from Elizabeth's face. "Cappy! Surely you aren't saying we're going to quit!"

He shrugged and spread his hands in a helpless gesture. "Honey, the bank is going to be at the door tomorrow morning." He indicated the boat and the equipment. "By this time tomorrow, everything is going to be under lock and key."

They all looked toward the sinking sun and felt the hope run out of them like water through a sieve.

"This close," Cappy murmured, closing his eyes. "If we could have found one bar, just one, I know I could have convinced the bank to give us an extension. But..."

Richard stood and looked down at Elizabeth. "Do 'e believe me? Do ye believe three tons of gold bars are down there?"

"Yes," she said without hesitation. Then she understood. Standing, she bent for her flippers then pulled down her mask. "Let's go."

"Are you crazy?" Cappy and Tim said in unison. They looked at each other then Cappy continued. "It's almost dark. You've spent too many hours underwater today as it is. You're asking for trouble! No. I can't allow this!"

Richard and Elizabeth stood facing each other, their fingertips lightly touching. The moment was one of such perfect accord that neither had to signal it was time to go.

They entered the water together, holding hands.

Three hours later, when Cappy was pacing the deck, frantic with worry, two pair of hands broke the surface of the waves.

Each pair of hands held a gold bar.

Chapter Thirteen

Near dawn Elizabeth woke to find that Richard was not in bed beside her. He had left the fragment of his pipe stem on the bedside table. She hadn't realized he had kept it. Slipping from bed, feeling an uncomfortable sense of foreboding, she tied on a robe and finally discovered him outside on the beach throwing stones at the horizon.

"Richard?" She stepped up behind him and touched his shoulder. His muscles were tight, as hard as carved marble.

After a moment he covered her fingers with his hand, but he didn't look away from the last vestiges of starlight sparkling on the waves.

"Whatever it is...talk to me," Elizabeth whispered, staring up at him. He should have been ecstatic, but he wasn't. Richard had hardly spoken a word since they found the gold, had not participated in the impromptu celebration at the No-Name Bar. She leaned her sleep-tousled head against his shoulder, alarmed by the tension and resistance she felt. "Please, Richard. We've come so far. Don't shut me out now."

For one terrible instant she thought he would not respond, thought he would maintain the strange reserve he'd exhibited since she had glimpsed him sitting on the sand examining his iron chest. "Richard... please."

Gradually his body relaxed beneath her fingertips and he turned and wrapped his arms around her waist, holding her so fiercely tight that Elizabeth almost winced. He buried his face in her hair.

"How could I know it would be so devastating?" He spoke in tones of anguish, his voice almost inaudible. "I was concentrating on the bloody damned gold. I didn't let myself think how it would feel to find me cannon and Mr. Greene's sword. To see again me pipe and Rachel's necklace... Lord Almighty, gel! 'Tis like a blade in me guts!"

Elizabeth pressed her forehead against his throat and felt him tremble.

"Until yesterday, this life wasn't real. Can 'e understand? I thought it was, but it wasn't. 'Twas more like a vivid dream, or maybe I told meself 'twas a dream to keep from losing me bloody mind."

"Oh, Richard."

He lifted his head and stared at the horizon. "Rachel is dead, Lizzy. She's gone. And Tom, her husband. And the Reverend Mr. Goodnight, and Mr. Washington and Mr. Franklin. William Halsey and Charles Berry are dead. Everyone I knew is long dead, and their children and their grandchildren. I can deny it till hell ices over, but the truth is every soul I ever cared about is dust in forgotten graves. 'Tis an agony." His eyes squeezed shut in a pale face and his expression tightened into a mask.

She had to strain to hear his next words. It was as if he spoke more to himself than to her.

"The difference betwixt now and the night I washed up on your beach is that I am awakening. I'm beginning to understand 'tis not a dream. This is real." Grief hoarsened his voice. "This is real. 'Tis the other world—my world—that is only a dream."

Elizabeth's fingers flew over his face, his shoulders, trying frantically to offer comfort where no comfort was possible.

"I have to go home, Lizzy."

"Home?" she whispered, her fingers digging into his shoulders. "I don't understand."

"Nay," he said gently, stroking her cheek. "Not home as in returning to me own time. That isn't possible."

Elizabeth saw the defeat in his eyes and understood he no longer believed the wind and the tunnel would return for him. His hopelessness both stung her and broke her heart for him.

"I need to return to Boston."

"But—why?"

Streaks of pink and indigo illuminated the sky before he answered. "I must find a way to accept this reality. I have to stand on familiar ground, ground I once knew, and know it is no longer *my* ground. Ye said me house still stands, preserved by Rachel's hand. I want to see it. Nay, gel, I *need* to see it, to stand in me own parlor."

"Are you...are you saying you would return to your own time if you could? Even now?" Elizabeth heard the catch in her voice, tasted a surge of panic.

"Ah God, Lizzy, I miss it so. I long for me own house, me own chair, for the heart's ease of familiar faces and familiar things. I long to comfort me grief with the sight of Rachel and her Tom. Can ye understand, gel? 'Tis no reflection on ye or your times. It's just...I..." He shook his head.

"You're homesick," Elizabeth said in a dull voice. She could not help him.

"Aye," he said softly. "And I need to know."

"Know what?"

"If the wind and tunnel came for me. Or if I'm stuck here, as I fear I be."

Elizabeth's breath caught in her throat. "Would that be so terrible?" she whispered, hurting inside. "Being stuck here?"

He stared into her eyes as if seeking an answer. But no answer came.

Elizabeth's heart pleaded with him to say the words she longed to hear, the words she had expected he would say after they found the gold. But he didn't. Tears glistened in her eyes. "What will the house tell you? What will you learn from it?"

"I don't know," he said finally, pushing a hand through his hair.

"Do you think if you're standing in your house that the wind and the tunnel will come for you?"

"Elizabeth, I don't know. I just know that I have to come to terms with a reality that hasn't seemed real until now. I feel lost and adrift. I'm floundering, gel."

Elizabeth stared up at him, pulling her robe more tightly around her body. "You said there were words you wished to say to me after we found the *Black Cutter*." She hated herself that her pain was so great that she was willing to sacrifice her pride too. "Is this what you waited to say? That you want to leave me and return to your own time?" Her mouth tasted like ashes.

Gently he lifted her chin, forcing her to meet his eyes. "Me brave, beautiful Elizabeth. Nay, gel. Those are not the words I held beneath me tongue. I thought improving me finances would free me to speak me heart. I erred. I am not a free man. I'm snared in a dream, Lizzy, fighting to find me own reality.''

A light breeze teased the tears on her lashes. ''I think I would have gone with you.''

''Nay, gel, I was wrong to ask it of ye.'' Pain roughened his voice. ''This is your time, your life. This is where ye belong and where ye must remain. If the wind and tunnel had returned, I would not have taken ye with me. I know what it is to live outside one's own time and I don't wish that pain for ye.''

Elizabeth grabbed his arms and gave him a shake. ''Listen to me. This is a good reality, damn it!'' She dashed a hand over her eyes. ''You have a future here, Capt. Richard C. Colter. You're going to be a wealthy man, a partner in Golden Dreams. You have friends who care about you. And . . . I love you.''

''Lizzy—''

''No, don't say anything.'' Pride roared back to life and sparked in her dark eyes, warning him. ''I don't want you to say a single word out of obligation or pity or a sense of reciprocity.'' She closed her eyes and swallowed the tears clogging her throat. ''What I want most in this world is your happiness, my dearest Richard. I mean it. If . . . if the wind and the tunnel return while you're in Boston, then step into it if that's what you want.''

Nothing had ever been as hard to say.

''But I don't want to be your second choice, Richard, a consolation prize instead of the thing you most want, which is to go home.'' Her chin lifted. ''I don't know where that leaves us, I only know that's how I feel.''

Richard stared down into her eyes for a long time before he kissed her, gently, tenderly. When he released her, Elizabeth stumbled backward a pace and gathered her robe at her throat. She spoke in a voice thick with pain, knowing his pain was equally as great.

"I'll make your plane reservations."

ASIDE FROM TAKEOFF and landing, the airplane flight was not as terrifying as Richard had imagined it would be. Once he grew accustomed to gazing out the window, he used the flight time in an attempt to come to terms with himself.

He knew he had wronged Elizabeth and he deeply regretted it. On several occasions he had led her to believe he would declare himself once he was financially able. But he had not recognized the uncertainties and complexities churning inside him. Until he saw the *Black Cutter,* he had not realized how the dream state had deteriorated and how frighteningly real his life here had become.

Instantly his mind reared back from that thought. And suddenly he was hopelessly lost in a maelstrom that whirled reality and unreality into a confusing, indistinguishable stew.

How could he declare his love when he could no longer distinguish what was real? Was Elizabeth real? Was he? Was anything real?

As the plane descended toward its final approach to Logan Airport, Richard pressed his face to the window. The strangeness of his situation and his present existence was such that he genuinely expected to gaze out a twentieth-century window and look upon an eighteenth-century town. It jolted him when this did not occur.

The Boston he saw beneath his plane window was not the Boston he had known. But once he recovered from his shock at how large the city had grown, he recognized it. Not the buildings or highways that sprouted like strange vines, but the topography. There was Castle Island, connected now to Dorchester. There was Bunker Hill, where his father had perished.

Moving like a man in a trance, and after a half-dozen false starts, he managed to deplane, then hail a taxi that eventually swerved to a stop in front of a sign announcing Colter House.

Richard dropped a handful of bills into the front seat, then stepped out of the taxi, his pulse thudding in his ears. His hands shook and his ears rang.

His first impression was that his house had shrunk. Even if it had not been hemmed by high-rise buildings, it still would have appeared diminished to him, not as he remembered. Over the passage of two hundred years, the brick had darkened and the windows he had taken such pride in seemed to have narrowed. The view from his front porch was different. Once he had been able to glimpse the commons to the west and from his back garden he could see Griffins Wharf. Griffins Wharf was gone now. In every direction the view was blocked by tall buildings.

"The next house tour begins immediately, sir."

"There were cobbles in the street. And flowers here in front. The oak was but a sapling." He scrubbed a hand over his face.

A young woman eyed him with concern. She wore a costume from Richard's era. No woman of Richard's acquaintance would have worn an evening gown at ten in the morning. He wondered wildly if the young woman realized she was committing a scandalous breach of conduct.

"Are you here for the tour?"

"Aye," he murmured, amazed to discover his voice still functioned. Reaching for his wallet, he extracted a five-dollar bill and paid the donation she requested.

There were other people inside the foyer, but Richard didn't notice them. He noticed the smell. After all this time, his house still smelled of lemon paste and the scented wallpaper which had been in fashion when he had had the house built. Surely he imagined it, but he thought he inhaled a faint echo of his pipe tobacco and the lilac-scented toilet water that Rachel loved so much.

"My name is Susan Dawson, I'm a history major from BU. I'll be your guide today. Colter House was built in 1786 by Capt. Richard Charles Colter. Captain Colter was a dashing figure," Miss Dawson said, smiling as if she had known him personally. "He was a successful privateer, famous for capturing rich prizes in the Caribbean. His ship, the *Black Cutter,* sank with all hands on board in 1792. If you've watched the news lately, you'll know that a salvage company in Key West, Florida, located the wreck of the *Black Cutter* just this week."

"They found a fortune in gold bars," someone added.

"Captain Colter's sister, Mrs. Rachel Fairbanks, inherited the captain's house and lived here until she died in 1829 at the age of seventy-one."

Richard closed his eyes. The reality he sought pierced him.

"Mrs. Fairbanks bequeathed Colter House to the Massachusetts Historical Society, with the proviso that nothing in the house be altered or changed until the year 2000. Everything is to remain exactly as she left it, down to the items on the tabletops, desks, and so forth. The Society may clean and repair as needed, but we are not permitted to replace or rearrange any item. Therefore we ask you not to touch anything, no matter how tempted you are. And please stay out of the roped-off areas.''

Miss Dawson frowned at Richard. ''May I get you a glass of water, sir? Are you ill?''

''Nay.'' He waved a hand, then thrust it into the pocket of his topcoat. His fingers trembled like loose bones.

''As long as you remain outside the roped-off areas, you are free to wander as you like, or you may stay with the group and I'll answer any questions I can.''

Richard waited until the group moved into the summer parlor. His stomach cramped and rolled; his hands were damp and hot. From where he stood he could see into the front parlor, the one Rachel had kept closed except for company or receptions. The carpets which had once been so vivid were sun-faded and worn, the colors muted and dull. He stepped onto a plastic runner laid atop the carpet and entered the room.

It was as he remembered. The furniture, the fireplace tools, the wall hangings. His own portrait above the mantelpiece. Stepping forward, Richard looked to see if the family bible was opened to the Colter family genealogy. It was turned to Judges: Chapter Five, Verse Six was underlined. He stared at the last phrase of the verse and his stomach lurched.

. . . and the travelers walked through byways.

What had that phrase meant to Rachel? It was no coincidence that this page was showing and underlined, she had arranged each item and prohibited any alteration.

Pulse thundering, feeling slightly dizzy, Richard entered the dining room and studied the table. Three place settings occupied one end of the table, one of them a child's setting. The china bore the Fairbanks' crest. The arrangement struck him as odd, as a child would have taken meals in the nursery. Then he understood. Rachel was telling him that she and Tom had had one child. At the far end of the table was a single place setting. Here the silver and plate was stamped with Richard's seal. He stared at it and his vision blurred.

Miss Dawson's voice startled him and he blinked hard.

"As long as she lived Mrs. Fairbanks laid a setting for her brother, as if she expected him to walk in the door at any moment. It's a charming anecdote, don't you think?"

Richard couldn't answer. But he knew this would not be his last visit to Colter House. He would return tomorrow and the next day and the next, looking for clues, looking for... he didn't know... reentry into his life?

He toured the rest of the house in a trance, his eyes hot and burning. Finally, almost dreading it, he entered his study. There was his chair and stool, his books, his globe, his desk. Nothing had been changed. His pipe rack was where he had left it last, there was even tobacco in the box.

With all his heart, he longed to sink into his favorite chair, light one of his pipes, then open his eyes and find himself home. He could almost hear Rachel's light step on the staircase and the musical chime of her laughter. He could almost smell the lilacs in his back garden and the scent of Mrs. Kingsbury's cherry pies.

It wasn't until the next day, when he returned, that Richard thought to inspect the papers so carefully laid out on his desk. His heart almost stopped, then raced when he saw a letter penned shortly before Rachel's death, her old-fashioned writing now faded on yellowing paper.

December 10, 1829

My dearest Richard,

Thirty-seven years ago the Reverend Mr. Goodnight brought me the terrible news of your death. Ye will smile, my dearest, when ye learn I scandalized the good reverend by labeling himself a liar. If ye were truly gone, I would have known it in my heart.

Where are ye & where have ye gone? Every day for thirty-seven years I have asked myself these questions. Some days I curse that ye left us without a word. Other days I envision a great adventure in a strange and wonderful land. On fanciful days I see ye here, a ghost figure growing older as I do, so filled with substance I believe we could speak if ye only wished it. I imagine ye riding up to the gate and I touch a necklace, garnet, that ye gave to me in an earlier dream.

I have always known things, my dear Richard. I leave this letter in the sense that one day ye shall read these words, a fancy others view as evidence of an old woman's decline.

A message runs through my mind when I think of ye, as I do so often. Mayhaps ye will ken it, for I confess I do not. We choose our own reality.

Do not mourn me, dearest, for I do not mourn ye. My life was long & rich & full. In my heart, I believe the same of ye.

God bless & keep ye & yours.

Your loving sister, Rachel.

THE *SANTE ORO BUZZED* with fast-paced comings and goings. Elizabeth chipped away at an avalanche of paperwork; Cappy scurried around obtaining necessary permits and leases, working with the state officials. The telephone rang incessantly, media people swarmed over the wharfs. Excitement crackled in the air.

"Everything's coming together beautifully. So why are you looking so glum?" Cappy asked, ducking into Elizabeth's office for a moment of quiet. He studied her tired eyes. "Has he called?"

"I talked to him yesterday."

"He is coming back, isn't he?"

Elizabeth pushed away from her desk and shoved a wave of hair out of her eyes. "I don't know. He's confused and lost, Cappy. And so am I. I don't know if I want him to come back."

"Honey, you can't mean that. Colter loves you and you love him."

Elizabeth leaned back in her chair and closed her eyes. She didn't think she had slept a wink since Richard left for Boston. "Do you have any idea what it's like to have a rival like mine? Another time period, for God's sake? I don't know if I could stand a life knowing that Richard was with me only because he couldn't have what he really wanted."

Cappy sat down and leaned forward over her desk. "That's nonsense, Elizabeth. Colter told me that he'd take you with him if he ever went back. You are what he really wants."

She shook her head. "He changed his mind. I think he sensed my reservations, my fear." They fell silent, Cappy because he couldn't think of anything encouraging to say, Elizabeth because tears closed her throat. Finally she blew her nose, then said, "There's something else that's bothering me. I think about it every minute. I haven't told anyone because it's so weird.''

Cappy stared at her, then burst into laughter. "Elizabeth honey, what could be more weird than a two-hundred-year-old guy jumping through time and space and landing on your beach?''

She frowned. "How about history books that say one thing one time and something else another time?'' When Cappy stared at her, she sighed. "I have a book at home, *An Early History of the Caribbean*. Sometimes it says the *Black Cutter* went down with all hands. Other times it says there was one survivor, the captain.''

"Honey, that is not possible. Words printed on a page can't change.''

"I know," she whispered. "But I swear it happens. Last night I reread the section about Richard. Now that section reads that four months after the *Black Cutter* sank, Richard was rescued off Key West Island by a Dutch merchant ship that returned him to Boston where he became known as a somewhat eccentric inventor. He never married, never sailed again. He never spoke of his time on Key West Island. He died in 1825 at the age of sixty-five.''

Cappy's eyes bugged. "Good God. That gives me goose bumps. You aren't dreaming this, are you?''

"I wish I were!'' Tears gathered in her eyes and spilled down her cheeks. "Don't you see, Cappy? It means he went back. He went home.''

"Wait a minute," Cappy said, rubbing his bald head. "Okay, the history books don't *always* report that Colter survived and was rescued, right? Isn't that what you said?''

Elizabeth nodded. "It's the weirdest thing. I'm going crazy, aren't I?"

"Maybe...maybe Colter's fate isn't decided yet. Could that be? Would that explain it?"

"You're asking me?" Elizabeth gave him a wan smile through a glisten of tears. "Hell, I don't know. I don't understand any of this. I think I'm going out of my mind. I want to scream and rage and hold on to him. I want to shout into his wind and scream that it can't have him! Other times I feel like I have to let go, that love is unselfish and giving, that I would love Richard best by releasing him. Cappy, tell me what to do."

He stared at her. "Honey, I don't have a clue."

Elizabeth glanced at the calendar on her desk.

She didn't tell Cappy that it was two hundred years ago tonight that Richard was rescued by the Dutch merchant ship. She couldn't bear to speak her worst fear aloud. It hurt too much.

Chapter Fourteen

Elizabeth didn't know how long she had been sitting on the beach, staring at the dark horizon. She didn't remember twilight fading or the stars appearing, but it was full night now. The marl beneath her jeans and bare feet had begun to lose the day's heat and turn cool.

How would it happen? Would Richard walk through one room in his house and discover he had stepped from the twentieth century back into the eighteenth? Or was the wind and the tunnel an integral part of the process?

And how would it be for her? Would someone in Boston phone to report him missing, or would he simply fail to return? Would he have time to leave her a message? Probably not.

Tears ran down Elizabeth's cheeks as she hugged her knees and stared unseeing into the darkness. There were so many questions. And so few answers.

Would she awaken tomorrow and find history rewritten? Would she discover that peanut butter had been invented in the late eighteenth century by a privateer named Capt. Richard Colter?

There was only one thing in this whole crazy weird business that Elizabeth knew for certain. She loved

Richard. She would always love Richard. There would be no other man for her. After him, other men would seem pallid and dull, drawn in shades of pastel.

She heard a sound above and behind her, and as she roused herself to glance over her shoulder the light went on beside her balcony door.

"Richard?" For an instant she couldn't move, then she jumped to her feet, watching him stride down the steps to the beach. Her heart flipped over in her chest. "Richard!"

Every nerve in her body urged her to run to him. But she didn't. Seeing what he was wearing held her back.

He wore the clothing he had arrived in, his linsey-woolsey breeches, his woolen stockings, the handmade shirt with flowing sleeves. In his hand was one of the swords from above her sofa.

Elizabeth stared at him and her heart pounded into overdrive. He was large and powerful and magnificent, her brazen pirate lord. Never would he wear other clothing that suited him so well, never would he look this handsome.

He strode forward, halting on the sand before her and his bold, smoldering eyes devoured her.

"Why are you dressed like that?" Elizabeth whispered.

"I'm not certain, gel. 'Twas a compelling urge. But this is what I am, an ill-clad and ignorant traveler from a faraway time."

"You're so much more than that." The words stuck to the roof of her mouth. From the corner of her eye she watched a glow form out on the water and her heart froze, then accelerated, knocking against her rib cage. She couldn't bring herself to look at the glow directly.

She kept her gaze riveted on Richard's face, storing his memory for a lonely future, loving him.

"I'm dogmatic, opinionated, set in me ways. I'll never be fully reconciled to the idea of sharing me heart and hearth with a twentieth-century woman. Ye shock and amaze me, gel. Ye irritate and goad me fair crazy. Ye won't keep to your place, no matter what."

Hot tears flooded her eyes. The glow at the edge of her vision expanded like a window opening on daylight, on another time. Distant voices carried on the sea breeze. Did Richard see it too? Did he hear the voices?

"I'm dogmatic and opinionated myself, Richard. You and I would always have struggled over who would be boss and neither of us would have won." Her voice choked, swimming through tears. And she spoke rapidly, knowing their time together was running short like sand through an hourglass.

She longed to hurl herself on him and clasp him against her heart, yearned to surrender to his deep, urgent kisses one last time. But she didn't dare. Tonight Richard was larger than life, imbued with a strange energy she could almost see.

A faint radiance pulsed around his body as though he were charged with an unnatural otherworldly electricity. Tiny fingers of fire lightning skittered along the blade of the sword.

Elizabeth wet her lips and stared up at him, her heart in her eyes. "It's happening," she whispered. A skiff of wind flipped a tendril of hair across her cheek.

They held each other's gaze for a moment, for an eternity, then turned together toward the window of illumination lighting the night sea. Two hundred yards offshore, a fully rigged merchantman bobbed on a daylight sea. Elizabeth's hands flew to her mouth and she gasped. Although she expected the ship, the actual sight and reality of it shocked her. The men on the ship lowered a dingy to the water. Others shielded their eyes from the sun and pointed to where she and Richard stood.

When she whirled and looked behind her, the houses along Manhattan Cove had faded to sepia outlines. Their shapes lay superimposed on the landscape like the faint negative of a photograph yet to be taken. A bonfire blazed where her house had stood but a moment ago. Behind the fire was a mangrove swamp. The Key West of Elizabeth's time shimmered and faded against the night, giving way to a stronger reality from another age.

Wind gathered and rose around them, sending leaves and scraps of paper tumbling along the shoreline, etching caps on the incoming waves. Richard's hair flew around his face as did hers.

"Lizzy!"

As if Richard's shout was a signal, the wind increased in force and sound, building to a fury, whirling loose sand and a strange sweet smoke around and between them. A howling sound built in Elizabeth's ears. Her shirt fluttered and molded against her breasts. Richard's sleeves billowed and flapped; he braced his body against the forces tearing at them.

As Elizabeth watched in terror darkness gathered before her, even as the radiance bathing the sea expanded. The darkness coalesced into a spinning, swirling channel shaped by the howling wind into a tunnel at the end of which lay the Dutch merchantman and the dingy rowing toward them.

"Richard!"

She screamed into the wind, but he didn't hear. He stood facing the tunnel, his eyes staring and mesmerized by the strange colored lights that flashed and fizzed and beckoned along the tunnel walls.

Elizabeth ducked her head and struggled against the howling wind. She threw out her hand. "Richard! Take me with you! I love you! Don't leave me behind!"

But she saw his face. And she knew he would not take her into the maelstrom.

Hypnotized, he stared into the whirling, roaring tunnel, his golden head the only spot of color in the flying darkness. "Richard!" The wind swallowed her words. Tears streamed down her face and flew away.

All he had to do was step forward. Two paces and he would pass through the spinning tunnel into the light that had now reached the shoreline. Two paces and he would return to his own time, to his own life, to all that was familiar and comfortable and dear.

Strangling on tears, desperately scrubbing her eyes to see every detail of him, Elizabeth abandoned her fight against the wind and her own fate. Submitting, she made herself step backward, away from the terrible joy transfiguring Richard's face.

"Go, Richard! I release you!" Tears scalded her cheeks. She felt the wind clawing at her heart. "Goodbye, my love. Remember me!"

The wind spiraled into a high scream. The tunnel whirled and flashed and beckoned with beguiling power.

Richard stood wide legged before it, lashed by the wind, his knuckles white around the hilt of the sword.

Electricity crackled and flashed around his body. His hair was a halo of white fire.

He threw back his head and shouted.

"Elizabeth! I need ye! Elizabeth, come to me!"

"Yes!" Fighting like a tigress, she battled the furious wind, struggling to gain each foothold, stretching out her hand until Richard caught her fingers and pulled her hard against his body.

"Take me with you!" she screamed.

His powerful arm clasped her to his chest. He held her with his left arm and with his right arm, he brandished his sword.

"I say nay!" he bellowed, roaring his refusal into the howling fury and madness, raising his sword like a shield against the radiance glowing across the sea. "I . . . choose . . . this world!"

Raising his arm, he drove the point of the sword deep in the marl between himself and the tunnel.

The wind roared to a screaming crescendo of noise and light. The radiance on the sea blazed into a nova so bright it blinded them. A gale ripped and tore at their hair, their bodies. The tunnel whirled and crackled, fizzed and flashed in front of them.

Then it was over.

The wind and the tunnel, all of it, vanished so abruptly their ears rang with the sudden silence, their eyes ached from the abrupt transition to blackness.

Gradually Elizabeth moved from Richard's side and looked at the sea. There was no Dutch merchantman, no light from another age, another time. Starlight rippled across a calm night sea. When she peered behind her, she saw the houses rimming Manhattan Cove, saw the familiar porch light shining above her deck.

Her knees collapsed and she sank to the cool marl. Richard knelt in front of her, his hands on her shoulders. She felt a tingle pass through her body, then it too was gone. She hurled herself into his arms. "Oh, Richard," she whispered. "You could have returned home, back to your own time."

"Wherever you are, my darling Elizabeth, that is my time. I love you, gel." He pulled her into his arms and held her so tightly she thought her bones would crack. "I love you!"

She pulled back to look into his face. "But I thought you were saying goodbye when you first—"

"Because I said ye shock and amaze me? Ye irritate and goad me fair crazy?" He grinned down at her and brushed a strand of dark hair away from her cheek. "That weren't goodbye, madam, that were surrender. Despite the appalling suspicion that I'll never be the unchallenged lord of me own manor, I came here tonight to ask for 'e, Mistress Rowley, if you'll have me."

"But I thought...Richard, I saw you staring into the tunnel and there was such joy on your face. I thought you were going to step forward and I—" She bit her lip to halt the tears that shimmered in her eyes.

He brushed his thumb across her cheek. "'Twas joy at having the choice, darling gel. If I hadn't been given the choice, all me days I would have wondered...and so would 'e."

Elizabeth flung her arms around his neck and covered his gorgeous bronzed face with hot kisses. "I love you! Oh, Richard, I love you so much!"

"I love 'e too, madam," he said, laughing. "Now compose yourself, I have words to speak to ye."

"You just said them," Elizabeth said, laughing and crying. "But say them again and again. I'll never get tired of hearing them."

They knelt on the sand, holding hands and facing each other in front of the sword Richard had driven into the sand. Richard cleared his throat.

"Me dear Mistress Rowley. Over the term of our acquaintance, I have noticed a steadily deepening affection toward your small sweet self. Upon reflection, I have decided it would please me mightily if ye would consent to honor me by becoming me wedded wife."

Elizabeth gazed into his smoldering blue-gray eyes. "Say it again."

"I love ye, madam," he said in a low, intense voice that trembled with emotion. "I love 'e beyond all time and measure and have loved 'e from the moment I first saw ye. I love the way your eyes flash dark fire and the way you stamp your little foot. I love your courage and your bold spirit. I love your generous heart and your quick, sharp mind. I love your body and the way ye feel against me naked skin. I will still be loving ye with me dying breath. Ye belong to me and I to ye." His eyes traced the contours of her trembling mouth. "Now put quit to this suspense, woman. Will ye have me or no?"

"Yes! Oh, Richard. Yes, yes, yes!"

He sprang to his feet and scooped her up into his arms, bending his head to plunder her mouth. He grinned down at her. "In my time, we would now visit all our relatives and share our glad tidings."

Elizabeth wrapped her arms around his neck and leaned to kiss the corner of his lips. "In my time, we visit the bedroom and share ourselves," she said in a throaty voice.

He carried her toward the stairs leading up from the beach. "This is our time, Lizzy, me love. We'll make it so, gel."

"Aye, Captain," she whispered as he carried her up the stairs and into the house. "I love you. I'll always love you."

Until the end of time.

WELCOME TO

The quintessential small town,
where everyone knows everybody else!

Each book set in Tyler is a self-contained love story; together,
the twelve novels stitch the fabric of the community.

"The small town warmth and friendliness shine through."
Rendezvous

Join your friends in Tyler for the tenth book,
CROSSROADS by Marisa Carroll, available in December.

*Can Dr. Jeffrey Baron and nurse Cecelia Hayes discover
what's killing the residents of Worthington House?*

GREAT READING...GREAT SAVINGS...AND A
FABULOUS FREE GIFT!

With Tyler you can receive a fabulous gift, ABSOLUTELY FREE,
by collecting proofs-of-purchase found in each Tyler book.
And use our special Tyler coupons to save on your next
TYLER book purchase.

If you missed *Whirlwind* (March), *Bright Hopes* (April), *Wisconsin Wedding* (May), *Monkey Wrench* (June), *Blazing Star* (July), *Sunshine* (August), *Arrowpoint* (September), *Bachelor's Puzzle* (October) or *Milky Way* (November) and would like to order them, send your name, address, zip or postal code, along with a check or money order for $3.99 for each book ordered (please do not send cash), plus 75¢ postage and handling ($1.00 in Canada), payable to Harlequin Reader Service, to:

In the U.S.	In Canada
3010 Walden Avenue	P.O. Box 609
P.O. Box 1325	Fort Erie, Ontario
Buffalo, NY 14269-1325	L2A 5X3

Please specify book title(s) with your order.
Canadian residents add applicable federal and provincial taxes.   TYLER-10

Take 4 bestselling love stories FREE

Plus get a FREE surprise gift!

HARLEQUIN®

Temptation®

Rebels & Rogues

Jared: He'd had the courage to fight in Vietnam. But did he have the courage to fight for the woman he loved?

THE SOLDIER OF FORTUNE
By Kelly Street
Temptation #421, December

All men are not created equal. Some are rough around the edges. Tough-minded but tenderhearted. Incredibly sexy. The tempting fulfillment of every woman's fantasy.

When it's time to fight for what they believe in, to win that special woman, our Rebels and Rogues are heroes at heart. Twelve Rebels and Rogues, one each month in 1992, only from Harlequin Temptation.

HARLEQUIN
·HISTORICAL·

CHRISTMAS

·STORIES·1992·

Capture the magic and romance of Christmas in the 1800s
with HARLEQUIN HISTORICAL CHRISTMAS STORIES
1992, a collection of three stories by celebrated historical
authors. The perfect Christmas gift!

Don't miss these heartwarming stories, available in
November wherever Harlequin books are sold:

MISS MONTRACHET REQUESTS by Maura Seger
CHRISTMAS BOUNTY by Erin Yorke
A PROMISE KEPT by Bronwyn Williams

Plus, as an added bonus, you can receive a FREE keepsake
Christmas ornament. Just collect four proofs of purchase
from any November or December 1992 Harlequin or
Silhouette series novels, or from any Harlequin or
Silhouette Christmas collection, and receive a beautiful
dated brass Christmas candle ornament.

Mail this certificate along with four (4) proof-of-purchase coupons plus $1.50 postage and
handling (check or money order—do not send cash), payable to Harlequin Books, to: **In the
U.S.**: P.O. Box 9057, Buffalo, NY 14269-9057; **In Canada**: P.O. Box 622, Fort Erie, Ontario,
L2A 5X3.

**ONE PROOF OF
PURCHASE**

Name: _____

_____

Address: _____

_____

City: _____

State/Province: _____

Zip/Postal Code: _____

HX92POP   093 KAG